A
SUFFRAGIST'S GUIDE
TO THE
ANTARCTIC

A SUFFRAGIST'S GUIDE TO THE ANTARCTIC

YI SHUN LAI

A
atheneum

New York London Toronto
Sydney New Delhi

An imprint of Simon & Schuster Children's Publishing Division
1230 Avenue of the Americas, New York, New York 10020
This book is a work of fiction. Any references to historical events, real people,
or real places are used fictitiously. Other names, characters, places, and events are products
of the author's imagination, and any resemblance to actual events or places
or persons, living or dead, is entirely coincidental.
Text © 2024 by Yi Shun Lai
Jacket illustration © 2024 by Beatriz Ramo
Jacket design by Karyn Lee © 2024 by Simon & Schuster, LLC
Map illustration © 2024 by Filippo Vanzo
All rights reserved, including the right of reproduction in whole or in part in any form.
Atheneum logo is a trademark of Simon & Schuster, LLC.
Simon & Schuster: Celebrating 100 Years of Publishing in 2024
For information about special discounts for bulk purchases, please contact
Simon & Schuster Special Sales at 1-866-506-1949 or business@simonandschuster.com.
The Simon & Schuster Speakers Bureau can bring authors to your live event.
For more information or to book an event, contact the Simon & Schuster Speakers Bureau
at 1-866-248-3049 or visit our website at www.simonspeakers.com.
Interior design by Karyn Lee
The text for this book was set in Sabon LT Std.
The illustrations for this book were rendered digitally.
Manufactured in the United States of America
First Edition
2 4 6 8 10 9 7 5 3 1
Library of Congress Cataloging-in-Publication Data
Names: Lai, Yi Shun, author.
Title: A suffragist's guide to the Antarctic / Yi Shun Lai.
Description: First edition. | New York : Atheneum Books for Young Readers,
[2024] | Audience: Ages 12 and up. | Summary: In 1914 England,
eighteen-year-old American Clara lies about her age and citizenship to
land a coveted spot on an Antarctic expedition, but when the crew is
marooned on an ice floe, Clara's mission to advance the women's suffrage
movement takes a back seat to survival.
Identifiers: LCCN 2023003081 | ISBN 9781665937764 (hardcover) | ISBN
9781665937788 (ebook)
Subjects: CYAC: Antarctica—Discovery and exploration—Fiction. |
Survival—Fiction. | Suffragists—Fiction. |
Americans—England—Fiction. | Great Britain—History—George V,
1910-1936—Fiction. | LCGFT: Historical fiction. | Novels.
Classification: LCC PZ7.1.L2317 Su 2024 | DDC [Fic]—dc23
LC record available at https://lccn.loc.gov/2023003081

For Jim, who has never expected anything less than bravery.

For Roz, without whom this book would not be.

For Livia: Go forth.

And for Dad, in fond remembrance of our own

real-life Antarctic adventure.

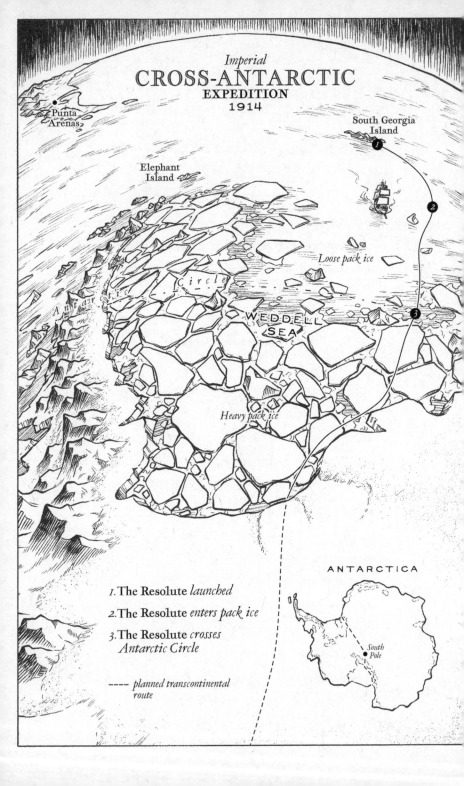

Imperial
CROSS-ANTARCTIC
EXPEDITION
1914

Punta
Arenas

South Georgia
Island

Elephant
Island

Loose pack ice

Circle

WEDDELL
SEA

Heavy pack ice

1. The Resolute *launched*

2. The Resolute *enters pack ice*

3. The Resolute *crosses
Antarctic Circle*

- - - - *planned transcontinental
route*

ANTARCTICA

South
Pole

ANTARCTIC EXPEDITION FEARED LOST!

Staff Editorial, *London Daily Times*
1 November 1914

Amidst the carnage of the Great War, another strike against hope: Sir Douglas Henderson's much-anticipated crossing of the Antarctic continent is presumed doomed, with all crew members assumed deceased. As there has been no communication from the expedition ship *The Resolute* since mid-October, one must assume the worst.

The news from the expedition was already bleak, with colder-than-usual temperatures in the Antarctic spring setting the timeline back by weeks. The ship became locked in sea ice a mere hundred miles from their desired destination on the Antarctic continent. Then the oil for the engines that were meant to propel the expedition sledges across Sir Douglas's beloved "Blue Continent" was reported hopelessly frozen, rendering the sledges useless even if the crew could manage to make shore. Who knows what other bad luck has befallen the expedition since it last sent word?

Among the missing crew is Canadian Clara Ketterling-Dunbar, the only woman on crew and first-ever woman on any polar expedition. This newspaper has found *fact* that she is a member of the Women's Social and Political Union, that group of dangerous suffragettes angling for a voice in what is rightfully a man's world!

Sir Douglas would have been well advised to not overlook the old truism that women on board are bad luck to begin with.

Imperial Cross-Antarctic Expedition, 1914
Diary of Clara Ketterling-Dunbar

18 November 1914

(Day two marooned on the ice.)

Wind E x SE. Visibility good.

Biscuits and berry preserves for breakfast.

Patience poker with Higgins.

Read some of *R* volume of encyclopaedia.

Two days since the sinking of *The Resolute*, and already there is the frisson of panic among our crew, only barely masqueraded by light boredom. The Boss says we must wait until some leads open up for our lifeboats to make a move, but all around there is nothing but solid ice, interrupted by more ice: ridges, hummocks, and hillocks.

19 November 1914

(Day three marooned on the ice.)

Winds calm. Visibility middling.

Tinned ham, tinned peas for dinner. Tinned Victoria sponge for pudding. No. Not really. In my admittedly limited knowledge, no one has yet invented tinned Victoria sponge.

Surely, the leads will open as we head into the Antarctic summer. But Wilson says this is the coldest year yet. He is not hopeful.

Spoke briefly to Figgy whilst between chores.

Figgy: We're doomed, aren't we?

Me, fighting down my own panic, loudly: Don't be ridiculous.

Figgy, staring angrily all around him, flinging arms up in the air: Ugh! What would a woman know about an expedition, anyway?

What he doesn't know is that I can't ever betray the extent of my fear.

Never was a wide open space so terrifying.

(Day four marooned.)

Winds easterly. Floe is, damn it all to hell, holding very firm.

Predict will be here for some time yet—not even the tiniest lead to be seen anywhere.

Trying to keep my counsel, because God knows what would happen if the crew saw a woman "getting hysterical."

21 November 1914

(Day five marooned.)

If one is to keep a diary, one must ensure that it will be of use to someone. Billings is already keeping the wind log; Wilson is tracking the floe; Higgins is still taking pictures despite the fact that many of his glass lantern plates are God knows where on the seabed of the Weddell by now; Givens is painting pictures, just in case Higgins runs out of film, and also for those patrons of the expedition who would rather look at paintings than photographs or glass lantern slides; Cook has all his recipes written down. Whatever is the point of one more voice among the many?

Perhaps a new project will distract me from my rising fear.

Hang it all; diaries be damned; I am now writing:

A SUFFRAGIST'S GUIDE TO ANTARCTICA.

Hello. I am Clara Ketterling-Dunbar, and I'll be your guide through the Antarctic. I am one of twenty-eight crew members of *The Resolute*, rest her mast and timbers, and I write to you from a for-now-warmish tent sat on a large ice floe roughly one hundred miles from the shore of the Antarctic continent itself. I am American. I am eighteen, although I have told the crew I am twenty-one. This is the first time I have admitted these two facts on the page.

Of the crew, only The Boss and MacTavish know of my origins. Everyone else believes me to be Canadian; the sentiment toward Americans is not of the most *favorable* caliber, shall we say. And, probably most importantly, *no one* knows much of my activities in England before we embarked on this accursed expedition.

I am far too aware of everyone's feelings toward Americans; much as we have dragged our feet in getting women the vote, we have also shamefully been incapable of providing leadership in the Great War, which, so far as we know, is either still ongoing or has ended in the time since we have been away from civilization—and therefore, from most news of the world apart from what we were able to receive on our wireless before we went out of range. We had just pulled away from Liverpool when the order came for England to go to war; pulling into Portsmouth we had readied the ship to be turned over to war concerns, but the King himself encouraged us to "proceed" for "God and Country."

(I am still parsing this; for the life of my American soul, I cannot quite comprehend the import this seems to carry for everyone else on this ship. Even our Aussie, Higgins, seems besotted with the phrase, although he's just as likely to use it when he wins a poker hand as he is for matters as weighty as world war.)

One day soon I hope this will actually be a guide to Antarctica for women. For now, we may generously refer to it as a guide to the Antarctic *area*, as our expedition has yet to reach our goal of the Antarctic continent. One mustn't be too fussy when one is talking in such grand scales: Antarctica is a very, very large place, expanding and shrinking according to the whims of the ice pack and floes clustering near its shoreline.

Our ship's geologist, Wilson, would argue with me here. He would say land is land and should not be confused with ice, but I much rather prefer the imagery of a place breathing and growing and shrinking with the seasons. Anyway, this is not a geologist's guide.

Antarctica is so large, in fact, that we had planned to take four whole months to walk from shore to South Pole, where we would meet another crew and restock our rations and then all together complete the trek across the continent, but our lack of ship seems to have scuppered that plan. I hope our other crew will not hang about too long, like a sad suitor waiting for a date that will never come.

I digress. Let me begin by saying that, should this diary be found without me, you would do well to disregard everything before this entry. What comes before now seems to my eyes to be a hackneyed, homely recounting of life aboard *The Resolute*. Plenty of other diaries on this expedition will recount the card games, our monthly haircutting nights, the lantern-shows of life in exotic locales. . . .

From here on in I will endeavor to provide you with an honest recounting of everything you need to know to survive here.

Let us begin with the most important item of all.

The Ship.

Ours is called *The Resolute*. Although she has left us for her watery grave, I will speak of her in the present tense, because I do not much feel like admitting her departure.

Your ship is your home. Treat her well. Her various parts will become living room, sitting room, bunks. Her decks may become gaming areas on the days, say, when one is locked in ice and cannot go anywhere. Her decks are also housing for our many, many dogs, which I will come to a little later.

We are now six days on the ice, since our *Resolute* went

down, and I fear I will never be able to unhear the shrieking and groaning of her keel as it was slowly crushed by sea ice, the booming cracks of her hull as great shards of floe pressed their ways into her belly. It resonates in my sleep.

Oh, I'll never forget it. As our beautiful barquentine—our home for the last four months—went down, the ice floes that had worked so hard to stave in her hull just closed over where she'd gone down, knocking against one another like so many dominoes, as if they'd finally defeated their nemesis and were celebrating. The gently rippling water made it apparent there would be nothing left to mark that she'd been there, that she'd protected us from the elements so gracefully, without asking anything in return but that we take care of her.

I am reminded of our rage, in the days after our letter box–bombing campaign, to see no coverage in the press whatsoever: so much had happened, and yet, there seemed to be no evidence of our actions. Everything seems fruitless then, doesn't it, if there is no public record? It would be weeks yet before we heard from a well-placed source that Parliament had gone so far as to direct the press to delay all mention of the actions of the suffrage movement whilst they gauged our impact; it was a far cry from the days when we were press darlings—a most abrupt, unwelcome shift. (Is it churlish for me to want the battle for women's rights to have just as much coverage as impending war? Is it not, after all, a civil war of sorts?)

I stayed to watch the place where *The Resolute* had gone down for some time, even when the floes stopped making their eerie racket and had gone on to float placidly, in desultory fashion, to other waters. I wanted to somehow mark with my eye—take a picture with my memory, as Mama has encouraged me to do so many times—of the place where our home had gone down. But of course, water does not allow for that. Everywhere one looks it is the same now; the patterns in the floes move constantly, and if you take your eyes off a spot for just one second, you cannot find where you were looking again.

I must leave this for later. Cook is calling for me.

(Nota bene: Cook stomps everywhere, such that we joke that he may one day posthole himself into the water, and then where would we be? "Time for dinner, Clara," is his normal call, followed closely by, "Come help me with the biscuits?" as if he is asking, but we all know by now that he isn't asking. Cook does not ask when it comes to matters of the stove.)

Biscuit duty calls, damn the biscuits. I am weary of them.

22 November 1914

I feel a renewed sense of purpose upon recasting this diary as something useful. May it prove of service to any woman who comes after me. Let me resume with some good information about some of the people you may encounter on the ice.

Your **expedition boss**. We actually do call ours "The Boss," but your moniker may vary depending on your feelings. Ours obviously also has a Christian name; he is called Douglas Henderson, and he speaks not very much and moves like silk. One can never hear him coming. Extent of this trait yet to be fully gauged, as everything sounds louder on the ice, out in the open.

When The Boss speaks, one pays attention. Your expedition leader will likely command the same attention, although this may be entirely due to his—or her!—level of experience and the British love of all things hierarchy. Ours has been to the Antarctic twice and the Arctic once, twice as assistant expedition leader and once as expedition leader. No word on what qualifies one to be an assistant or leader. One does not ask such questions. Indeed, if one is to believe the seasoned members of the crew, one should never have a need to ask questions of The Boss, ever.

This is familiar territory. At the Women's Social and Political Union, Emmeline Pankhurst, the founder of the organization and until recently my hero in all matters suffrage, would have nothing other than total obedience to her methods, which made her unilateral decision to lay down arms in favor of serving the British war effort truly infuriating. You can see how a young woman could be so frustrated that she signs on to a cockamamie expedition to the Antarctic!

But I digress. We are still speaking of bosses and their usefulness.

I don't yet know if The Boss's apt command of our crew is due to his style of delivery or his message. The Boss's favorite message to me is "Leave it, Clara." He delivers this command quietly but sternly, as he does most of his commands. It comes out of the side of his mouth, like I'm a toddler underfoot and he can only be half-bothered to address me. The first time he did it, I had to pause to make sure I had heard correctly. It had been some time since I let anybody talk to me like that, and he had that pipe sticking out of the side of his face, so I didn't truly believe he'd said it. But then he beetled his eyebrows and took the pipe out of his mouth and said it again, clear as crystal glasses: "*Leave* it, Clara."

Well, I blushed clean to the roots of my hair, which was unfortunate. I always blush when I'm angry, and everyone mistakes it for something other than what it is. Tate, who was standing nearby when it happened that first time, turned his head away, like he couldn't stand to see me blushing. Good man, that Tate. The suffragists would have liked him. They'd have called him sympathetic, and for a man, that's the highest praise one can give.

I remember very clearly what I did that first time to make The Boss tell me to leave it. We were on the deck of *The Resolute*, although really, where else would we be?

Figgy was making an absolute shit of getting the dogs squared away in their kennels for our voyage. How hard can it *be*? The dogs have different faces, different bodies, different moods even, and you can tell them apart like day and night, but there was Figgy, looking at the names painted above the kennels and vainly trying to search in the dogs' shaggy scruffs for the names stitched onto their collars, all while they nuzzled and yipped and made their racket.

I was coiling up the ropes then, and I watched him glancing back and forth, back and forth, until I just couldn't stand it anymore.

I dropped the end of the rope midcoil and was about to go over and just do it for him, and that's when The Boss said it. "Leave it, Clara."

I jumped. The man moves so quietly. If you're lucky you'll catch a whiff of his pipe before he gets to you; it's the best way to tell when he's near. I stared at him for a second, and that's when he said it again, unmistakable.

By then I'd figured out that one does not cross The Boss without very good reason, so I went back to working the rope. Ever since then, his voice rings in my head whenever I think of taking something into my own hands. "Leave it." I bite the inside of my cheek and think quick of something workmanlike to distract myself with.

The second time it happened, watch was changing over and I was frustrated at having to actually go *wake up* the next watchmen. The third time, it was my turn at poker and I'd already lost two lumps of sugar and a chocolate square to squirrely old Cook and our keen carpenter, Amos, respectively, and I believe I may have been *thinking* of accusing one of them of cheating. The fourth through nineteenth, who knows what I turned back to? It hardly matters.

The last time it happened was when our *Resolute* was cracking up. Wood was splitting right below our feet; we could feel it through our soles. We were all passing boxes in a line so they could be dropped over the side and down the chute Marvin and Hayes had rigged up at the side of the ship, and then I remembered the glass lantern plates Higgins had brought down to The Ritz for an evening's entertainment just a few days before the very cold snap, before the ice started growing, like the devilish beast it is, and closing in on us. (In those fraught days, The Ritz went from being just a place we gathered in the belly of *The Resolute* to a place of great comfort and even joy. How I wish we could recreate it on the ice!)

I stepped out of line to go fetch them, and wouldn't you know it, The Boss was right there. "Leave it, Clara."

"But Boss, Higgins's plates . . ."

He shook his great shaggy head. None of us had had a haircut in some time. Everyone had been worried *The Resolute* would crack, and one does not want any of your mates near your head with shears when they are on edge. "Whatever it is, leave it. You shouldn't abandon your place."

Sure enough, the line had backed up. To my left, Per was piled up with three boxes already, since the men on *his* left hadn't quite noticed I'd left the queue. And to my right, Hotchkiss was sniggering, like he couldn't wait to blame the breakdown of our operations on me or Per. Really, Hotchkiss would blame anything on anyone else. He's that kind of man. But he'd have been right to blame it on me, so I stepped back into line then.

I still think of those beautiful glass lantern slides, sitting in The Ritz, where we had our last joyful night within the embrace of our *Resolute*, slowly degrading in seawater, just waiting for someone to collect them.

Higgins tried to be cheerful about it, but I know he thinks of them too. A photographer, he told me, is the sum of his output. He has his camera still, but these particular slides were of back home in Australia, and I know he relished showing them and sharing a piece of his history with us.

I can leave it. I have had some practice since joining up with this lot. Why, just this morning, I have had to bite my tongue multiple times, as some of the men were arguing over who would get to read which volumes of the encyclopaedia. Twenty-eight crew members. Twenty-six volumes of the encyclopaedia. Surely not everyone wants to read at the same time, or even read Q or X at the same time, but it seems they are both very popular, perchance because they are short and interesting at the same time.

The Boss is calling a meeting. I hope it is to tell us what our literal next forward steps are. We have been living on the ice for near a week now, on a kind of semi-permanent knife's edge as we speculate The Boss's next move for us. Stern, our expedition's second-in-command, reminds us that The Boss does nothing without deliberation, but this seems to be taking a little longer than one would expect.

23 November

On days when there's very little wind and the blubber stove is belching black smoke into the air, I long for the open campfire Mama and I cooked over while we were camping.

Mama was perhaps unusual for her preferences whilst in the woods; where the fashion of the day was to bring as many accoutrements as might remind you of home, Mama chose always only to bring a frying pan and something to turn the fish and our forages with. She preferred even to not bring seasonings. She said the point of eating out-of-doors was to taste the flavor of the woods, the river, the earth. We only ever caught what we thought we could eat.

This is a good place to talk to you about **rations**, since The Boss has just now informed us that we are to be leaving some of ours behind for a hundreds-mile-long march to Paulet Island in a few weeks.

In truth, I was surprised at the kind of eating that was to be had on board a ship; I think I had prepared myself for biscuits, tinned gravy, and Kendal Mint Cake all the way, or something equally frugal. But our rations, up until fairly recently anyway, were something very closely approximating luxury, especially for life on an expedition. In fact, it's better than Mama and I ate on our many, many camping trips, although there is so much to be said for fried brook trout over an open fire and wild garlic scapes. There had not been much hunting in our first two months on board, as we were busy sailing. Fishing has not been entirely worthy, especially in these very cold waters, and I think it is this aspect of meat that had me the most intrigued: To open the larder and see a vast wall of jugged hare, tinned hams, to say nothing of all manner of root vegetables! To step aboard the ship and understand that there was a small *farm* on board, with chickens both for eggs and eating and two fat pigs! Then again, I also could not picture packing all of these heavy things on horseback or even on bicycle for a camping trip, so perhaps one cannot really compare after all.

Live chickens on a bicycle! Pigs on horseback! Really, Clara. The Antarctic life has my thinking addled.

Well, we had exhausted the chickens and their eggs by the time *The Resolute* sank, anyway, and good thing, too—if I had had to break some chickens' necks and leave them (*can* one march towing a crate of chickens?), I'd have done it, but it would have been terrible to bury that good chicken meat in the snow for some scavenging killer whales or horrid leopard seals to root up. (Would leopard seals eat chicken meat? To look at their faces on Higgins's lantern slides, one would think not. I can picture them turning up their pugnacious noses at chicken when they can have fatty, wonderful, fresh deep-sea fish that needn't be thawed, or fresh penguin meat.)

At our meeting, The Boss said, "Near everything we need is off the ship now. We shall, in the next few days, have to be making no small amount of serious sacrifice. The weather is fine now, and we need it to be much colder for any travel over the ice to happen." I stifled a snort. We are at the beginning of the Antarctic summer. Just what does he think will happen? "At the very least," he went on (The Boss is forever talking over my thoughts; I think I hear him in my sleep), "we will need to pack light to ensure we can travel well over softer snow."

The Boss paused for some drama, I think. He is well known on the lecture circuit for his command of dramatics. "In the next few weeks, we are making a run for Paulet Island."

I elbowed Givens. "How far is that?"

Givens furrowed his brow. "Two hundred miles, give or take," he said. He pulled off one mitten to chew on his nails, and I elbowed him again. "Put it back on," I said. He looked annoyed but did it; one must make a rigid habit of keeping one's extremities covered in this climate.

Most everything The Boss does and says is a little like this. A little far-ranging, a little out of everyone's normal consideration. I have learned not to question him so much.

I didn't question him when he asked me to sing for my

place on the ship, and if ever there were a time for a young woman to question a man's judgment, it was then. I almost shouted at him that I had not moved across the ocean from one suffragist movement to another only to cave to a man's whims, no matter who he was. Why, if he were a woman, he would be thrown into the loony bin for such a request.

But I bit my tongue, so sharp was my desire to see a world free from old society's rigors, and sang a sea chanty. Gwendoline, my very first English suffragist sister, had often sung by way of lifting our spirits after a particularly hard day of campaigning for our right to vote. And then, The Boss asked if I could play cards, patience poker in particular, and then he asked how many fish I had caught on my last trip and what kind.

At that late stage in his planning, The Boss had the air of someone who is easily distracted by the next greatest thing on the horizon. In my case, that could have been the next candidate to come along, and I wasn't about to give him a reason to doubt my commitment to the expedition and nothing but. So I sang, and told him not only of my skills at patience poker but also at whist and rummy, and even revealed a little of what I had learned from Mama about fishing and hunting. Everything I had read about The Boss said he had a flair for the unusual, and I figured if he wants to know whether a person is capable of entertaining herself and her crewmates whilst on a long boat journey, well, that is within his rights.

The expedition sounded batty from the get-go. Sail down to the Weddell Sea; land on the continent; *walk* across the continent to meet another boat, which was to take us all home after we've planted a flag for Merrie Olde England. All right, why not? In every possible scenario, it was going to be a damn sight more productive in terms of establishing a woman's place in society than just giving up, like the WSPU had decided to do "in order to support the war effort." I *ask* you: However will women gain our rightful place in society if we roll over at the first sign of challenge? However will we gain *respect*?

Emily Davison would have something to say about this, I just know it.

If she were still alive.

In any case, I suppose I should not have been shocked at The Boss's suggestion that we walk an additional two hundred miles to Paulet. What's two hundred more miles on top of the hundreds we were already meant to trudge, anyway?

Surely, The Boss must not intend for us to complete this expedition as originally planned. I believe he means to try to get us home as quickly as possible, although "home" feels fairly far away at this point, especially since the land-scape is the same as far as the eye can see—veritable plains of ice, snow, blue sky, and water.

"We'll never make it." Givens was grousing next to me.

"Shut it, you'll get nabbed for mutiny." I winked at

him, trying to jolly him out of his moroseness. Artists are *so moody*, even the ones who like to tinker with building whole makeshift kitchens.

He wasn't having it. "I'm just saying," he said, whispering now, "the ice won't firm up enough for us to walk on, hauling all our things."

"Shhhh!" Milton-Jones was glaring at us, and actually, The Boss seemed to be addressing Givens's worry right then. He was emptying his own pockets out onto the ice—scraps of paper, letters, some pieces of jewelry even. He held up a pocket Bible. "Given me by the Queen Alexandra," he said, and tore out a single page before dropping the Bible onto the pile too.

"Men," he said—I rolled my eyes; I was forever reminding him of my presence, it seemed, and I would never get used to being called a man—"we will have to travel light. Anything you can do without, I expect to be on this pile in two days' time, for in two days we strike camp and make for Paulet Island. Load everything else onto the lifeboats. Milton-Jones will take inventory."

What *is* it about men in eyeglasses that makes them look simultaneously all-knowing, insecure, *and* smug? You'd think Milton-Jones would take just a quiet kind of pride in his work and not worry so much about what everyone else thinks of him. He always looks so pleased when The Boss calls on him, like a cat, or a slug.

We were allowed to keep two pairs of mittens, two pairs

of socks, two pairs of woolens, two sweaters, and our coveralls, belts, and hats. Of course our diaries and pencils were a must as well as one set of eating utensils, a tin cup, and a plate. I gave up my Votes for Women motoring scarf, which was useless in the Antarctic cold anyway, and I offloaded the last of my Pankhurst buttons. (I have been thinking, anyway, that perhaps we do not stand for the same things. I bet Pankhurst has women picking up after men and the mess they've left behind to go to war.)

It has only been a few hours since this announcement, and the pile draws me to it as a matter of sheer curiosity, a kind of archaeological dig: the men have been hoarding things I never knew they were squirreling away, novels and pictures and fancy-dress items. The Boss spotted Figgy's banjo on the pile and made him take it back. He says Figgy's banjo playing keeps our spirits up.

I wonder if Figgy was made to perform at *his* interview.

Chutney has only today had the bright idea to call our camp "Dump Camp." Let it not be said that our crew is not witty, even if in the most obvious of manners.

Oh, yes, **hoosh**. You need to know about hoosh. This is a thing you will be eating day in and day out, probably not for main meals unless things get really bad, but definitely for elevenses and for teatime: it is a kind of porridge made of pemmican and biscuit and snow. The pemmican came to us premade, any kind of dried meat and fat in a cake. I understand our American natives first introduced it to us.

You chuck that into a pot with the biscuits and some snow to help break it all down. Cook does not seem to measure these; he just breaks up all the pieces as things heat up and then we get it served in our tin cups.

Be forewarned; if you do not scrape the sides clean with your spoon or fork and you do not take care to scrub your mug out with snow right away, the hoosh will form into a kind of frozen cement on the sides of your mug, and then your tea and Trumilk will all taste the slightest bit of hoosh for some time.

This lesson may or may not be brought to you by personal experience.

24 November

Today seems to be a good day to tell you about the **weather conditions** you will experience on Antarctica; despite the time of year, the wind is blowing every which way, and today we are hunkered down in our tent: me, Per, Blackburn, Givens, Chutney, and Amos. Burch is nowhere to be seen, a fact that caused us some alarm, but then Givens came tumbling in just as the wind started up, saying he'd heard Burch was playing poker with tent number four, so that was less cause for worry. Thankfully, our camp is fully set up now after a little hiccup this morning, which I will detail to you later.

I have learned the following information from Wilson (lithe, bespectacled, literally professorial; your expedition is also likely to have one of him serving in a geology or meteorology capacity, and you may also jokingly and flatly refer to him as "the Prof." Ours has been on an Antarctic expedition before and made the weather his métier).

Even though there is *some* predictability to seasons on Antarctica (warmer temperatures, in the high thirties, even, in the summer months), you are likely to experience weather events like blizzards and high winds no matter what the season. Precipitation is less likely, given that Antarctica is designated a desert and therefore experiences very little of the stuff, but the winds will kick up everything that is loose around you and send it flying, creating what is commonly known as whiteout conditions.

This is what we call it when you cannot see beyond your own hand, held at arm's length directly in front of you. In order to effectively guard against critical things like, oh, getting hopelessly lost between tents, we stake out guidelines with rope between each and every possible destination:

- The loo
- Each tent
- The kitchen/galley
- Common area/eating area
- General gathering point, for all-hands-on-deck emergencies, or your muster point.

One keeps a firm grip on the guideline with one hand so as to not get lost in the sometimes-driving snow and wind. With this system, one can be sure to arrive at some kind of safety, even if one has to navigate with one's eyes screwed shut against the weather. Truly, the winds are vicious here and one does not always see them coming, shearing through all manner of woolens and mitts and hats and balaclavas. You mustn't leave any bit of skin exposed for very long; it will quickly become frostbitten, and the pain one experiences as the skin returns to normal, if you can catch it in time, is like tiny fires everywhere just beneath your surface. It is a singular experience.

We are always a little on edge due to the weather. (For more depth, you may want to consult Wilson's diaries.) Here I shall only say that negative forty degrees Fahrenheit is truly pointless weather to measure. And that *The Resolute* was much warmer than our tents, even if it was sat in a bathtub of seawater. One must never, ever forget the constant threat of the air around us. One now performs the most basic biological function in a state of low fear that taking too long to urinate will mean one's bottom, fanny, or willy will literally freeze off. Gone are the chance encounters with your fellow crew; all meetings should be planned to take place in a tent or in a sheltered area so that one does not dillydally outdoors for a second longer than one needs to. Even fully covered up in our mittens and hats and double layers of woolens, we are at risk for exposure. Sunlight is a trickster; it can be bright and perky out but well below freezing, although there are rare days when we can take our meals outside, keeping our extremities bundled up. (Mama would say that it is critical for a body to get sunlight; over the weeks we don't get any, I often think of her, tilting her face luxuriously to the sky, humming a little under her breath.)

In order for there to be as little literal crossing of ropes as possible/tripping over one another, a campsite must be very well mapped out. This also means taking the long way 'round in a snowstorm/high wind, but that is still better than getting lost. We are forever balancing our outdoor time with the need to not get separated from camp and crewmates. This I learned from Keane, in a camp-planning lesson this morning with the Villain, which I will tell you about now, as everyone else seems to have fallen asleep.

(I don't know how they can sleep so easily. I hear every loose guideline, guywire, and fabric flap in the wind, and hope that others are notating the ones they hear in their tents, so we can go about tightening everything when this blasted wind is done. Every time the wind blows, the guy-wires stretch, which is no good for preserving our tents. I suppose the snoring may drown out the noise of the flapping. The crew has mostly good-naturedly ribbed me about my own snoring, which is apparently considerable.)

The Villain in your crew may bear a passing resemblance to the one on our crew, or he may be entirely different. Indeed, as Gwendoline reminded me constantly in the weeks before we came to an impasse in theory and therefore the end of our friendship, no one person is a monolith.

In our case, the Villain is one John Hotchkiss. He is well educated (Eton?) and speaks with the sure tones and the receding chin of the landed gentry. Of the crew members, he considers himself of the highest class and of the best taste and is, therefore, inextricably linked in my head with men of my father's ilk. He is more at home in a gentleman's club than on a ship, but his father's sponsorship of our expedition has bought him a place, whether for adventure or experience I have not bothered to find out.

He is handsome enough to look at, in the fashion of an immature boy, although one can easily see how his beauty will fade, and with it and every passing day in our company, his sense of propriety. At first, you may find he only taunts you with some kind of backhanded, unwanted compliment—"Why, Miss Clara, I would not have thought a lady of your *caliber* to be interested in such rough work as *this*," or, even better, "Step aside, Miss Clara, a woman of your *stature* must not trouble yourself with such roughneck men's work." This latter would be said with a glance at your bosom, which then slides inexorably down to your nethers, and a kind of jolting wink and nudge to whatever men may be nearby. After so long in close quarters, the insinuations will become more marked; the leering will likely become more obvious; the buffer you will have to build around yourself must grow in commensurate fashion.

Over time, you will understand that this Villain must have some acolytes nearby. (Villains do not operate in vacuums; bullies do not survive by themselves.) Months in close quarters is quite enough for you to know who those acolytes are. You must make every effort to keep sharp around these men—they will *almost* always be men, although we encountered more than a few women who would rather see us "in our place" forever, didn't we, in our ongoing fight for the vote?

One might be tempted to try to understand the motivation behind these attacks. Suffice it to say that the motivation will not consist of anything as simplistic and easily remedied as old wives' tales concerning the bad luck a woman brings a crew the minute she steps on board a ship; no, the motivation is something as broad and as silly as these men never having been shown what a woman can do when supported by her friends, or better yet, supported by a system of fairness and equity that will allow her to demonstrate her worth. Trying to disabuse a man so sure of his own position and his own moral and societal rectitude is a waste of time.

Witness my most recent interaction: yours truly had been tasked with helping **the Old Hand** to set up camp. He's grizzled, yes, but not old; experienced, but not overbearing with it; he has soft eyes and a consistently giving manner, even going so far as to offer the sole woman on crew his spare pipe so she can better fit in, and then going on to offer whatever else he might give to help her even after she turns down said proffered pipe.

This was the very first time one had set up a camp for so many people (well, yes, fine, for more than just me and Mama), and one was eager to get started with this new skill, for on the ice, one was realizing there is always more to learn.

(This will prove to be tiresome at times. But it will also prove to be a glorious, wonderful thing, as one will quickly realize that there is no end of wanting to prove oneself. Indeed, you will become increasingly frustrated, as it becomes terrifically apparent that you will never stop wanting to prove yourself to a group of men who seem doomed to believe the worst of womanhood. Worse, these men will prove to have very short memories and need to be shown time and again that you can hold your own.)

Probably the very best thing about the Old Hands—ours is called Keane, and he is from Ireland, county Donegal—is that they are surprised by nothing. Even their questions hold a kindly type of world-weariness: "Assumin' hoosh isn't a t'ing you thought'd appear on the dining table so much, eh?" And you can choose to either nod and answer firmly that you've had plenty of camping fare, thank you, sir, at which point the Old Hand will just hand you a tin cup full of the steaming stuff and leave you to eating. Or you might shake your head—even after months, one does not stop feeling abashed at how little one actually *does* know—at which point the Old Hand will grunt, shift his pipe from one side of his mouth to the other, and sit down to explain to you exactly what goes into it. And you'll listen, even if Cook has already explained it to you and you've even made it once or twice for the crew, because the Old Hand is kindly and always means well.

But when the Villain has been put on the same work detail as you and is on the hunt, by which I mean he is looking for someone to bully, the game gets changed up a little bit. Suddenly the Old Hand must become **the Protector**, and this is a role that always rankles you, no matter who is playing it.

It rankles because on this crew, it seems a Protector is always somewhere nearby, and you want to shout that you do not need a protector, that you can handle yourself just fine, but some part of you—the part that jumps at men walking behind you down a dark side street, the part that tenses every time you're the only woman in the room— knows that's not true.

(Higgins has been given control of the work rota again. I do not know if it is his innate mischievousness that encourages him to put me on crews with unsuitable teammates or his sheer doggedness to make a thing work, but I shall have to speak to him once again.)

"Assumin' ye've not set up a camp b'fore, Clara, beggin' yer pardon," said Keane, mashing request and apology into the same sentence, and I shook my head, but Hotchkiss was already there with an unpleasant rejoinder.

"You needn't be so tender with her, Keane," he said, sounding nasty already, "We all know she hasn't had any sort of real experience yet, isn't that right, Miss Clara?" (He calls me "Miss" to drive home the point of civility, when we all know he's truly incapable of it. By now near everyone is calling me just Clara. Even The Boss, who sometimes displays odd tics of formality.)

Keane glanced at me and raised his eyebrows; I shrugged, but inside I was seething. "I've had plenty of experience," I said, and I wanted to take it back, but Hotchkiss had already seized on the double entendre and decided to run with it.

Hotchkiss whacked Keane on the shoulder and barked the kind of jovial man laugh that's known worldwide, the one that's meant to encourage other men to join in on the target of their humor. Keane pretended he hadn't heard, but he shot me another dry look, which Hotchkiss ignored. When one is born into privilege, it comes with a kind of armor against even the most obvious of reproofs. "Get a load of that, Keane, our Miss Clara has a lot of *experience*, eh? Been around quite a bit, hasn't she? Wouldn't like to get in the way of all her *experience* now." Cue the waggling eyebrows.

He turned his attention back to me. I shivered involuntarily and cursed myself. "Look at that, we've sent a chill down her back. Wonder which lad she's thinking of. What of it, Keane? Which one of us do you think she has her eye on?"

Keane shoved a load of stakes and a hammer into Hotchkiss's arms. "Go and make yourself useful," he said, and then turned to me and kneeled in the snow. I kneeled next to him, and I pictured us forming a stalwart wall against Hotchkiss and his ilk. Behind us, I heard Hotchkiss sniggering, stomping away to stake out the perimeter of camp.

Keane glanced at me. "Yeh've had some experience with tents, now?" I nodded. Pitching a tent and setting up a smart campsite was one of the first things Mama taught me. "How big were your camps?"

I shook my head. "Not very," I said. "One tent, kitchen area with garbage site, loo area. Just two of us."

Keane nodded, economical. "'S a good start. Here's how yeh plan it for more." He used another stake to draw a rough diagram in the snow, mapping out how to create little avenues that our crew can follow from place to place, and how to plan it so there's good "traffic flow." His words, I promise! "You want about a third of a mile, a half-mile, between galley and loo, and you want to spread out the tents by about a fifth of a mile between them." That's what kind of knowledge fills up an Old Hand's head. Seeing the thing take shape, even in rough drawings, was like watching a mini city take place.

I am proud to say that I was able to contribute a little to the planning: I showed Keane my mother's trick for using our paces for measuring distances. It seems trite now that I am looking back on it, but in the end, it has made our tent-city planning that much more pleasurable—everything is at a good, even distance apart from one another, and we can feel certain we measured things for maximum efficiency.

I miss our *Resolute*, but one cannot deny there is so

much more fresh air out here on the floe. And more room to run away from Hotchkiss and his miasma of horrid insinuations.

Wind has finally stopped. I'll go check on the Dump Pile, see if we lost anything to the wind.

Cook is the person I have had the most experience with to date. You might suppose this is funny, a ha-ha laughing matter, although I can assure you I do not feel the same, even after months of enduring "dry British humor" about a woman's place on the ship. Indeed, some men look askance at me still, especially those who seem determined to hew to their calcified beliefs about what a woman is capable of and what she may endeavor to learn over her long life.

There are only two ways to remind these men that I can be their equal: One is to cross one's fingers and hope the questioning men are nearby in order to see one do the hardest tasks, providing that one is assigned to the hardest tasks. The other is to just knuckle down and get on with it, especially since The Boss has made it very clear that everyone has to pitch in at every task, whether it's mopping floors, giving one another haircuts, mending sails, or helping Cook in the galley. Keane tells me it has always been this way on The Boss's expeditions; he has some hang-up from being raised as the son of a merchant, as opposed to being born gentry. Even Milton-Jones, a commissioned officer in the Royal Marines, had to scrub at the floors. Even Hotchkiss, son of a viscount, had to spend time in the galley. From what I can gather, this is a most unusual arrangement, given that the whole of England is obsessed with social rank and landed gentry.

I would be remiss to not note that there were days when I felt I was being assigned to kitchen or haircutting duty more than the others. And it is especially galling when, after all these months, you have never been once invited to hunt for a seal, not even when they are shooting from an ice-locked ship that is utterly stable and hunting a clutch of seals that is dead asleep on a similar hunk of ice. Why once, they were sleeping so deeply that we could hear them snoring!

And yet, somehow, I was never invited to try my hand at this part of crew work. But one gets tired of asking, doesn't one, especially when there seems to be so much else to do.

I still remember the first time I killed an animal, on a hunt with Mama. I felt only the slightest qualm, as from a very early age, Mama had told me where the meat that appeared at the table came from. She only ever did this when Papa was out, which was frequently enough for me to understand her message, and for me to notice his regular absences.

We started with trapping. Rabbits were plentiful on both our Philadelphia land and on Mama's land, and I learned quickly to field dress both rabbits and birds. And each time we caught or shot one, Mama would say a few words, not exactly amounting to prayer, but expressing thanks all the same. I suppose it is for this reason that I do not find myself balking at the thought of shooting an animal. Why should I, when I happily grind its muscle and tendon between my teeth to fuel my own strength?

To hear the crew tell it though, you'd think I had never once considered where meat comes from.

So many times women have been called silly. Really, through sheer lack of consideration, it is the men who are far sillier.

Now that we are on the ice and looking to trek to Paulet in a few days, I am angling for a spot on one of the pulling crews, which will drag our three lifeboats on sledges. Eight or nine men will be hitched to each of our boats, which will be packed with as much kit as is humanly possible to pull. The dogs will pull the remainder of our kit on additional sledges.

I feel certain The Boss will assign me to one. Now that we are off the ship, there are so many more opportunities for me to contribute. Maybe now I'll stop being the go-to person for haircutting and sewing.

Maybe if I wish hard enough for it that will happen. More likely for me to stalk Higgins and see if I can't make that happen.

Later

Have spent all day stalking Higgins to no avail. He moves like a sprite, nimble, which I suppose would make sense for a photographer. On *The Resolute* he was everywhere—up on the mast, up on the riggings, hanging off the bow, always looking for flattering angles from which to photograph our ship.

I will try again tomorrow, but for now I will continue filling you in about Cook.

Our Cook is just as you would expect him. Portly, but firm. His head is shaved clean, for fear of dropping bits into our food, and so it is forever covered by two woolen caps so he may keep warm. His eyes are close-set and sharp, like little bright blue beads, his teeth on one side worn down by his ever-present pipe, although one would wonder why he does not worry about dropping tobacco and ashes into our foodstuffs.

Due to the pipe, he talks really only out of one side of his mouth; due to his busy hands, the pipe is held in place nearly entirely with his teeth. He is not given to many words, and for this I am grateful: it is preferable to work in the kitchen, I think, if one does not have to speak too much, especially when one is being asked to look after the biscuits; oh, ye gods, the biscuits.

But I secretly enjoy the biscuits. Biscuits are a thing I can make with my eyes closed. Mama and I made them all the time when we were camping. Salt, flour, a little bit of water, cooked on a stick over an open fire. Besides, it's often warmer in the galley, even with this new one on the ice: Givens has rigged up some kind of ingenious little stove with a chimney on it to replace Cook's normal range, which is at the bottom of the Weddell by now. The smoke funnels up and over the sailcloth walls we've erected around this makeshift galley. Smokewise, it is a marked improvement over what we had on *The Resolute*. Everything-else-wise, not so.

I miss the ease with which one could move around, even if I found it cramped when I first stepped foot on *The Resolute*. And I think we had all gained a kind of operating competence in *The Resolute's* galley, even Per, who is a ninety-pound weakling and who seems to be all arms and legs with none of them in tandem with the other three limbs. Moving to this new galley is starting all over again.

Still 25 November

I forgot to note: this year, President Wilson has designated tomorrow as our official American Thanksgiving, and this is the day we were to have been celebrating, not that I can tell anyone this. Sentiment toward the United States was very bad when we left. "Cowards" and "heartless" were character traits prescribed to Americans, since the US had refused to commit to the war one way or another.

I hardly know what I would have done if we had been told to turn around and contribute to the war effort, even though I now recognize our being allowed to gallivant around the Antarctic while the rest of our world is at war (the United States excepting, of course) to be yet another gigantic stake in territory driven in by privilege. Oh! Everyone has gone off to war, but this merry crew of men will flex the bounds—with the express permission of yet another powerful male!—of "contribution" and go off to mess around in icy waters, even getting marooned on the ice.

There hasn't been much talk of the war at all, although it seemed destined to be one that would change all our lives. No, we are too taken by our own minute struggles, and, since near everyone's memories are of life just before war, the men moan daily about things that seem inconsequential.

Almost everyone's memories. *My* recollection of England before we left is of marching on Parliament, of asking the question, over and over again, in meetings and campaigns of government hopefuls, "Will the government give women the vote?" We stood up and asked until we got thrown out. And then another of us would stand up and ask, until she got thrown out.

Repeat.

And therein lies the fine-lined difference. Everyone here believes in *a* mission, to the point of bodily harm. But our aims are quite different, coming as we are from such different origin points.

We have been playing a little football on the ice. Although we played a few times down the length of *The Resolute*, there is a certain unbridled joy in booting the ball as far as you can, without fear of sending it over the side of the ship into the water. No one has yet begrudged me a place on the football pitch, but this may just be because I have proven myself exceptionally good at it, and anyway, there are very few stakes involved in a game of football.

The men seem surprised by my skills, as if any mere fool could not hitch up her skirts and boot a ball around. On the ship we just set up some crates at either end of her for goals. Here, we rig one from sail cloth or any old items we can find to mark the lines.

Keane informed me, however, that this is not the best way to play the game. "Er. Clara, y'need to pass the ball to your mates, see? It makes for better play."

I shook my head. "But if I see a through line, a clear way forward, shouldn't I try to win?"

Keane pulled on his pipe for a minute. I waited. One does not rush Keane along; one waits. "Clara, truly I wonder how you ever got along before this, wantin' as you do to do everything yerself, like."

Well, I was not expecting that. "Isn't the point to win? And if I can, shouldn't I?"

Keane shook his head, and McNish, one of the able seamen and a great fan of football at home in England, laughed outright. "T'point is for your whole *team* to win, lassie! Not just one person, hey?" he said. And then, before I could agree or disagree or even nod or shake my head, McNish barreled on, sounding as passionate as I'd ever heard him before. "The point is *play*!" he bellowed, and then, as if outraged, smacked his fist into his palm, grinning, nevertheless.

"I . . . I *suppose*," I said.

McNish grumbled. "And anyway, you can't always be the one to score. Sometimes you are too far down the field and you need someone to help you along the way."

Keane took the pipe out of his mouth. "Just pass the ball, Clara. It's the right thing to do."

I nodded. Pass the ball.

This seems a good time to introduce you to **pastimes of Antarctica**.

Here I must tell you that there are a great many more opportunities for enrichment than one might suspect.

Firstly, the aforementioned football. When the air is warm and the sun is out, the top layer gets slushy on our pitch. We have to move it from time to time just to ensure that we do not tramp too much in one area. Wilson says the ice is plenty thick here, but one never knows, especially with the killer whales about. They can smell very well, and they can sense when there is prey on the ice above them, and we do not want them thinking we are prey.

We saw a pair one time from the ship. They had cornered a seal on a small ice floe, and they were rocking the ice back and forth, back and forth between them, nudging it with their evil snouts and making wavelets upon which the floe would tip and spin. The poor seal hung on with its claws for literal life, and when it couldn't, it would slide helplessly to one end of the ice before one of the pair would tip it again, and the seal would slip toward the other side. It was clear they were toying with it, the brutes.

After they had terrorized the seal to their liking, they just left. The poor thing lay panting on the ice, its glossy sides heaving with terror, its nostril flaps opening and shutting as it tried to decide whether it should risk a swim to another larger floe or if it should stay where it was. It lifted its head once in a while, looking about for the killers, but they didn't come back, and eventually it floated out of our sight.

"Poor pup," said Riggs, one of the sailors. I jumped, so taken had I been with watching the seal. He broke the shotgun he'd been carrying over his arm.

"What . . . what is *that* for?" The Boss wasn't keen on loaded firearms while the ship was moving.

"I was going to shoot the poor thing, weren't I, if that turrible game'd gone on much longer. It'd have been better." He nodded and left.

We do hear the killers sometimes, breaching and huffing in the water off our camp. It's hard to tell how far away they are, as the Antarctic air is so still and silent when it's not moving at blizzard speeds, and our floe is large enough in at least one direction that we know there must be seal holes. No gun could fire a large-enough caliber bullet to kill one of these whales with one shot, and their jaws and those wicked conical teeth are too strong—whoever came into reach of one would surely be done for. I fear seeing those great ugly heads pop up through one of the weak spots on the ice, so we stay far clear of even *making* any weak spots.

Can you imagine a more ignominious way to die? "Well, old boys, we were just playing at a game of football, when suddenly a great big mouth appeared and dear Clara was gone from the pitch."

No. No thank you.

Another regular pastime is exercising the dogs. We do it every day if the weather allows, because otherwise they get ornery and bite people, and a bite here could mean losing a hand entirely. I took them for a run with Givens today. It is a stretch to exercise all thirty at a time, so we hitch ten of them to some traces and go as far as we can. We can describe decent enough loops around camp, and our lighter exercise sledges, not weighed down with all our kit, allow us to surmount the smaller of the ice ridges and heaves we encounter. But there are huge ones that we do not bother with, especially in the direction of our route to Paulet. I am sure The Boss has seen these and has a way around them, so I will keep my counsel for now.

Of all the dogs, I like Crabbers the best, for his agreeable demeanor and gentle face. Lucy is a true mother—she takes care of every pup whelped, even those not her own, and it is not unusual to find her carrying away someone else's puppies in her mouth. Marcus is a great fat bore, but he is good company, and Figgy, whom I named after Figgy out of sheer frustration that Figgy-the-person still cannot truly tell any dogs apart, is just now beginning to lose his puppy fur and grow some of that rough sledging-dog fur. He is always shivering, so I am glad for him.

Other pastimes: We published a ship's magazine each fortnight we were on board; that was a diversion. Every other Friday night we had a variety show, wherein the men got gussied up in whatever they could dress up in, mostly dressing up as women and singing in falsetto, which they find absolutely hilarious.

Funny, the call for me to dress up as a man and sing a tune in my best baritone is considerably less popular.

Every Saturday night we have "Wives and Sweethearts," which is where our captain, Phillips, simply says, "To our wives and sweethearts!" The men formerly answered back, "May they never meet," which everyone seemed to think was uproarious even whilst glancing surreptitiously at me. I shrugged and ignored it, but one night it was announced that instead of answering back, everyone would go around and say a little something about someone they loved whom they'd left at home.

Predictably, Hotchkiss scoffed, but when it came his turn, he gave a moving tribute to his mother. I laughed into my sleeve. I don't see this tradition continuing, however. It is one thing to be toasting whilst you are in a nice, warm dining room; quite another when you are sat outside in near-freezing weather.

Later, as *The Resolute* became mired in ice, we added another pastime, which Higgins called "sallying," whereby we would run from portside to starboard en masse, trying to rock her out of the ice's grip. It was funny, until it wasn't anymore.

Our printing press is at the bottom of the Weddell with

The Resolute and Cook's stove and Higgins's glass slides now, so we shall have to think of something else if we do bring back our magazine.

Very tired all of a sudden. Think will have a nap.

26 November

The rota has come out for the march to Paulet. I am not on
a pulling crew. I am, with Per and Blackburn, one of three
who runs along behind each sledge, one for each of our
lifeboats, pushing and guiding it so it does not run off the
track (what track? Everywhere there is snow and ice) and
picking up loose items as they fall and cramming them back
onto the sled.

Well, I marched right over and confronted Higgins
about the rota. He looked truly surprised. "Don't you
worry, Clara. Everyone will have their turn."

I just stared at him. "Are you sure?"

He nodded. "It's a long march, trust me."

"*Sure* sure?" I asked again.

He snorted and rolled his eyes the tiniest bit, clicked
his tongue. "Clara, no one has time for this. The rota is the
rota; why are you angling for this hard work, anyway?"

Well, I was surprised. "Do you think I can't do it?"

He answered a little too quickly for my tastes. "Of
course I think you can do it! Why would you think I think
you can't do it?" Higgins's eyes went a little shifty then, but

I still couldn't bring myself to ask the questions that needed to be asked: Have I proved myself worthy of this crew? Do you trust me?

In the end, I just stalked away, trying to make a dignified exit. Higgins cannot understand; he clearly has never been doubted in his life. I know for sure he's not had to weather months of tiny reminders of one's low status in society.

I am fully disgusted; what a sad, useless job. Part of me wanted to chase after Higgins again, tell him of the many times I had walked up hill and down dale with Mama, hauling the fruits of our last hunt, or the times we had ridden our horses till they were wet with sweat and she and I laughing with exhilaration, nearly falling off our mounts for the tiredness in our legs and backs. And, I wanted to ask him, if I could summon such determination for sheer joy's sake, did no one think I would muster the same energy when the stakes were so much *higher*?

Can one possibly find such innervation, such emotion, trudging behind a dragging boat, when one would rather be leading it?

I think not.

But no. Here I am, doomed to pick up after a boat on sledges.

Our pile keeps on growing, by the way. People keep finding items they feel they can do without. Empty picture frames seem to be a popular item; it seems the men are taking out the photographs of their sweethearts and wives and children and tucking them into their diaries for safekeeping rather than lugging around the frames.

What an odd pretension. Wouldn't you have thought of such a thing before you packed yourself onto a ship for God knows how long?

Big wind during "nighttime" hours. Temperature lower by a couple of degrees this morning; we are readying the life-boats and sleds to be pulled to Paulet Island. We have three lifeboats: the *James Connick*, the *Dudley Stanwick*, and the *William Jenkins*, all of which are named after our beneficiaries, who all, by the way, look oddly alike, sporting similar beards, like every financier in Great Britain.

Milton-Jones is dashing around like a cockerel in heat, barking at us to hurry it along with striking camp and storing our tents. The dogs are sitting in front of their kennels, wondering why they're not getting their morning exercise. They don't know that they'll be helping to pull all our kit soon—enough exercise for them all.

This is a good time to introduce you to the concept of the **expedition dogs.** If you are planning an expedition, you will definitely want dogs along. If you hear anyone talking of horses, immediately suggest something else, *anything* else: The horses' skinny little legs posthole in the snow, and they panic very easily. You do not want to deal with a panicked horse. Several expeditions in the past have used horses and failed miserably; one wonders why the men who were planning these expeditions did not think to ask a seasoned horsewoman whether or not bringing prey animals to the ends of the earth was a good idea.

Plus! Horses love to be warm.

(Oddly enough, horses are probably among the top ten things the crew complains about missing, along with their sweethearts, cream biscuits, and proper walls. It's a strange, motley assortment of nostalgia.)

Here are the things dogs are good for:

1. Companionship. Many is the time when a girl is lonely and wants for someone to talk to who is not a man. So one saunters down to the kennels and picks a wide, furry face to commiserate with. Their expressions may be inscrutable, stoic even, but they are listening. Their great ears pivot to and fro if you talk to them. Crabbers's head swivels this way and that with each new word he learns; Lorelai likes to bury her wet nose into your neck, in the manner of one longing for affection. It is a most joyous sensation when one of the pups puts his nose very close to your ear and whuff-whuff-whuffles gently into it. It does not tickle so much as invigorate, and if you think this is odd, then you have never had it done to you.

2. Warmth. All our dogs have great coats of fur. Take off your mittens without fear of frostbite or discomfort,

plunge your hands into their ruffs, enjoy the feeling of heat from another body trickling into your extremities. The dogs do not mind, I promise. When one has been crying out of sheer loneliness and rage, nothing beats the ruff of a patient, big dog, nor the shorter, fluffy hair of a young one.

When you are selecting dogs for your expedition, do not pick the dogs with short bristly hair; they will die of exposure. When a new puppy is born, you must be sure to bank lots of hay around them, or maybe if you are an Old Hand you will take three or four puppies and carry them around in your clothing, between your skin and your woolens. You will say it is because they need to be kept warm, but we know better, because we catch you talking into your shirt collar when you think no one is watching.

3. Exercise. Sled dogs need exercise, so you will get exercise as well. Trying to control a team of sled dogs is much harder than you think it is. Your entire back and stomach will become strong from keeping yourself upright on your sled as the dogs jerk and herk all over the track; your arms will gain odd little ropy muscles right down to your wrists from fine-tuning the guide ropes and harnesses.

Your mind, as well, will be exercised: You will plumb depths of frustration as you try to corral the most unruly, roly-poly puppies into some semblance of a respectable pulling team. You will learn new language around sledding—Gee! Haw! For left! And right!—and you will swear an unladylike amount. All of this is so you can reap another benefit of dogs on board, which is . . .

4. Efficiency. The dogs will make short work of everything. You will be forever marveling at how strong they are and how quickly they can pull a thing; at how fast they dig a hole; at how speedily they eat their meals and then evacuate their bowels; how little time it takes for them to get into a yelling, nipping match with another dog; how expediently they stop their yelling; how expeditiously they can make a person feel loved.

5. Work. Yes, you will work around the dogs. They make a god-awful mess, their poop is forever having to be cleaned up, their hair gets matted and must be brushed regularly. . . . At times one is like a lady-in-waiting to Delilah, Ramses, Ozymandias (do not let the artist of the crew name your dogs, if you can help it. Then again, the dogs that Cook has named are Lumpy, Bacon Butty, Nuts, and Porkchop, so you will have to work with your preference, I suppose). Hay in kennels needs to be fluffed and aired, or you may find yourself entertaining ideas of sewing cushy, stuffed hay beds for them out of spare canvas. Of course, this is when there was canvas

to be spared, before the extras went down with the ship, and in any case, you remind yourself you'd do well to stay away from any self-imposed sewing tasks, since some of the crew already believes this is all a woman is good for, anyway.

28 November

Everything's packed up. The cold has held and The Boss says we should actually try to leave tonight, to make sure we take advantage of the slightly colder temperatures. I don't much understand how that works: there shouldn't be too much difference, since the sun is still out for most of the twenty-four hours. I shall ask Wilson a little later.

Anyway, Keane himself says it makes a difference, and of anyone on this ship, he's been on the most Antarctic expeditions, so I can at least trust his judgment.

I only *hope* I will be able to fulfill my life's métier of picking up things that have fallen off of lifeboats—however shall I manage, woe is me, etcetera.

Later

I did end up scooping a few things up when they inevitably fell off, this particular boat having been packed at least in part by Chutney and Figgy. It was a misery, although staying in the rear of the boat made it so that I was out of the wind, and my fingers, which I could keep tucked into my fists within my mittens as we trudged, do feel a little bit relieved for it.

It hardly matters, actually. After all of today's labor, the ice ridges have proven to be close to—but not *quite*, loaning to a sensation of some accomplishment—insurmountable. The sleds and lifeboats both are usually too long to sit in the infrequent valleys between the big ice ridges. These ridges are severe and steep enough that getting the cargo over them is a lot like pushing something against a wall. Between the dogs and the men and the few of us who are assigned to guiding, we made some very small paces forward, three quarters of a mile in total, Billings said.

There were a few times in between that we'd be lucky and press forward fifty feet or so, but all those stretches served to do was raise our hopes. Humans are funny this way—the tiniest bit of progress and we think we can conquer the world.

The Boss is making our three quarters of a mile out to be some kind of victory, but we can literally *see* Dump Camp from here. Our pile looks *huge*; why are these sledges and boats so damned heavy still? The ridges around our caravan are too big for us to make any kind of decent camp, so we are retreating to Dump Camp for sleep, leaving two of us here for overnight watch.

Still Later

Guess who drew first watch at Three-Quarters-of-a-Mile-from-Dump-Camp Camp? I'm sat on the *Dudley Stanwick*, atop our stuff, and the sharp view of Dump Camp is even more mortifying from here. I can actually pick out who's who by the way they're walking between Cook's *other* makeshift galley (Givens's invention is somewhere beneath my arse) and the tents. Milton-Jones is my watchmate tonight. The man can *talk*. So far I have heard about his wife, his father, his wee daughter, his garden at home in Henley-on-Thames . . . fortunately, our watches take place in tight pacing circles around the watch area, so we can keep from freezing. The walking helps to stave off the ennui some.

It is odd I have never drawn lots to be on watch with Milton-Jones before, or maybe I have just simply blocked it out of my head; being on watch with Milton-Jones is like Milton-Jones being on watch with himself.

Finally I could not take it anymore. "Milt," I said, interrupting him mid-philosophical nostalgic wax, "what do you think of our walk to Paulet?"

There was a pause. "Well, I can't rightly say, Clara," he said finally. He looked somehow both deeply uncomfortable and supercilious then, and I wanted to smack him. I could virtually see the stiff upper lip the Brits are so famous for appearing on him, even below his impressive mustache, which he spends some minutes each morning smoothing and grooming. Sometimes I wonder if I'll ever get a straight answer from my crewmates—it seems they lock down the minute they sense any kind of discomfort, or they hide in a sloppy joke or lazy sarcasm.

"Come on, Milt," I said finally, when it became apparent he was aiming to stop his commentary there. "You can tell me. There's literally no one around for . . . three quarters of a mile." I grinned. "Let's just discuss for a moment, crew to crew. I promise I won't turn you in for doubting The Boss."

Milton-Jones took his glasses off and swiped at them with his sweater sleeve. This is a technique I have seen him use before when he doesn't want to answer a question or isn't ready with a verbal riposte. "It's not *quite* that," he said, finally. "It's just that—well, you're a *girl*, excuse me, a *woman*, and I'm not sure you're meant to be troubled with all of that."

If I haven't mentioned it before, Antarctic nights are *cold*, even the ones where it's light out all the time. Our fingers are very often on the verge of freezing; my eyelashes, I'm sure, must be much shorter by now for having nearly frozen off most of the time. So let me tell you, it is really something when I say that my internal temperature dropped by what felt like a few degrees when I heard him say that.

I tried to process what he was saying and got no further than goggling at him. Finally, I said, as evenly as I could, "Milt, that's just not *on*. I mean, I mean . . ." There was an uncomfortable pause while I tried to figure out how to express my discomfiture and disappointment without crying, which I really did feel like doing right at that very moment. I flapped my arms. "How can you say that?

The Boss was very clear when I signed on that I'd have equal part in everything. And don't you remember what he said to us the very first day we all came on board? He said I was to be treated just the same way you'd treat everyone else."

"Of course I remember," Milton-Jones said, sounding aggrieved, like how dare I question his memory. "I'm not entirely sure he can be taken at his word, however."

My mouth dropped open. Milton-Jones, *actually* second-guessing The Boss—this *would* be close to mutinous behavior, if it ever came to light.

He was still talking. "You can't deny that he looks after you."

"I . . . surely he looks after all of us equally!"

"Well . . . maybe. I'll not argue that point. But I think you'll be deluding yourself, Clara, if you don't admit that people see you differently than they see the rest of the crew."

I set my lips. "*Men* see me differently from the rest of the *men*," I said, trying for even and coming out wavering with anger. "Let's be clear about what's what."

Milton-Jones nodded. "I'll grant you this point," he said. I waited, but he didn't seem to have anything else to say, and I told him I needed a minute to think, which is why I'm sat on top of the boat, writing, freezing my fingers off while he paces below.

Just another hour or so until our watch is over and someone comes to relieve us, and then it'll be time for a nap, then breakfast, and back to hauling again. Or tucking, on my part.

I'm finding it very hard to countenance that even after all we have encountered this expedition, the men do not want to "overburden" the woman.

Most infuriating? They put *Amos* in a set of traces. Despite the fact that he is very good at carpentering, he is the eldest of our crew, and, apart from Per, who is barely sixteen, the slightest.

Also, for a carpenter, Amos is oddly clumsy, although I suppose for pulling things this doesn't really matter. But when one is bitterly disappointed one looks for all the shortcomings, doesn't one???

I suppose I should thank Milton-Jones for being so straightforward. I should, but I can't just yet. I am too annoyed, to think that my hard work thus far has gained me no status and no further consideration beyond my gender.

I can do anything, I want to tell them. At least let me try. If they only knew of the things I had been a part of in London! If only they knew just who on this crew had cut the telegraph wires, who on this crew had stood in front of Parliament to ask for the vote.

Over the five short months I had with the WSPU, the marks on my body became something of a map of our experience. Ink stains on my fingertips from helping to fold and deliver copies of our newspaper; callouses from typing; bruises and cuts from being shoved and heckled whilst standing our ground at speaker campaigns and from standing guard near our sisters on their soapboxes, as they worked so hard to deliver greater understanding to people who would oppose our suffrage.

The external marks have faded now, but my legs are strong from marching and my voice is strong from demanding attention from politicians who will not listen.

Why, even though the WSPU had largely ceased its activities by the time we left for Antarctica, the last set of bruises, from being pushed out of a campaign meeting, had only just healed entirely. The fading cut over my eye was not from bumping sloppily into a doorframe as I lugged my kit down the stairs of my bedsit, as I had excused it to much of the crew, but rather from trying to dodge the swinging baton of a raging policeman as he reached past me to evict Gwendoline from yet another meeting.

Every suffragette I know has these marks on her body.

Curses! Got my monthlies. Was back at camp after watch, though, when it happened, so I went to see MacTavish to see if he could set aside any more cotton batting for my supplies. And I wanted to talk to him about what I'd learned from Milton-Jones.

"Well," he said, hands busily working at picking through the cotton to make sure there weren't any poky bits, "can you blame them? They know nothing of who you are. You've not bothered to really talk to them of yourself much."

"Not necessary," I said automatically. "I'm here to work, to see the Antarctic, not to make friends." And, I added to myself, which one of the men would be impressed at any of what I'd done with the WSPU? Which would admire the smashing of windows, the shouting down of politicians? Which would have admired Emily Davison, our sister, who died what ended up being a most ignominious death while trying to hang a Votes for Women banner on King George's horse? I'd kept my mouth shut so far about my involvement in what some called a terrorist organization, and I wasn't about to expose myself to an unfair court of public opinion just yet.

MacTavish, unaware of my private thoughts, quirked a smile at me. "Well, that's not entirely true, is it, Clara?" I didn't answer, but he answered for me. "You're also here to prove yourself, aren't you?"

Sometimes, when a thing is too close to the truth, saying it out loud makes it grow teeth. I couldn't answer for fear of saying too much.

MacTavish sighed. "Well, there you have it," he said. "The men don't know you're here to prove yourself— although to *whom*, I'm not sure even you're clear. And you've not made it easy for them to approach you. You're like one of those cactus plants. Prickly. Hard to approach."

I couldn't stop myself from yelping, even as I was thinking about whether or not I knew what I was doing in Antarctica. Surely I didn't need to be here to prove anything to *myself*. It was the rest of the crew that needed just a little *push* to see what we women can do. "That's bullshit, Doc, and you know it. I pull my weight around here." Even as I was talking, the creeping fingers of confusion were crawling up my neck. I'd told myself I was there to find equity, but what if it was impossible to find *especially* here?

"That's completely not what I said, at all." MacTavish shook his head. "Setting that aside for the moment, Clara— on the ship was one thing, one skill set. Out here, on the ice, it's another.

"They've not had the chance to see any of what you might offer. Can you shoot? Can you fish? Can you haul gear? *I* know the answer to these questions," he said hurriedly, "you've told me what you and your mother got up to in those Pennsylvania woods." He paused for a second, thinking. I've always liked this about the Doc. He is so considered, not like a lot of men I know.

"*I* know," he said again. "But they've not yet seen it."

To be fair, The Boss hadn't asked for any proof, and I am beginning to get the feeling that maybe even he, the most egalitarian of men, has only ever seen me for what he thinks a woman can do. That maybe he has not allowed for the probability that I can do all these things, equally well, and maybe even better, than a man can.

MacTavish continued on. A man *will* fill any dead space, if only just to hear themselves talk out loud. "It's almost like, on the ship, there was a limited amount of skill set that everyone needed. Everyone was *inside*, which is traditionally the woman's domain anyway." He held up a finger, probably because he saw I was about to let loose. "So everyone was about on the same pitch, do you see? And maybe you even had an advantage of sorts, because you were already better at those things than men are. We are not trained to do these things, like cleaning and tidying up and mending and cooking and cutting each other's hair."

I waited. It felt like something was coming, still. "Perhaps everyone already expected that things out here, away from the ship, would be . . . well, different."

I worked the needle through the muslin on my sanitary napkins while I thought. "What . . . like *how*? They thought they were going to have *carry* me or something like it? They were going to have to feed me? I'd stop being useful and they'd have to find me a fainting couch and smelling salts?"

"Not quite." MacTavish started to bundle everything into a canvas sack, stitching a couple extra needles into it. "I think that's probably enough for the week, wouldn't you say? There, just in case you need to sew up some more." He worked at the sack for another minute longer. "Aye," he said finally, "I think that might be it. They aren't sure they can depend on you."

"Hmph," I said. "It's more accurate to say they think they know my role on this ship better than I know it. Better than even The Boss knows it! The absolute cheek of them!" I stuffed my supplies into the chest pocket of my coveralls. It made a huge lump, like a third breast, or like a fat chicken ready for slaughter, but I didn't care. "Which is just what I should expect, isn't it?" I couldn't keep the bitterness from my voice, and I turned to go.

MacTavish gripped my shoulder, and I had to work hard to keep from wheeling on him. "Clara, don't be too angry," he said. "People's natures are what they are, and their beliefs are sometimes so strong that they don't believe a thing after they've seen it with their own eyes, even." He patted my back. "For what it's worth, *I* don't worry about you. I know a woman's strength. You don't witness a woman giving childbirth without having some understanding of what a woman is." He gestured at my parcel. "Even your monthlies are impressive. They are inconvenient and painful, and yet, you soldier on, month after month, year after year."

I stared. "Doc, I suggest a little less patronizing would be useful right about now."

MacTavish's face collapsed, and I felt like I had kicked a puppy. "I was just trying to . . . ," he said, and trailed off.

"Oh, Doc. Don't. Just don't." I stomped off to our tent. At least Per is off on watch for the next few hours. Blackburn is probably off doing something *manly* with the rest of the crew, so I can have the next hour or two to stew.

I was going to write to you here a section about getting to know your ship's **surgeon**, or **doctor**, but really all you need to know is that you will inevitably end up telling them all manner of things you did not expect to tell a rowdy Scotsman of farming origin.

Sometimes they disappoint. Other times they are just trying to be the best they can be. This will drive you to infuriated distraction because it still ends up in disappointment, and then you wonder if you might be in some danger, having imparted all manner of confidence to a mere man.

Later

Back at it again. Push, shove, guide the sleds and boats. Tuck in loose objects. Managed another half mile, much worse than yesterday. Dump Camp is a little farther off in the distance, but we are still not even two miles from it after literal days of pulling. I wonder when The Boss will call it. Surely he must.

I remember once in August when Mama and I were out for a week camping in the Delaware Water Gap. I was eight, and we kept on hunting for firewood, but it had been a wet week, and so we eventually just had to give up and retreat home. Mama said, ever so cheerful, "Well, let's just try for another week, shall we? Next time we will remember to pack our own kindling, at least, or warmer clothing, so we can stay out all night even without a fire."

The point is, I think it's time to pack it in and wait out the next few months.

Later

The Boss has called it. Good man. Hotchkiss is grousing about it; he wants to be the man who keeps on pushing ahead in any kind of situation, no matter the hardship, no matter the lack of efficacy. When we had our individual bunks on the ship, at least one could pull the curtain across it and maybe shut him out a little bit, but here on the ice, where everything is wide open and all the voices carry, we cannot help but hear him complain.

He reminds me of the boy who came calling for my hand in marriage. His parents were with him, and it was one of the rare times when Papa was at home. Of course, this boy and his parents wouldn't deign to speak to just Mama. He was a mewling, pimply sort, barely out of the carriage in terms of the way he acted and the things he'd experienced. I found very little to speak to him about, although to hear our fathers speak of it, that hardly mattered.

Mama put her foot down. I don't know what she said to Papa, but it must have had some effect, for I never saw the boy again.

I will never understand this about Mama—how it is that she did not want to join up with the fight for women's rights? Why, if she had her own votes, she might not have had to submit to Papa as she did until he died. If she had some say in how things were going, she might have had a happier life. And maybe we would not have had to spend time fighting off the advances of a clearly unsuitable match. When I pressed her to come along to London, she only said that she was happy to leave the fight to younger women, and that she'd be happy if we won the vote. She said she only wanted to lead a calm, happy life.

How perverse! Can one lead a "calm, happy life" seeing every day the vastly improved rights men have over women?

Cook is ringing the bell for chow. He popped by earlier to see if I could help with dinner, but I had mending to do and could not spare the time. Chutney has gone in my stead, which is just as well—his stew is always well seasoned, whereas mine seems to leave everyone moaning for pepper.

30 November

I tried again to teach the boys to mend. Their reluctance was illuminating.

When I asked them, they glanced at each other, conspiring already. Blackburn spoke for them both. "Yes, Miss Clara, only a moment before . . . this task we have."

"Mm. And what task would that be?"

"A thing. Something Wilson has suggested for us." I looked askance at this; Wilson likes to perform his experiments alone, and last I saw him he was neck-deep in melted snow samples, looking for signs of life

"Well, this will only take a minute." I pulled out needle and thread and a scrap of spare muslin, and the boys practically jumped.

"Oh, no, Miss, not the mending again."

"Per, it will go so much faster for you if you just learned to do it yourself instead of leaning on others to do it for you."

"Our mam always done it for me."

"Your mum's not here now."

"Yeah, all right! But you are, and you'll be me mam, woan'cha?"

Per fluttered his eyelids, and I cringed. I'm afraid I started shouting. "No! Don't be ridiculous! I'm not here to be anyone's mum. Now you'll take five minutes and learn to do these idiot stitches, or . . . or . . ."

"Or what?" Blackburn was at his best when he was defending Per. "Or what, Miss?" He squared his skinny shoulders and glared at me.

I completely caved. "Would you talk to your mother this way?" I put on the voice I'd heard my governess drop on me a few times.

They caved, too.

Their stitches are horrible—good enough for sails, not nearly fine enough for socks. Well, we'll just have to keep on at it. I pointed out that Mahoney does all of *his* mending, and Per shouted, "Yeh, but he's private-like! Don't want anyone else touchin' 'is socks or nuffink!" I pointed out that Milton-Jones also does his own mending, and they said, "Yeh, but he's like an old lady!"

Finally, I decided I'd had enough. "I'm not doing it anymore," I said. "Either learn or go around with holes in your socks and be seen as unwilling to help where it's needed. And while you're at it, you can cut each other's hair from now on."

They positively gaped. I thought it was because they'd never heard me be firm before—at least, not about stuff like this—until Per said, "But then—what'll ye do with all your free time?"

"What do you mean, what'll I *do*?" I said instead. "Do you ask Givens or Higgins or Mahoney what they're doing all day?"

"Well, ain't it your *job* to mend and cook and cut hair?" This from Blackburn.

"You know," I said, "you should know better. From the beginning The Boss has said everyone has to chip in."

Long pause. "But you're a *woman*." This from Per now, who looked truly befuddled.

I closed my eyes and took a deep breath. "I *know* that. Thank you for reminding me. I'd clean forgotten." I curtsied.

Per sniggered, and Blackburn cast him a glare and doubled down.

"So what *else* are you going to do, then?" He did not seem to be able to let it go. "Can ye even build things?"

I thought back to the many fires and shelters I had built over our camping trips. "I can."

"Can you hunt?"

"Small game and large."

"Hunh." Per was looking back and forth between us now, and I didn't much like what that meant. It looked like he felt like he was going to have to choose an allegiance, and that my answer to whatever Blackburn said next was going to determine that loyalty.

"Can ye *fish*?" This last sounded like a Hail Mary.

I stifled a laugh. "Can I *fish*." I thought of all the hours Mama and I had spent tracking stags. Fishing is the easiest of all the sports, requiring only patience and a sensitive touch.

"Well, yeah. Can ye?" This time, it was Per asking.

"I can fish," I said, patiently, trying not to shout. "Let me tell you about the way I grew up."

In a way, I think I grew up like many young ladies in my age group: I rarely saw Papa and spent most of my time with Mama. But most young ladies' mamas, I gradually realized, were not the same as mine.

My mama was an expert horsewoman and bicyclist. She was nearly always in divided skirts, having not much use for the many layers of petticoats and corsets that were all the rage then. I was but three when she took me on my first camping trip; I remember, just barely, first experiencing the rush of the river, the smell of the air, the light of the campfire. Later, we'd go off for weeks at a time on camping trips, traipsing about the scraggly property that was a part of Mama's dowry. Papa never came on these trips, and by the time I was old enough to notice, I was also old enough to not care.

But Mama, despite all her skills and fieldcraft, did care, and it was finally obvious to me the day we came back from a swooping, rollicking gallop in the hills around our home, ten years ago. I had my horse tight to Mama's horse's flank when I heard her bark, "No!" and she pulled up Buttercup's reins sharply, causing the mare to rear at the unexpected pain in her mouth. Mama hung on, though I nearly knocked into

Buttercup, and I heard her muttering under her breath even over Buttercup's annoyed snort. "No, no, no—it's too soon."

In our forecourt stood Papa's motorcar and three or four more beside it. Papa never came home alone.

"Mama?"

Mama's face had constricted; her brows beetled down. Her lips, red from the wind and so recently parted in a broad, joyful grin, went thin. I suddenly wondered, had Mama always reacted this way at the prospect of a visit from Papa?

"Your father is back," she said, needlessly, and nudged Buttercup into a fitful canter.

Later, I pieced together that it had been six months or so since we'd seen him, but it's a funny thing about childhood—from one month to the next, your awareness can grow by leaps and bounds, so that something you did not notice at all last month can suddenly take over all of your consciousness—say, for instance, the day you realized the weather around you may not be the weather at all in Spain, or even the weather in Florida, which is much closer but might as well be a world away for its different precipitation and habits and even animals. We'd never seen an alligator in the wild in Philadelphia or the Gap or even in Fairmount Park, and Mama said there are often alligators in the streets of West Palm Beach, just out for an evening or morning constitution.

But then, if you are a child, for the next months you

cannot stop thinking about how everything is different somewhere else, and how your world is very, very small.

It was like that when I realized that Mama was not happy to see Papa, and maybe had never been happy to see Papa whenever he was back from wherever he'd been. I could not stop thinking about this once I realized it.

That evening, I paid close attention to her. I noticed, for instance, that she came downstairs not in her favorite divided skirt, but in layers of skirts and petticoats and a shirtwaist with a painfully small waist. I noticed that she wore a shoe with a taller-than-usual heel, rather than her normal comfortable slipper, and I noticed her hair was pinned up in extravagant whorls. I noticed she did not smile like her usual self, but rather that she quirked only the corners of her lips upwards, even when Papa greeted her.

This was not the mama-and-papa relationship I had read about in storybooks.

I also noticed that she tried to send me to bed as quickly as possible, saying that I had caught a sniffle while out on our gallop. She cut her eyes at me when I opened my mouth to protest, so I went straight up to bed, but not before I heard the loud women who were gathered in our library and their male companions.

"Oh, don't be like that, Mathilda," I heard Papa say. "Let her stay and meet my friends."

"No, Frederick," Mama said, and that was that.

Later that evening, when my governess had gone to

bed, I crept back to the landing and tried to listen for some snatches of conversation. Papa got loud when he drank, and I had never known him not to drink. His friends were no different.

"Oh, no," I heard Papa say, "we just have the one girl, isn't that right, Matty?"

Silence from Mama.

"We've been trying," Papa said then, "but dear old Matty's delicate body just doesn't seem to want to keep them alive, does it? Must have a thing against little boys."

Some murmuring from the rest of the group. I hoped they were saying nice things to Mama.

It was only much later that I would learn about miscarriages. And still later until I understood that Mama had had two before she finally carried me to term. And that, some months earlier, she had lost a third baby, most likely planted during Papa's last visit.

But I did know that Papa was being cruel to Mama. You could tell from the tone of his voice.

I didn't need to hear any more, and I crept back to my bedroom. But Mama had been badly hurt. Barely fifteen minutes later I heard her swift footsteps and her door close ever so gently. When Papa wasn't home, Mama closed every door with a joyful clap.

I could hear laughter from downstairs, and I went to her room, opening the door without knocking. "Mama?"

Mama sat at her dressing table, staring into the mirror. In one of the novels I'd recently taken to reading, tears might be streaking down her face, but this was not happening here. Mama had her head propped on one hand, her face sliding into her palm. She looked cripplingly tired.

"Yes, Clara. Come in."

I was too big to crawl into her lap by then, but I sat on the floor by her, my head in her lap. "You know, Mama," I said to her, "Alva Vanderbilt got a divorce, and she is just fine! All of Marble House is hers if she wants to be there. She could knock around in that great big house all by herself, free as a bird, if she wanted. She could have her friends over for tea. Go where she pleases! I've heard she even hosts suffrage luncheons!"

Mama half laughed. "Oh, my darling," she said. "Miss Alva is a *Vanderbilt*. Richer than Croesus! They can do whatever it is they prefer." She stroked my hair listlessly, and I'd have done anything to have her fingers busily braiding my hair as she did each time before we went riding, just to give her something to do that wasn't so desultory. "But this is not for us. Those of us who are not so lucky must still abide by society's rules. It would not be possible for us," she said.

She pushed me back then and slid onto the floor next to me. "Clara," she said, quite earnestly, "if you marry, marry for love. But first, find a place where you can cast off the arbitrary rules of this society. Find a place where women are equal, find a land in which you can be seen for and measured by your own merits, and not just as a woman."

I remember being distinctly perplexed: If, in one's own home, one couldn't be equal, where else would one go? I looked to Mama for the answer, but her gaze was on something else by then, and I left her to go to my own bed.

But I did not sleep. I waited, crouched by my door, until I was sure Mama had gone to sleep. I waited even longer, until I heard Papa's guests being installed in the guest suites farther down the hall. And then I went down to the library.

Papa was still there, his face hidden by the wing of the chair he liked to sit in when he was home. His legs were stretched carelessly out to the fire, and I could smell and see the pipe smoke. He coughed, a wet racking sound, and I shivered, but then I crept farther forward, holding my breath against the miasma of smoke and stale booze.

"Papa," I said. The word sounded odd on my lips. "Papa." I tried again, louder.

He stretched his neck, so that one eye peered around the edge of the wing. I saw it glistening in the firelight, and I recalled the story of St. George and the dragon. This must be like what St. George saw; now I was catching a glimpse of my own fearsome beast.

"Well, there she is," Papa said then, and I tried for a smile.

Papa outright guffawed. "So, she smiles," he said, as if I were not in the room. "Come here. I hardly know you."

My feet were growing cold on the parquet of the floor, but I went closer still, the question I wanted to ask him giving me strength. Even then I had no special feeling for this man, no sense that he belonged to me.

He stretched out a long, skinny arm and crabbed his fingers around my wrist. They were stained with what I know now to be tobacco, but at the time they just seemed discolored. I snatched my wrist back then. I could hold my question in no longer.

"Papa, why do you make Mama cry so?"

A long silence. "Mouthy, like her ma," he muttered, and I felt an ember of hate begin to grow in me, although I would not have called it that back then. I only knew I still needed to know.

The fire popped and Papa stood, hooking an elbow on the mantle. It was like he was looming over me. His shadow, from the fire, stretched even longer. His eyes were hooded in darkness now. "I do not make her cry," he said. "It is her own uselessness."

I did not know what to say to this.

Papa went on. "It is her place to please me," he said. "And when she does not please me, she *should* cry, should she not?"

I wanted to say something, anything. But I couldn't, and very shortly afterward, he made a disgusted moue with his face and sent me back up to bed. It was the penultimate time I would speak to him, but I already knew I did not want any part of a world in which it is one human's place merely to *please* another.

Irony is not my strong suit. But I'd have to be deliberately ignorant to overlook the fact that I've gone to the ends of the earth to pursue a place free from expectations—and yet.

This is a good place to tell you about relations on board an expedition ship and on expedition.

It may be that, by the time you read this, there will be many more women on expeditions. I hope this will be true. If we do not get the vote, this would, at least, be some small comfort. But I only have this one experience, and so I will tell you: even if there are other women on board your expedition, you must stay vigilant of stupid things like men feeling like they are stronger, faster, and smarter than you are. For this kind of thing, it helps if you can find yourself an ally of some kind. Your best ally is likely to be your expedition leader, because he has clout and leverage; everyone must listen to him or suffer the consequences: docked pay, or merely the jaundiced stare of a Boss who is not pleased with you.

Your second-best ally is likely to be the ship's surgeon. He is the person who will be the most well-rounded, as he is likely to have had to mix with all manner of patients. He will have seen the most of the human condition, and, in my experience, is likely to see any member of the crew in toto—that is, brains, experience, origin, sex, and all. This you may find as invaluable as I have found.

Barring that, you will have to befriend the popular crew members. Watch very carefully in your first few days to determine who they may be. (One might say I have made a hash of this, as I seem to have mostly befriended MacTavish, whom the men are quite beholden to admire, and Per and Blackburn, who are but boys, and so do not hold much social sway. Well, we will be here for some time yet. Perhaps I will improve upon my social standing.)

When you have identified your allies, you must then walk a path even narrower than that which society has chosen to prescribe to women: You must ask for help *only* when asking for help would not undermine the role you hope to occupy on crew. You must stick close to the allies, so you are assigned the same tasks they are; you must then get in the way so that your allies will not conveniently forget that you are just as strong, just as quick, just as clever and curious as any old man on crew.

That's in theory, anyway. It is proving to take longer than I expected for the men to recall these things as a matter of course. Perhaps later in this diary I will revisit.

As to the other kind of unwanted attention you may encounter—yes, there will always be those men who believe women are only there as sexual objects (this is different from women only being there as ornamental objects, which is slightly less dangerous).

I have no good advice for this one. You must simply endure, as women have been doing for centuries. Your allies should help. They may physically get in the way of a lurid glare. They may choose to open their mouths and tell the offender to shut it. You must never, ever be alone with those who would believe women are there only for sexual entertainment. On the ship it is very rare for any of us to be alone, but you must never be caught in some dark corner by yourself.

You might choose to make yourself ugly. On an expedition there is no choice, really: one's opportunities to bathe and attend to a proper toilette are not a priority. You might choose to adopt a manner unbecoming to a potential suitor. You might choose less flattering clothing, although a less flattering getup than two sets of woolens crammed beneath coveralls and big lumpy hats jammed over one's head would be hard to imagine.

Put your head down and work.

Never. Be. Complacent. Your biggest adversaries on an expedition are the weather and the men. You can do something about each of these.

Nota bene: some of you may be wondering whether one isn't remotely attracted to any of the men on board an expedition. It's true, there may be some fine specimens on board, but one would do well to remember that no one signs onto these things to find a mate.

It would be overly romantic to believe that one's mind is on anything but survival on these expeditions, especially if one finds oneself in the minority. Equally, it would be disingenuous not to mention that one may find oneself the subject of interest from one quarter or another.

The interest may be obvious, say, a hand creeping ever closer to one's own in an already-packed mess situation. One deals with this equally overtly, by picking up the wayward hand and dropping it back on the offender's side of an invisible line.

The attention may be covert, say a hand creeping over one's knee under the mess table. Here, too, the answer needs no subtlety. One picks up the encroaching appendage and drops it back in its own lap. You may even find yourself the subject of attentions that seem minute, but are grossly offensive: snide phrasing, perhaps; a nasty double entendre; a long leering gaze. Do not be talked into overlooking these; they are just as overt, attacks on your feminine form.

In none of these situations should one avoid confronting the issue head-on: I find a long, hard stare at the person attempting the overture particularly useful. One needs only one additional firm word: "No."

This interlude brought to you by hard-won experience. Experience is also here to tell you that neither overt nor covert nor sly offenders seemed to be bothered; rather, I seem to have won a modicum of respect for this method. And honestly, what did they think would happen anyway? That the two of you would go off and find a berth of your own someplace, snuggle up to play happy domestic bliss in the most undomestic settings on earth?

Should everything fail and you find yourself urged to make romantic overtures to anyone, you only need to remember how long it has been since anyone on your expedition has had a proper bath. And, likely, you will want to check your priorities: Are you here to find a mate, or are you here for something bigger?

Mama's birthday.

Happy birthday, Mama!

I miss you. I miss our talks. I miss the little things, like breakfast; I miss the big things, like camping.

I miss the little things like admiring your very efficient morning toilette—hair swept back in either bun or braid, a quick tooth clean and face wash, and off for the day!—and I miss the big things, like your teaching me every language you know and encouraging me to read in them.

I miss the horses and the bicycles and the picnics, you always by my side.

And strangely, I miss your coming to England with me. Can one have nostalgia for a thing that never happened? I know you would have eventually discovered the same fire I did. I know it is there still.

In honor of Mama, I asked Higgins once again to let me try to pull the sledge this time. (See "relations on expedition," above.)

Higgins pulled at a lock of his hair, looking at the work rota, thinking, while I stood there feeling like a little beggar girl. Never mind; it'd be worth it if I could just try. Finally, he nodded and made some scratches and arrows on his page. It was almost as if, now that we weren't *going* anywhere, Higgins had decided it was all right for me to have a go.

Mahoney helped me to strap in. It was me between Mahoney and Givens, and even though us and the six men strapped behind us were almost tipped into the ice, all the way forward, the sled felt like it was riveted to the ice. Hotchkiss, looped into the traces behind me, grumped as expected—"*Look* at her! Why, she isn't even on the ground, they're *lifting* her, don't you all see it?"—but the men next to him shouted at him to get on with pulling.

When the *Dudley Stanwick* finally started moving, it went quite smoothly for about fifteen feet until we hit the slightest, smallest bump, what looked like the tiniest ridge in the ice.

And then she jerked to a stop, and we had to start the whole exercise all over again. The few times we were able to hitch the sled over humps and hummocks felt like reasons to celebrate, but there wasn't any time or room, nor any energy for that. I almost wanted to go back to the back of the sled, shoving things along and tucking things in. But Hotchkiss and his cronies were in my head, almost willing me to give up, so I just kept pulling.

Never have I felt such numbing fire in my legs before. Not when we tramped with all our food and hunting gear and fishing rods and clothes up to the cabin that one week-end, choosing to try something new; not when we bicycled for eight hours on end, exploring the countryside; not when we rode our horses into the backcountry at a full gallop for an hour over rough terrain. Not even—and I am loathe to admit this—on our march in Washington, my very last activity with the American suffragists, when I was called upon to physically fight for our right to be there.

Nothing has ever felt like this before. Even now, a few hours later, my arms hang loose from my shoulders and I wonder if they'll be of use anytime soon.

My shoulders themselves feel all cut up beneath my sweater and my woolens; my hands, from being out in front in the wind, seem to crack each time I flex them, to draw more blood flow into them.

Mahoney helped me out of the traces and nodded at me. "That's done, then," he said. "Same again tomorrer?" I nodded. Sweat ran into my turtleneck and froze there. I shivered.

I fumbled my feet out of the way of the traces so I wouldn't trip, and started the walk back to Dump Camp, still a half mile away. Someone caught up with me. I was too tired to turn my head to see who it was, but I knew soon enough.

"Well, Clara, old girl? Have you quite done with this . . . exercise of yours? It's time to leave the pulling to the real men, wouldn't you say?" Hotchkiss has a particular smell about him, one that I can always track. Tobacco, sure. Sweat, like everyone else, but there is something peculiar about him, a musty fungus left to rot in the cellar.

I grunted and thought, if only he knew how hard it actually is to be a woman. Has he ever seen the work the laundrywomen do? Or how much one must argue just to be granted an education? I didn't stop walking. I pasted a smile on my face and said, "Doing what I can. Just like everyone else."

He snorted and spat. A most unpleasant sound. "Well, I wouldn't say you can say that you're the *least* bit like everyone else, old girl," he said. "Not at all."

I had had enough. I turned and faced him. "Look, is there something you want, Hotchkiss?"

He backed up, hands held up in mock terror. "Oh ho! Our cat has claws. I did wonder when our pussy would start to spit."

I rolled my eyes and gestured for him to go ahead of me. "Look, you're obviously walking faster than me. Why not just go ahead?"

Hotchkiss narrowed his eyes at me. He opened his mouth to say something, but MacTavish arrived then, clomping in his boots like he was in a hurry. "Hotchkiss," he said, and Hotchkiss nodded at him.

"Doc."

MacTavish turned to me. "Well, Clara, good pulling today."

I nodded, weakly.

Hotchkiss barked. "Hah!"

MacTavish glanced at him. "I forgot to say," he said, "The Boss wants to see you, Hotchkiss."

"Is that so?" Hotchkiss seemed skeptical, and so was I.

"Yes," said MacTavish. "You'd best get going."

Hotchkiss seemed to think MacTavish was having him on, but he didn't want to find out. He marched in the direction of Dump Camp.

"Boss didn't really ask to see him, did he?" I said, when Hotchkiss was a good distance away.

MacTavish shrugged. "Who can remember, with all we have to do?" He grinned at me, practically sparkling with mischief. He changed the subject. "So. Today."

"Yes. Today."

There didn't seem to be anything else to say, and in any case I was too tired for it, and trying to ignore the pains and various raw bits that kept on presenting themselves on my body. I kept my eyes on the horizon where Dump Camp sat, looking homey, and we continued on walking in peace, or as much peace as you can experience in a place of this much extraordinary landscape.

This is a good place to tell you about **the landscape on Antarctica.**

Your vision will never, ever be the same. I feel I will forever be comparing every white, every shade of gray, every clarity of sky and purity of air to what I have borne witness to so far. It is impossible to ignore the absolute striking otherness of the snow and ice and sky and water here. I don't know how the men feel, but I never, ever tire of observing it, of trying to remember it.

I know that Givens's paintings and Higgins's lantern slides, even after they've been colored, will be but pale comparisons, and so I try to fix these images in my head, to take a picture with my brain. If these images in my head become ever more vivid as I grow older, they will still never match the original.

The blues are sometimes so pale it feels as if you are looking at pure light. One wants to be squinting all the time, it's that bright. The horizon is so, so big, almost as if you are looking past the curvature of the earth. The storms, when they roll in, can be seen from miles away. The ice is so white it almost seems clear, and it forms such extraordinary shapes after years in the wind, that one cannot easily imagine how humankind will ever exhaust the store of inspiration available to us. Indeed, I feel we can never match it.

Some of the frost forms like little blooms—Higgins calls these ice flowers and never seems to tire of making pictures of them in all kinds of light and manifestation, at all stages of growth.

The icebergs are yet another marvel. There are so many different styles and forms of them. And then one thinks rapidly of the *distance* involved in how the eye perceives the behemoths—an iceberg can be seen from very far away, and so one does not really comprehend the size of it until one is closer to it. It is a thing of awe, a thing to make one feel so very inconsequential, and yet, so fortunate to be alive.

Wilson has tried many times to explain how these things are made. But the scope of history involved in making just one berg, from glaciers to their movement to tongues to the calving of great pieces of ice that eventually float in the salt-water of the sea and become icebergs . . . we crew do not seem to have the attention span for such things, or rather, we lack the scope of reference needed to comprehend them fully.

But imagine—if I, who have had my scope of reference pushed beyond the mere idea of "white," "blue," "ice," and "snow," believe myself to be limited, just how much you, a new arrival, will feel expanded merely by being here.

These are the things one contemplates when one is trudging in companionable silence toward a hopefully hot meal and a not-so-warm reindeer hide sleeping bag.

By the time MacTavish and I got back—it must be admitted I trudged more slowly than everyone else, and MacTavish was good enough to accompany me—the rest of the crew had eaten. Tinned ham, peas, potatoes. Trumilk and a precious portion of Kendal Mint Cake for dessert. Good enough. Higgins asked if I wanted a game of patience poker, but I was not above begging off with women's troubles, and he let it go.

Extraordinary thing, this. One mention of lady troubles and everyone's eyes go shifting somewhere else, as if one has a giant horn continuously growing out of one's forehead that only everyone else can see.

⁊⁊

Today we shuffled all our stuff back to Dump Camp from out there on the ice. Part of me felt as if it would have been easier to carry it all back piecemeal, by hand, by individual dog, rather than put ourselves in the traces again and heave those loads, but I'm sure there's already been tons of calculations done on that score already. (Aside from being an excellent navigator, Billings is very good at eyeballing things like weight and effort, time and distance . . . I suppose that kind of skill just comes with practice.)

A few good things came out of this hauling, though— all our belongings and goods are back in one place, and now that we are back at Dump Camp for the foreseeable future, we get to pick out all the things we left behind. Of course, we will only have to dump it all again when the leads open up enough for us to get back in the boats and make an actual water-run for Paulet, but . . .

I confess I missed my likenesses of Mrs. Pankhurst and even my Votes for Women motoring scarf, so I dug those out of the pile.

Tomorrow, another day in the traces.

We are to be back by midday for a meal together regardless of whether our supplies are fully back at Dump Camp. The Boss said he will tell us more about our future plans over our luncheon.

Later

Well, it's not much of a plan. The Boss says it's time for us to exercise our patience. We are to "put on a stiff lip and keep each other's spirits up," which I suppose means more banjo nights from Figgy. Maybe we will even resurrect our ship's magazine again, to which I have contributed one or two stories anonymously and would like to do again. I find it titillating to consider that maybe one day I will be outed as the Melville of *The Resolute* expedition.

The crew seems to have enjoyed my work, anyway.

Dump Camp has been rechristened "Camp Patience."

Oh, it's useless to pretend that I am at all happy with this move. "Wait and see" is the kind of thing that drives people to bizarre behavior. Look at what happened to me: I signed up for an Antarctic expedition!

I fear the worst from this delay. Even at the moment The Boss announced Camp Patience we could sense the restlessness of the crew, their disappointment. People who want forward motion will find a way to take it.

In late April 1913, riding a wave of rage and disgust, I made the decision to sail for London and the WSPU. It had been a month since our fateful parade in Washington, DC. A month since men lining our parade route had seen fit to honor us by spitting on us, pushing us to the ground, and sending over one hundred of us to the hospital. A month since the policemen of Washington had turned their backs on us. A month since Alice Paul's group of suffragists had seen fit to push Ida B. Wells, a champion for women's rights and Black women's rights, to the back of the parade, *only* because of the color of her skin.

Five years since Papa, that emblem of entitled male behavior in my domestic world, had died.

Meanwhile in London, Mrs. Pankhurst had just been arrested again. Surely Mama would see the importance of becoming involved beyond merely being a dues-paying member of the National American Woman Suffrage Association.

"Come with me, Mama. It is beyond time for us to fight harder than ever for the vote."

Mama shook her head slowly. "Clara, the Pankhursts are not well known as a reasonable part of the fight for women's rights. Do you not want to be a part of something more . . . legitimate?"

The words were out of my mouth before I could take them back. "'Legitimate?' Mama! What is *legitimate* about the way women are being treated today? What is legitimate about officers of the law laughing and jeering as women are trampled beneath the feet of hooligans?" I took a deep breath. "What is legitimate about the way Papa treated you?" I shut my eyes and shook my head fast fast fast, to shake the image of his standing so casually, arm draped over the mantle like he owned the place, when it was Mama's dowry that allowed him to live there, to take advantage of the heat from that very fireplace, to drink the wine he liked so much.

I felt rooted to the spot. I had never before talked to

Mama about exactly what had happened the day of Alice Paul's parade, the brave step she thought she was taking as a leader in women's suffrage. "You cannot . . . you cannot know what it is like, to see your friends and colleagues struck down—to see them get up time and time again only to be spat on, all the while hampered from their true strength by something as mundane as petticoats and corsets!"

Mama cast a quick, nervous look around, and I read in that gesture all I needed to know: Mama could not understand, but I tried once more.

"Mama, the Americans are not ready for us. We are not ready to fight for true equity. What of the fact that our movements have not been able to unite? We have women who want a federal amendment and women who want state amendments; we have the temperance union. We have the scores of colored women fighting for their voting rights, but we refuse to help them gain them! We need *more*. We *need* the Pankhursts, and I aim to go and learn what I can from them."

Mama tried to speak but did not seem to be able to form the words, and my fury collapsed. I took two steps forward and threw myself onto the chaise longue next to her, just like I had when I was a child. "Mama, please do try to see. Pankhurst is as angry as we all should be."

She shook her head slowly. "Pankhurst," she said, "had the support of a loving, faithful husband, one who believed in her, and that can be everything."

I opened my mouth to say it had been five years since Papa had passed from our lives, but she shushed me. "Clara, I am *tired*," she said, finally. "And I feel I have so much living to do, finally so much more of myself to discover. I do not have it in me to enter another battlefield yet."

"Mama," I said, "you may stay here in your conservatory, and you may think that you are finally living a full life. Now imagine what it might be like if you had the vote. If you could say, feel, that you are truly equal."

She shook her head again. "Abstract, lofty goals," she murmured. "For now, this is real to me, do you see? This is enough. And anyway," she went on, just before her eyes drifted back down to the page, "waging the kind of war the Pankhursts are bent on engaging in is certainly not the way to convince me."

"I'm going, Mama," I said, after a moment of silence.

"You have my blessing," she said, firmly.

Mama's life was not for me. My life is not for Mama.

I left Mama there that afternoon in the conservatory, and since then I had never done more than send her brief letters assuring her of my health—and eventually, of my travel to Antarctica.

Her return telegram was brief. "Go and fulfill," she wrote. "Write upon return."

Mama was not entirely wrong. The WSPU *was* waging war, with Pankhurst as our general. She ruled with military might, and we all fell into line or were asked to leave.

But they taught me to *fight*. When you have watched a jujitsu expert of only four foot ten upend a strapping young police constable who outweighs her by at least fifty pounds, and when you have lovingly been taught to do such a thing yourself, you will have understood some semblance of true power. Of course, I have not told the men on our expedition this. I tell them about the battles Mama and I fought against many a trout in the Delaware Water Gap; I tell them about the early mornings we spent stalking deer in the woods; I tell them about the hundreds of campfires I have lit and sustained.

But I do not tell them about the battle for women's rights. For me, it is bigger than anything I have ever undertaken. But to them, it is merely a novelty, or even something to disdain.

Dammit all, Cook is calling. Will tell him I don't want to help cook tonight, that I will do it some other day. He must find someone else.

Still Later

Infuriating! I told Cook I didn't want to be stuck on kitchen duty tonight, and could he please get someone else to help?

He put down his ladle and outright laughed at me. When Cook laughs the whole camp pays notice, and I flushed from head to toe, I am sure, to know that everyone probably already knew that I was in the galley with him.

"Lass, what do you think this is? Some kind of

esssssspecial training school where you can choose what kind of events and classes you want to participate in? Garde-manger at noon, and then soufflés at three in the communal kitchen? But only if you like? Oh, no, lass. *Everyone* chips in here. Do you not remember? On the ship, everyone did what they were needed to do, and tonight I need you here in the galley."

"But Cook—"

"No." Cook had picked up his ladle again and wasn't even looking at me anymore. "Look, Clara, we've got a quarter of the men trying to organize our next move and half the men trying to set up our camp again so we can be safe and happy while we wait. I need you where I need you. Be a good girl now, and start the biscuits."

Ugh! I took a deep breath. "Cook, please tell me why you can't have someone else do it."

He glanced up at me again, beady blue eyes sharp. He winked. "Yer a lass, ain't cha? Who better?" He laughed, deep and ironic, and I . . . I set my teeth and got to mixing biscuits.

The Dump Pile is smaller now, but it is still sizable. We've fallen into a funny little habit where we're using it almost as storage. We haven't unpacked anything properly from it, and whenever anyone is missing anything, someone gets the bright idea that there's probably a duplicate of the item at the pile.

It's become a running joke: "Bright idea, man!" Or, in my case, "Bright idea, Clara!" I can't decide if I want to be called "man" or not. The loneliness sometimes is crushing.

I'm surprised that Milton-Jones hasn't already inventoried it all. He loves to keep track of things—always writing in his diary.

Of course, that's all a lot of us are doing now—writing, or sitting in the sun, or reading the books we've salvaged from *The Resolute*. There really is talk of starting our magazine back up again, and I have given a few more haircuts.

I wonder what the WSPU is doing right now. Farming? Making munitions? Otherwise—and once again—picking up the slack of men?

Hmph.

This is a good place to tell you about your **personal expedition kit.**

You will be issued certain kit. These will likely comprise five sets of woolen long underwear; two sets of mittens and two woolen caps, in case you lose one; and five pairs of long woolen socks plus a balaclava. None of these will be sized to women, so you will indeed end up doing a fair amount of mending and sewing at the beginning just to make sure you can move about in your kit the best you can.

You will get two sweaters, a set of Burberry coveralls, two good pairs of boots, and a good reindeer-hide sleeping bag.

You will also get one plate, one bowl, one cup, and one set of fork, knife, and spoon. You will get a few blank notebooks to serve as your diaries and multiple pencils, for if your expedition leader is as shrewd as mine, he will have sold all the publicity rights to the expedition well ahead of time to raise funds, and you will be expected to notate your experience for posterity. Well, I am not intending on handing over everything I write here to some yellow journalism rag; I am planning on turning it over to a woman-run press who will do everything they can to make sure we women are prepared for every expedition we may ever find ourselves on.

You will also find yourself outfitted with a penknife, which you must keep sharpened at all times. They are ludicrously useful.

Obviously, do not forget to pack our women's needs. Do not worry about hair ribbons or things like it for keeping your hair back; the first thing I did when I got on board was to cut all my hair very short. Let me tell you, it caused quite a scandal, although no one ever said anything out loud. It was all sideways glances, until The Boss told them to get over it and gave them a five-minute period to stare as long as they liked. Higgins laughed and laughed—having traveled to more lands than most of the crew, he has seen women with much shorter hair.

As previously mentioned, you might consider packing a beloved book or three—one of the odd joys of this expedition has been swapping books with my crewmates. The books most in demand now are the various novels the crew brought along with them. We read to one another sometimes, which makes the whole expedition recede into the background . . . one can imagine for a few minutes that we are in a sitting room someplace, drowsing off a meal. But one's level of alertness can never be compromised, and so it isn't too long before we are up and scrabbling for something else to do to improve our camp, even if there really isn't anything to do.

The Dump Pile is, in fact, serving as a kind of library. There is a little section set off from the other things, four or five upturned crates where we all go to drop off books we have read and pick up new ones.

3 December

Lately, downtime does not seem to be an unusual occurrence. But that means this is as good a time as any to tell you about some of the **day-to-day tasks** you will undertake on an expedition.

We have already spoken about the haircuts and the biscuits and the mapping out of camp; here I will use the space to tell you about some of the things you will have to learn to do in order to help the expedition run smoothly.

First, camp must be trim and tidy at all times. This means that if you are in one place for more than a day, you should make it your task to go around and check that all the guywires on your tent are tight. This should happen every single morning after the temperature changes of the night. You should also, each day, ensure that the fabric of the tents is in good shape. If it is starting to wear through in places, you should patch it straightaway.

You should also endeavor to keep the areas around each tent as clean as possible. Garbage should be buried in one area; the latrines should be dug, filled with snow, and redug in another location weekly, if at all possible.

The dogs must be exercised and brushed, and their kennels must be cleaned.

The daily watch is taken in shifts of four hours. There are two of us on watch at any given time; this is a convention we have carried over from our life on board *The Resolute*.

I would be lying by omission if I didn't say here that I started this list by way of wanting to believe that we are busy all the time. But the truth is, there are plenty of times when we are sat around, idling, reading, playing cards, or, in my case, hankering for a hunt and pining over one's previous lives, even as we know death is lurking just outside the camp in the form of bad weather, or even as our muscles are on high alert, looking out for the evil snout of a killer whale or the crest of a rogue wave to break up our floe.

I went and asked Milton-Jones if he would take me hunting. He did not even consider, did not even really look up from scribbling madly in his diary. He said he wasn't sure of me at all, since he'd never seen me shoot. "Well," I said, "would you have asked that of Per? *Have* you asked that of Per?"

He finally looked at me and stammered a bit then and said, somewhat stiffly, "No, I've not."

"And do you want to know why that is?" I was building up a head of steam and didn't wait for him to answer. "Because you didn't *need* to. Even Per has already had several chances to take down seals in the time we've been together. No one seems to even want to let me shoot at the ones that are sleeping! Why do you think that is, Milt? Have a think about that!"

"Er." Milton-Jones's mustache bobbed, which I took to mean he was swallowing uncomfortably, which I very much appreciated. "Er, we've not had cause to go hunting in some time, have we?"

I sighed and rolled my eyes mightily. "Well, yes! That is the whole *point* of hunting, so we will not ever be caught in a position to have *cause* to!"

He regarded me. Well, I think he did, anyhow. The sunlight glancing off his spectacles makes him hard to read. Finally, he bent to scribble in his notebook, as if he could not be bothered to pay me any more attention, and said, "Young Per is also not a woman. A woman's blood, it is said, runs hotter than a man's, and the animals may be able to smell us coming."

It's one thing to hear something outrageous like this from a mere member of the public. It's quite another to hear it from a member of your crew. I did the thing where you stare at someone furiously, trying to channel all the rage in your head into one mean glare whilst no useful words at all come out of your mouth, and then I stomped off to where a random group of crew members were hanging out their laundry, it being a decent kind of day weatherwise, and shouted, "Oi! Which one of you believes that you can smell a woman?" Barkley sniggered, and I blushed. I didn't quite think through what I was going to say before I opened my mouth and this unfortunate nonsense came out.

I opened my mouth again. "Oh, hell! You know what I mean! Don't be idiots!" To which there was more sniggering. MacTavish finished hanging up his skivvies and took me firmly by the wrist. "Clara," he said, "just the person I needed to see."

I must stop him from rescuing me in this fashion. Having him fight my battles for me is no way for this to go.

"Now, what's bothering you so?"

Between flushes of embarrassment and anger, I somehow stuttered out the story. He just shook his head. "Och, that Thomas," he said, looking truly despairing. "If he does not want to do a thing, he will think of all manner of excuse."

"I *thought* so!" I said, feeling vindicated.

"No one questions him, hardly, because he was a Marine officer, and he is so used to having his word taken at face value. I half think he spouts silliness just to test and see who will take him at his word."

"I *thought* so," I said again, feeling smug, and busily reviewing my memory for any other lies Milton-Jones might have told.

"But then—hmmmm." MacTavish pulled at his beard. "Clara, *are* you done with your courses?"

I tell you, I went hot with fury and cold with anticipation all at once. "I . . . why would *that* matter?"

"Oh, Clara, do not worry so much nor be embarrassed. It is said that sharks can smell a drop of blood a mile away in the water. I was only wondering if maybe a sea leopard or some other keen predator like it might also be able to smell your courses."

I just stared at MacTavish.

Oh, but I was mortified. *Mortified!* To imagine that others *can* smell me, even if it is only an animal! I hardly know what to do with such a feral thought, and yet, it is not entirely out of the realm of possibility.

I shook my head and swallowed my indignity. "My courses are nearly done, MacTavish," I said, "so hopefully someone will take me out, although I won't be asking Milton-Jones anytime soon."

He nodded. "Now mind, I'm not saying it's a real consideration. I'm just saying that if I'm thinking it, then there may be other men who are thinking it too—and so we must consider it."

I waved my hand, maybe hoping I could just magic him away for a second. I could not wait to be done with the topic of my menses. It had been hard enough watching The Boss struggle with it when he realized that he'd hired a woman for the expedition, and that she would likely have her monthly courses over the course of the time we were on the ship and on the ice.

He'd set a special interview with me just for the purpose of addressing it, in fact: a telegram had arrived for me, by courier, a week or so after he'd told me I'd won a place on his expedition. And it *did* feel like that—winning, I mean. Henderson was renowned for his prior Antarctic expeditions, and I was to be the very first woman on any of them. He'd told me to be ready for press and interviews, but he was keeping quiet until the rest of the crew had been hired, and now I worried he was calling me in to tell me he couldn't take the risk of bad press, or that the rest of the men had said they didn't want a woman on board, or something.

I dressed in my most severe, most practical dress, and I went downtown, with my heart feeling like it was thudding painfully in my throat, to the Kensington offices, wondering what my new boss wanted of me, and whether or not I'd still have a boss after.

When I got there, MacTavish was there too, although I didn't know he would be our ship's surgeon just yet.

"Miss Ketterling-Dunbar, meet MacTavish," The Boss said, watching me over his spectacles. "Ship's surgeon." I wondered if he'd expected me to react somehow.

"Pleased to meet you," I said shortly, extending my hand to be shook. MacTavish's eyes widened as I gave him my best Mama-grip. She'd always hated the way "ladies" offered their hands for shaking, as if they'd fall off their wrists at the slightest pressure. MacTavish attempted to lift my hand and bowed his head, but I kept a firm downward grip—there was to be no kissing of hands here. This was not a social call.

His eyes twinkled, and I knew then we'd have a good rapport. I gathered my many skirts to wedge myself into the office chair they'd set out for me. Probably the most exciting thing about the expedition then was the need to wear trousers every day. I'd read a magazine article once about camping by an experienced woman camper, and on her packing list was four or five skirts and petticoats, and not a *single* pair of trousers. Ridiculous.

The two men made a heroic attempt at small talk, moving from weather to politics to my health, and eventually I couldn't stand it anymore. "Gentlemen," I said, as politely as I could, "I have much to prepare in the brief time before we leave, so if there's something you specifically needed to discuss with me . . ."

The Boss glanced at MacTavish. MacTavish raised his eyebrows back at The Boss. It was everything I could do to not burst out into giggles, since it was obvious that they had called me in to talk about something unmistakably female in nature, and therefore of utmost embarrassment to at least one of them, and also that they were not yet equipped to speak of it in plain terms.

"Erm. I grew up with four sisters," said MacTavish.

"On a ship, we are not always equipped for every need," said The Boss at the same time.

I waited. "Gentlemen," I said again.

The Boss cleared his throat. "Erm. I was very happy, as you know, to have met you at your interview and assessment," he said. "But the good doctor here has reminded me that a woman has . . . er, specific, that is, highly womanly . . . needs that may not be met by the facilities on the ship. . . ."

This was going in a direction I could not afford it to go. I'd given the men too much rope, and they were about to hang me with it, along with my chance to go to Antarctica.

I wanted to hold up my hand, but I'd been told once before that it was rude, so I stilled it on the handle of my infernal parasol and relied on my voice. "Let me just stop you there, Mr. Henderson, with utmost respect. You are referring to a woman's monthly courses, are you?"

(As much as I wanted to set them right so we could have this ugly business out of the way, I also could not resist the urge to make them at least admit this biological function they were dancing so ungracefully around.)

"Er, yes," said The Boss, and I thought to myself that I would scream if I had to endure one more stiff upper lip "Er."

MacTavish was watching us carefully.

"Well, then, let me assure you, I have far more experience than either of you at being a woman, and six years dealing with my monthly courses—my menstruation, if you want to be exact about it. No one in this room is better equipped than I to deal with them, and no one on the ship will be. So I suggest you let me go on being the expert at this, and rest in your own assurance that my monthly courses will disrupt your operations as much as they do mine, which is to say not at all. And—" this time I did hold up my hand, for I could see The Boss was about to interject, "Let me remind you that I also have six years of experience dealing with the maladies you will have likely heard 'plague' a woman during her monthlies."

MacTavish leaned forward.

"These are nothing more than a mild ache near my womb, and they are dealt with with a steady mind, deep breathing, and occasional clutching of the midsection and doubling over in agony, whilst commandeering the attention of *everyone* near me by shrieking, so that they may hear my suffering." I smiled, to show I was joking. MacTavish's lips curled in a smile around his pipe. I went on. "Let me handle it as women have always done, sirs."

The Boss grumbled. No one said anything.

"Surely," I finally said, "you're not now worrying about the supplies that help women to manage our menstruation?"

Affirmative grumble from The Boss; mere curiosity from MacTavish, who clearly must have seen or a least read about a few of the methodologies one could employ.

I sighed under my breath. "Will you begrudge any of your other men their needs, or creature comforts, even? A special blanket, perhaps, or a lucky pair of shoelaces, a few favorite books or a deck of cards? A photo of their loved ones? No? Food? Water? No? Then don't begrudge me my needs, either." I was talking fast, worried they would interrupt me. This I could not afford.

MacTavish finally nodded. The Boss glanced at him.

I suppressed another sigh. "Would you like me to exit the room, gentlemen, whilst you discuss among yourselves?"

"No need." MacTavish was firm. He turned to The Boss. "I think you can put your worries to rest," he said.

There was an awkward moment, and then Henderson slapped MacTavish on the shoulder, nearly sending Doc face-first into the desk that separated us. "Didn't I tell you, man! A real frontierswoman we have here!"

I didn't bother to correct him. Pennsylvania is about as far from the frontier as you can get. Men will believe what they want to believe.

I left that day feeling as if I had some support, that we could move forward through this expedition without having to worry about such trifling matters. And, true to The Boss's reputation of shrewd showmanship, by the time we were to set sail, he had secured a multi-thousand-pound investment from a medical supply company that included six months' supply of sanitary napkins for me, which, true to male-oriented accounting, only lasted three months. Ha! Ha! Ha! (Press interviews, clearly, did not address this latter part of the sponsorship.)

God forbid a woman have to deal with real life.

I suppose I can forgive MacTavish for forgetting the confidence with which he spoke of my aptitude at handling my menstruation that day. So much has changed now that we are not on the ship anymore, and hot water to wash my cloths with clearly does not come as readily. But I have managed by myself—I just ask Cook for a little time each day of my courses to prepare my hot water from ice and snow, and I've never even had to ask for more than my fair share of soap. I suppose women just conserve better than men do; Mahoney always seems to be short of the stuff, and Chutney is always asking around to borrow someone else's, which just makes me shudder. I've heard the men talk of finding slivers of soap in their sleeping bags, which is just strange. I keep my soap in a net bag made from one of my old silk stockings. It never gets lost, and it lasts much longer when we do need to bathe.

In any case, MacTavish suggested now that I go back and ask Milton-Jones to take me on a hunt again.

"Why would I do that? He's already said no, and in very specific fashion."

"I'm sure you just caught him at a bad moment." But MacTavish sounded unsure, and he hadn't seen the absolutely shocked look on Milton-Jones's face when I asked him the first time.

"Don't you want him to take you?"

"Well, yes! He's the best shot of all of you here."

"Well, then, go and tell him what you've been telling me—that you want to contribute. Give him a chance."

Give him a chance! Surely it was more about everyone

giving me a chance at my rightful place in the crew as an equal.

Anyway. I'll try him again a little later. One can't but be told no, and anyway, there are others to ask I suppose, although none as well equipped.

Later

I've learned some things I simultaneously didn't want to know and probably still needed to know. When I finally tracked down Milton-Jones again, he was at the Dump Pile, pawing through it, moving all manner of things to and fro, making notes in his notebook. All in all, not an unusual sight—Milton-Jones has made such a nuisance of himself over our stocks that our original quartermaster has simply passed over the job to Milton-Jones. Why The Boss didn't see fit to give him the job in the first place no one seemed to know.

Milton-Jones seems to be both excellent at the job and terrible at it—we see his long figure hunched over his notebook and busily counting all manner of stock so often it creates a question in our heads—if he counts accurately, why should he have to do it over and over again?

I cleared my throat, so as not to startle him out of count. He held up his finger, counting under his breath, and I waited.

"Clara," he finally said. He didn't even really look up. He pushed at a stack of boxes that seemed like they didn't want to go. "Lend a hand, will you?"

"Oh, sure." I stepped forward and began shifting boxes. The ice had crusted around the bottom of each stack, and they no longer slid as they did when we first placed them here. Imagine doing this in a skirt. Or a corset. Ridiculous. I can't imagine I'll ever go back to those, no matter where I end up in life. The boxes finally slid to one side, and Milton-Jones peered behind it. "Nothing there," he muttered, and made another notation in his book. He sighed deeply and sat on top of another box.

"Well, that's it then," he said, almost to himself.

"What's *it*?" I pushed over another box and hitched myself onto its edge. For the life of me I couldn't figure what he was looking for or counting.

"Hm?" Milton-Jones glanced at me as if he'd only just noticed I was there. He was scribbling in his notebook again, flipping between pages, cross tabulating, it seemed. He pushed his spectacles up on his nose. He was silent a moment longer, and then he seemed to come to some kind of decision.

"You mustn't tell anyone, but our stores are not where I'd like them to be," he said, sounding glum.

"What, here? No, they're not here," I said, laughing. "Most of them are back by the galley, so Cook doesn't have to trudge back and forth, of course!"

"That's just it," he said. "I had hoped there was more here, to supplement what's already over there—maybe something we overlooked, or something Cook had moved back here for space's sake, but no. What's over there is what we have, and it's not enough."

"Enough . . . ammunition? Diaries? Spare parts for watches? Dog food?"

He nodded slowly. This was like watching molasses slide downhill a muddy slope in January. I restrained a sigh.

"Yes, food," he finally said. "But not just for the dogs, for all of us."

I felt myself go perfectly still. For the first time since I'd been on the expedition, I considered what "not enough" meant. "That can't be right, Thomas." Urgency required the use of Christian names, even to an officer of the Marines. "Surely The Boss would have said something if that were the case."

"The Boss—" Thomas shook his head. "The Boss doesn't want us to ever feel like there's any reason to get our spirits down," he said, looking very down spirited himself.

"No, I don't believe that's true," I said, hopping off my box. "Come on, let's go tell him. He'll want to know, surely."

He shook his head again. "He has to know, but he won't want to know. On the last expedition he was on, the men nearly didn't survive for a variety of reasons, and The Boss is convinced that low morale was one of them. He'd risk so much to ensure everyone was happy and functioning at highest spirits."

I'd read something about this—only three men of thirty survived that expedition, The Boss being one of them. They were all suffering badly from scurvy and other physical ailments. It was said that the expedition leader was so rigid, that he insisted the officers and the crew sleep in different parts of the cave they had finally found to shelter themselves in, just to preserve some misguided sense of hierarchy. It was part of the reason The Boss made us all pitch in at every level on *The Resolute*, although I still am of a mind to speak to him about the appearance of "female" tasks once a woman is on board. (May I have this resolved well before any other woman sets foot on an expedition.)

Some mean part of me always wondered about what would have happened in that cave if they had run out of food. If they had been down to eating one another, would the officers have turned up their noses at eating the sailors? I doubted it, very much.

"Thomas," I said now, "can you be sure?"

He nodded. Say what you will about Milton-Jones, no matter how much ribbing he takes from us, he always seems to take it all in stride. I could learn something from him, I suddenly realized. Milton-Jones is so sure of the position he occupies that he moves *with* the jibes. He knows people think him fastidious, and he simply owns that reputation, whether it's true or not (it is). He knows people find his habits strange, and he lets them think so.

If I were more like Milton-Jones, maybe I wouldn't be struggling so to acclimate to what the men think they know of women.

"I've counted until I can't count anymore," he said. He stood up, shut his notebook. "The Boss hasn't wanted to hunt until things seemed desperate. I'm going to tell him it's time."

He set off toward camp. I ran after him. "Wait, wait. Is this why you didn't want to take me hunting? You didn't want to go against The Boss's ideas?" Thomas's stride is long, and I had to move fast to catch up. My heart lifted.

"Hmm? When did you ask? Of course I'll hunt with you. I've been hearing stories of how much game you've shot on your camping trips with your mother."

I touched his arm. "Wait, Thomas, wait. You said you didn't want to take me because my blood would run too hot, or something, and scare off the animals."

He outright laughed at me. "Oh, Clara, you must learn not to take yourself so seriously. 'Blood running too hot'! Who'd have ever believed that? Now leave me be to speak to The Boss, and I'll see you for dinner."

Never let it be said that women are baffling. Never, ever. Never!

Later

Well, Thomas did not have to give The Boss the bad news, after all—it seems we have been granted a reprieve: We met the last watch on the way to The Boss's tent, and they have relayed news of a colony of penguins about three miles distant, on a floe connected to ours by a solid ice bridge. The watch has also informed us that The Boss has given us the go-ahead to hunt. Thomas's mustache wobbled in some relief at this news.

I hope the ice bridge will hold until we can get to the penguins. There's no telling how they came to be there, if they swam, if they were following food, or if they just floated. I hear they are curious creatures; I wonder if they will come around on their own to visit, walking right into a death trap. This is not a pleasant thing to ponder, although I *am* curious to try some penguin meat. I can't help but think it probably tastes like chicken, only a little briny?

Must go help pack for the hunt. My first hunt on the Antarctic! Surely it will be easier than shooting pheasant, since penguins cannot flush. And when they startle, it must be in a waddling kind of manner, unlike the quick, darting flush of a good brace of *flying* birds.

Still Later

Absolutely rattled. Just back from hunting. I am hiding behind a snowbank and hope no one will find me for some time yet.

I began to understand that this would be a much bloodier affair when Thomas handed me the packing list for the hunt: a portion of hardtack and pemmican for rations for the walk back, fourteen cudgels, and two rifles. I pointed. "*Two* rifles? *Fourteen* cudgels? But there are seven of us. Do you mean fourteen rifles, two cudgels?"

Thomas shook his head. "A few reasons." He counted off on his fingers. "First, we cannot waste ammunition on shooting penguins, as we need a good number of them to feed the crew. Second, they will startle too fast if they hear the guns. Third, penguins are best subdued by a blow to the head," he said. "The rifles are for seals and sea leopards." He shivered. "On the last expedition I got *chased* by a sea leopard. They move fast. If Mahoney hadn't been right behind me with his rifle . . ."

Well, having to a beat a penguin over the head was not at all what I had expected.

Hotchkiss, standing nearby, almost as if he were waiting for my unwitting reaction, sniggered.

"Well, Clara! Now we'll see whether you're really fit to be on this expedition," he said.

I opened my mouth to protest, but Keane got there before I did. He took his pipe out of his mouth and glared. "What would you do if she didn't meet your exacting standards, ya gobshite? Would ya boot 'er off the floe? Would you leave 'er on 'er own?"

Hotchkiss pretended to ponder, hand to weak chin. "Well now, old chap, that's an interesting idea, isn't it? Leave her to the killers for them to play with." He snapped his fingers. I fought the urge to yawn, wondering how long we'd have to watch this pantomime for, wondering why someone else didn't make him stop. "Then again!" he finally said, "A woman's good for a lot more than we've seen out of Clara just yet, so maybe it's best we keep her with us." One of the other men laughed out loud. Hotchkiss spat. "Old men like you—you always want to protect the women. She put herself here; she needs to prove herself."

I waited for Keane to lob back a rejoinder, but he just rolled his eyes and shifted a little closer to me. I wanted to tell him I didn't need his protection, but there was a sense of menace to Hotchkiss I hadn't noticed before: the whole time he was talking, he was staring at me, his eyes cold and hard.

"Shut it, Hotchkiss—and you, Vince, you shut it too, or I'll write you up for conduct unbecoming," said Thomas, unexpectedly. There was a blessed moment of silence in which Hotchkiss, as surprised at all of us at Thomas's outburst, shut it, but not before leering at me once more for good measure.

He licked his lips. "Nothing like a Royal Marine for interceding, is there? Well, excuse *me*, your *highness*." He dropped a mock curtsy in my direction. Vince punched his shoulder in congratulations. I turned my back.

"We have to put a stop to that; it won't come to any good," Thomas said under his breath to me.

I nodded, but really, what was there to do? I didn't want a knight stepping in to save me. It wouldn't change Hotchkiss's mind or his behavior. Getting written up for conduct unbecoming might dock his wages, but the idea of "wages" is so far away now. We won't get paid until we land back in Merrie Olde England again, anyway. If.

People feel how they feel, is how Mama always put it when the society ladies wondered out loud at how much time we spent in the outdoors rather than promenading in the park and looking for suitors for me at balls and teatimes. She said the same to the society ladies, only in much more obscure terms. Something about a healthy, well-rounded education for me. But they still only measured us by their own experiences.

I suppose it's not much different here.

While I was musing, we had come close enough to the penguins to begin unloading our sled and giving each man their two cudgels, one extra, in case . . . in case what? In case a penguin reached out and took one from you?

"One swift blow, Clara," said Keane. "Hit it hard; they have terribly thick skulls. Knock it once to stun it and then you must kill it with the second blow. Anything else would be inhumane. All right?"

"All right, I think."

Keane gazed at me a while longer. "It's for the good of the crew," he said. He put his pipe in his pocket, nodded at me, and went off to consult with the rest of the crew.

For God and Country, I thought, only I still haven't reached the point where I can say this with no irony.

I suppose now is a good time to tell you about the **penguins**. They are an entertainment source for the entire crew, when you are not hunting them for food. They move in great flocks. Watching them walk is a truly astonishing thing—they seem so human at times, with their gimlet stares and their questioning behaviors; it is not unusual to have one walk right up to you and distract you by nibbling at your trouser leg whilst you are trying to study them.

Some of the men, like Hotchkiss and his friends, take this as a sign of stupidity. To hear them speak of the penguins is to experience cruelty and small-mindedness. "Too dumb to know they're prey," is how they put it. I prefer to think of them as too innocent to have encountered a group of men whose sole mission is survival.

Wilson says it's true they have tiny brains, but he also expressed some remorse at having to kill such benign creatures. "They only seem to be curious about who we are," he said, sounding wistful when we told him we were off for a hunt.

There are several types of penguins one might come across in the Antarctic, but we mostly see the Adélie, the gentoo, and the chinstrap. On occasion, we see the emperor penguin, which is too majestic for me to even contemplate killing. It stands quite tall and feels very like a child.

Regardless of the species, all penguins travel in large numbers: rafts (when they're swimming), toboggans (when they're sliding on their bellies), waddles (when they're walking), parades (when they are large and marching). When they are just nesting, which we have not yet encountered since we have not yet reached land, they are said to be in rookeries. Truly, the number of ways one can refer to a group of penguins is myriad. The squawking and crooning of a group of penguins is truly the loudest, most invasive noise you will ever hear. Even more of an assault on the nerves is the smell of penguin guano. It is acerbic, primarily ammonia, and utterly eye watering. Even now, hours after our hunt, it lives in my sinuses. They say the sense of smell is the strongest of our five: Am I doomed to recall this awful day every time I smell ammonia? I shall never be able to feel clean again.

We could see the colony long before we got to it. There was plenty of time for my nerves to play up, imagining having to beat a penguin over its head. "We just wade into their midst?" I asked.

Chutney nodded. "They don't seem to notice much."

I gaped. "Don't they run when you start clobbering them?"

He nodded again. "They don't seem to see until it's far too late, but they *do* eventually see, so we'll move fast."

"Can I not . . ." I gazed at the rifles on our sled. Enfield Mark III. I knew it well. And it would provide distance.

Chutney grimaced. "No, miss. That'd terrify them. They'd bolt. And we'd just be wasting bullets." He smacked his cudgel against his palm. "This is the best tool I've come across yet."

Absolutely barbaric.

By then we were standing at the edge of the penguin colony. The noise, the smell, the overall ruckus in my head, wondering if I could manage to kill something at such close quarters. What I wouldn't have done for a hunt involving a good rifle and some distance!

Keane gave the signal to go ahead just as a penguin tottered up to my legs and began nibbling at my trousers. I closed my eyes, hoping to not meet its gaze, and swung, connecting with something hard. I opened one eye in time for it to fall at my feet, and then I took a step forward, closed my eyes and swung again. And again, and finally connected.

This second bird fell too, emitting a sort of surprised grunt as it toppled over. I hit it again.

I clubbed bird after bird—I entered a kind of fugue state, too similar to the state I was in during our march on Washington, where sound seemed to ebb and flow, and my eyes seemed unable to keep pace with the action around me—but still I went on, and when I stopped, the men were watching me, riveted.

All around me was a selection of half-dead penguins. Only one or two was truly dead. A good many more were twitching or moaning, and it was impossible to escape the fact of my ineptitude.

Hotchkiss started laughing, a high unpleasant call, and Keane flat out *barked* at him.

"*Shut it*, Hotchkiss. *Help* her." The colony, what remained of them, had dissipated by then, and Keane came toward me, following my wake of wounded birds and dispatching them as humanely as he could. From another direction Thomas was doing the same, and eventually the others fell into line too.

I was the last to react. The dying bird at my feet cooed weakly, and I used the butt end of my cudgel to put it to rest. I'd only killed two more birds by the time the men had done helping me. By then I was on my knees, feeling absolutely crippled with misery.

Thomas was closest to me, and he pulled a handkerchief from his chest pocket—a *handkerchief*, Thomas, really?—and waved it at me. "Come now, let's load these birds. The next hunt will be better." He looked around. "Everyone will be pleased with these, and you've done a good job aiming for their heads. You just need to put a little more speed into your swing, more snap in your wrist; that will help. And you need to swing *through*. Don't," he said, looking at me carefully, "pull back. Never, ever hold back."

The woman who taught us suffragists jujitsu had said much the same: Always follow through. I remember now how we could double our own strength just by using any attacker's momentum against them; a man rushing at you could easily be put on his back over your head if you only met him at the right place.

Thomas grabbed four penguins by their pink, leathery feet—even the leopard seals, I've been told, won't eat penguin feet—and swung them over his shoulders. "Come on now, time to get these birds home. Fresh penguin steak tonight!" I tried to hand his handkerchief back to him.

"Oh, no. You keep that till laundry day," he said, and laughed.

Between us, we'd managed to kill eighty-five birds before the colony had finally caught on to what was happening.

"Penguins are the reason some people are called bird-witted, I reckon," said Keane, locked into the traces next to me as we pulled the sled home.

"It was still an awful experience," I said, feeling weak and hating myself for it.

He nodded. "Needs must," he said, economically.

When we finally got home, Hotchkiss was quick to tell everyone what a hash I'd made of the thing. Barely bothering to keep his voice down, he said to a group of men, "Oh, lads! What an absolute ruckus she was making! Her nose was running something awful; I'd never heard such wailing, even out of the youngest babies in their prams!" Some of the men were laughing. Hotchkiss was positively beaming. "Soft, she is."

My first time out with the WSPU, we chained ourselves to the fences at Parliament, wanting an audience with the lawmakers there. I remember the faces on the constables we encountered that day, the words that came out of their mouths. They said we were sniveling, that we were better off at home; they asked if we wouldn't be happier nursing our wee ones. They pitied us, but I had never felt so strong.

This was like that. I was sure there had been no wailing and crying, but Hotchkiss was rewriting my story for me.

His voice followed me to the galley where I went to ask Cook for more tea. "I'd never *seen* such a sight. Why, if we were at home and she were at one of our dances I wouldn't want any part of it. Hardly worth a poke against a wall. It was truly unattractive."

I flushed with anger. Cook glanced at me, rooted in his apron pocket, and came up with a flask. "I've been savin' it," he said, "but you look like you need it. It *sounds* like you need it." He inclined his head toward Hotchkiss's voice. I sighed and held out my tin cup; Cook tipped a dram of whiskey into it.

I sipped—somehow warmer than just tea going down.

Cook was frying up penguin steaks. "Fruits of your labor, innit?" he said, beaming.

"Not quite, Cook—you hear what they're saying."

"Ah, it's nothing. Penguin skulls are like little rocks, Clara. We could break their backs more easily with cudgels, but we can't afford their innards leaking all over the meat, you know? It just takes practice. You'll be better next time."

Next time. Ugh.

Penguin steaks *do* taste like chicken, after all. They were delicious. And, prior to that, they were adorable to look at, and never must I think of the two in conjunction again.

The speculation of the primitive male brain about what women actually *do* and *are* has come to a head these past few days, likely in part because we have been eating well of fresh meat and sweetbreads. When one is sated and flush, one's brain seems to work overtime, worrying its way toward conclusions about things one has never understood.

It has come time for me to tell you **how the men on expedition are likely to view the lives of women,** if only so that you may know what to expect.

Here is what I have found out. Men in general seem to struggle to imagine our lives separate from theirs.

How I wish my friends were here now! How heartily would we laugh at these men and their lack of imagination. And then we would get right to work making sure that they know what we get up to, whether it be through articles in our newspaper or public meetings or just being ourselves! . . .

I like to think I have contributed to some of this today. A group of men was sitting about, talking about some memorable promenades and romantic places they'd like to take the women in their lives, when Wilson, noticing I had not yet contributed to the conversation—although wouldn't it be nice if they had asked me, the only woman, where I might like to be taken—asked me, "How about you, Clara? Is there a feller waiting for you at home?"

I took a deep breath and stilled my instinct to scoff. "No feller," I said, smiling brightly, but then I could not stop myself. "Life is too busy for fellers!"

Silence from the crew. "Too busy for fellers!" said Per. Per asks all the awkward questions. "What's that mean?" He then gasped, like a proper Victorian lady, and said with his hand over his mouth, "You're not . . . you don't mean . . . you don't mean you're a *Sapphic*, do you? Is that why you're not married yet?" He glanced around, looking absolutely scalded.

I kept the smile on my face, even though I thought just then of my suffragist sisters who did prefer the company of women as romantic partners. Whenever will their private lives stop being fodder for scandal and derision, and worse?

"It just means that my mother did not have a happy marriage, and she was damned if she'd see me locked into one too before I was ready," I said. I did not bother to answer Per's question.

There was a shocked silence, whether due to my swearing or the frank talk, I don't know. I shrugged to myself—men on our crew swear all the time; so can I. I augmented my smiling, and then Mahoney barked a laugh and didn't stop for some time. The others goggled. You never really can tell with Mahoney; he has his own barometer of what's funny and what isn't.

Finally he said, "Your mother sounds like a right smart woman. Women don't need us men anyhow, do you?"

"Well, my mother didn't think so, not after the experience she had."

There was more silence while the men processed this. I know all of them were thinking about how babies were made and how women didn't have babies without men and all of that. I was thinking about how even when women did all the hard work raising all these babies that men wanted, they were still stuck with no pension after their man died; and that a woman still had to go back to work two weeks after giving birth; and how Mama had been so beaten down after her marriage to my father that she couldn't even find the energy to fight for her own rights anymore.

Blackburn asked, "Well, if you weren't out promenading and going to dances and courtin' and all that, what were yeh doin'?"

I stifled a giggle. "What d'you fancy I was doing?"

Blackburn shrugged. "Dunno. Like, sewin' and stuff."

I sighed. "Surely you don't think a woman's life is all sewing things and patching things and making art for men to admire?"

He thought about this for a moment. "Well, now,

sometimes I see right pretty things from birds, things you might hang in a museum or summat."

I laughed. "What, like hair art?" Papa had hired someone to teach me the Victorian arts, although by the time I learned it was already considered old-fashioned. One of the most horrifying arts, frankly, beyond pinning butterflies and beetles to boards and labeling them, is whorls and floral designs made from human hair. I pulled off my hat, ran my hands through my shorn head. "You think I can make hair art now, anyway?"

The men laughed too, but then they went quiet, looking as if they really did want to hear more about the life of an Edwardian lady. All six men leaned forward with their hands on their knees, tea forgotten, steaming into the cold air, as if they were hearing a story they'd never heard before, and actually now thinking about it, they really had never heard it before. Not from me, and probably never from any other woman either.

Maybe no one had ever thought they'd want to know. I took a deep breath. This is perhaps a story they should know.

"My mother's people," I said, "were shopkeepers. They kept growing over the years—first with a little play area for the children who would inevitably come in with the women who were doing the marketing, then with a counter for postal matters, then with a telegraph machine. They expanded to one store, then two, then three, all the way out in, uh, Montreal from where they were in, erm, the countryside"—I remembered just in time that everyone thought I was from Canada—"and it was during that third expansion that my grandmother had my mother, Mathilda.

"Grandmama Lila liked to say that having baby Mathilda around made for a better workday, so she brought her into the store a lot, and that made her think that maybe women would like a place to stop in and have a chat with their friends while they were getting their chores done. So they built a little tearoom.

"And my grandparents hired women, all the time, to work the counter, to help with the bookkeeping—and they even invested in their futures. If one of the women wanted to learn, say, stocktaking or purchasing, Grandpa Henry or Grandma Lila taught her."

"Corrrrrr," said Per, and I didn't know if that was an admiring remark or one of shock, but I didn't care. I wished I had known Henry and Lila, but they'd died by the time I was born. Maybe if they'd been around to see what a mess Papa had made of Mama, she'd have had the support she needed to come with me to England and fight with the WSPU.

"My mother worked in the store from when she was twelve. But by then my grandparents had had my uncle Edwin, and according to the custom at the time, the store and most of its fortune would pass on to Edwin, even though my mother would go on to work in the store for many years after Edwin was born. And Edwin was eventually keen to try to manage something on his own. So when he came of age, the store passed to him—and anyway, my mother had been married off to my papa." I swallowed. "Who was not a very nice man."

Per and Blackburn twitched. Wilson looked away. No one wanted to hear exactly how not nice men could be.

"So, my mother turned to other things," I said. "She rode a lot, horses *and* bicycles. She inherited the family land in the country and a generous per annum allowance, and my uncle Edwin inherited the shops and the city homes; and so when she had me, she taught me the things that she had grown to know and love.

"Mama and Papa led very separate lives. Mine was with my mama, in the woods and in the library, and it suited us just fine."

Vince shrugged. "Sounds like what you hear of a lot of middle-class families," he said. "Doesn't sound like such a rough life."

"Mm," I said, evenly. "But it wasn't all sitting around and waiting for men, is the point. Nor does having married make it all easy."

Vince shrugged again. Dismissed it with a wave of his hand. "You had plenty of money and plenty of land. What's to complain about?"

I flushed, hot and angry, and I heard some of Gwendoline's last words to me, clear as the Antarctic day: "You'll never really understand," she'd said.

I took a deep breath. I had tried hard not to think of Gwendoline for some time. "*Obviously* I'm not the only woman in the world," I said. "Let me tell you about my friend, Gwendoline.

"Gwendoline is the first person I met when I went to England. Her father was a sailor; her mother worked in the laundry. And so Gwendoline also worked in the laundry, from the age of eight."

I remembered the first time I saw Gwendoline's hands, hard at work on our printing press, turning the crank. By then they'd been able to heal from her time in the laundry, but her hands were still prematurely wrinkled, always prone to chapping; painful, she said, in cold weather. I remember wondering why she didn't wear gloves to hide them, and what she'd said to me when she caught me looking one day: "Why should I hide my past? I'm proud of the work I've done," she'd said, "and frankly, you should be proud of the work I've done too." Gwendoline had looked softly at me, unrelenting in her gaze, until I'd perversely felt the need to cover up my own soft palms and manicured fingers.

The men were rapt, leaning forward, as if they'd never thought about the life of a laundress before. Which they hadn't, I'm sure, even though some of their mothers and sisters and aunts had worked for a living. "Gwendoline worked there until she was twelve, almost losing her arm to a mangle more than once; looking after her mother when she became ill, which was more and more often; taking laundry home with her for extra earnings. There was hardly time for even thinking about courting, even thinking about romance, much less thinking about hair art or"—I swallowed—"even riding horses or learning new languages."

I poked Per's stringy little arm. "Any of you ever lift a full load of wet laundry? Or handled one of those hot irons?" They shook their heads. "It's all damn heavy," I said. "Gwendoline was *strong*.

"But she was also deft with her hands, good at making small repairs and delicate stitches, and she became quite known in the laundry for it. People who sent their clothing in for mending began to ask for her. And Gwendoline wasn't just good with her hands, she was quick in her mind, too—before her foreman thought of it, Gwendoline thought to take her skills elsewhere, to a milliner's shop, where she began by making hatboxes and eventually graduated to finishing hats with their delicate little details." I mimed sipping a cup of tea with my pinky in the air, and the men chortled.

"By then her mother was quite ill and had stopped working; her father had been killed at sea years before. She worked from before dawn to late at night.

"And that," I said, seeing Hotchkiss approaching our circle to wreak God-knows-what havoc on this minor plot of peace I felt we had, "is what you do when you're a girl and you're not overly occupied with suitors. You are learning languages and reading and hunting and keeping up with your mother on her horse or her bicycle. Or you are working ever-long hours just to make things *go*, putting your body at risk every day, forgoing all the things you might be dreaming of, until you either get married off, at which point the work increases to include feeding your husband and whatever children society tells you you must now have."

Dead silence from the men, until Burch said, half laughing, "Cor, Clara, we only wanted to know what *you* did with all the spare time, not some washerwoman. We know what they do, don't we?"

I thought I wouldn't be able to speak without screaming. I thought maybe if I opened my mouth such invectives would spew forth that the men would never speak to me again. My heart pounded and my words stacked up in my throat, the true story of how washerwomen and factory workers and ladies alike banded together to throw rocks and to cut electrical lines and build kerosene bombs. How would that strike them, for what some washerwoman got up to???

I took a deep breath and tried to still myself, thinking of what Pankhurst would have said to a comment like that. Nothing, likely. She'd have looked away, as if it were but a fly to be brushed off one's hat, and I did so then.

By then, Hotchkiss had oozed his way into our midst. "All right, men," he said, "that's the end of nursery for you. Time to say goodbye to your nanny."

All my hard-won calm flushed away. I turned to face him, feeling dangerous. "Do you never shut your trap, Hotchkiss?"

Hotchkiss's eyes flashed. "Oh, the bitch has bite finally, does she? No dead penguins to snivel over, are there?"

I got up and walked away. "Where are you going, Nanny? Good job The Boss thought to hire one of you. The boys look happier near their nursemaid!" he called out fast before I could get out of earshot.

I turned on my heel and stalked back to him. Got right up in his face. Hotchkiss is barely taller than I am, and in my boots I have an extra inch. Gripped his collar. Got really, really close. Breathed in his stench—unwashed man, unsavory mind, bleeding arse of a specimen—and evenly, almost growling, feeling dangerous and stretched beyond my limits, I said, "You watch yourself, you low, low piece of shit. Don't cross me."

In my head, The Boss said, *Leave it, Clara*, but I was done leaving it. "You hear me?" I said again, for good measure. "Don't. Cross. Me."

I turned again and stalked away, and I was ready when he came running after me. I heard the ice squeaking under his boots, heard him panting, heard him yell, "Get back here, you lazy cunt, we have to—" but that was all he could get out before I spun around, got down low to the ground, just like Mrs. Garrud had taught us, and punched my shoulder right into his solar plexus. I lifted with my legs, feeling infinite—follow *through*—and flipped him over my shoulder. Effortless. He landed behind me, and I heard the wind go right out of him.

A sweeter sound I'd never heard. Certainly sweeter than the collective gasp I heard go up from the men I'd just been sitting with. "Clara, what did you *do*?" This was Higgins, and I *thought* I detected a note of admiration, but also of worry. For me or for Hotchkiss? I was not sure I wanted to know.

"Don't be stupid," I said. "*He* was running after *me*!"

"Aye, Clara, to tell you you're needed to help Givens and him with digging some new latrines. You're on a team together again." Higgins still sounded unsure.

"Oh, for *fuck's* sake! Not again."

On the ground behind me, Hotchkiss was still gasping. "Bitch," he wheezed.

I sent my eyes heavenward, bit my tongue. I bent down and extended a hand to Hotchkiss. "Get up, Hotchkiss, it was only a bit of play," I said, "and you called me a cunt. How did you expect I'd react?"

"Aw, he was only talking, Clara," said Higgins.

Hotchkiss turned onto his side, pretending he hadn't seen my hand, and I grabbed his arm instead, pulling him forcibly to a standing position. I whacked him on the shoulder, aiming for jovial, just like I'd seen him do to other men. "He's fine now, aren't you, Hotchkissy?" I added the pejorative just to give a name to some of my ire. Hotchkiss glared and wheezed.

"Get off! You think a girl would put me down? Not likely." He scoffed, or tried to, but that sent him into a coughing fit. He stalked, bent over, back to the staging area, with one or two glares backward at me for good measure. "Don't think this makes you better than me, you stupid dyke," he shouted. I balled up my fists.

Higgins put his hand on my shoulder, shook his head at me. "You shouldn't, Clara."

I shook off his hand. "He needs to stop."

Higgins glanced at Hotchkiss, hobbling across the snow. He quirked a smile. "Well, he might now."

I shrugged and followed Hotchkiss to the boats.

What I wouldn't give for a little less drama. How I longed for Mama's placid presence. For a split second, I wondered if she was right to want to avoid all this.

Even in her state of lassitude, I do not believe she would tolerate Hotchkiss for very long. But I am not Mama, and she is not the one who is here, stuck on an ice floe, with no options to flee.

We have been out of penguin meat for two days. Cook stretched it as best he could, but we are well and truly out now. MacTavish has been very clear: lack of fresh meat leads quickly to scurvy. Thomas has been doing his best to resist what I think is his natural urge to catastrophize, but we've been over and over the stocks, and the need is apparent even to my novice eyes: it seems the colder-than-predicted summer season has thrown all the animals off their normal patterns of behavior, and since that first mess of penguins, we have seen not even a footprint or any other indication of another colony.

Thomas has gone to see The Boss.

Later

Well, that went more badly than anyone would have expected.

I could hear Thomas stomping on the ice, moving like a buffalo just outside our tent where I was sitting with the flap propped open just a little—it can get awful warm in our tents, but the light through the tent fabric is a wonderful butter yellow that makes for perfect reading, better than the harsh glare of the light outside. I'd been perusing the Q volume of the encyclopaedia and was staring at a drawing of the Australian quokka, a mammal with an irrepressibly happy face and beady little contriving eyes, and I was just thinking about how lovely it would be to hold one of these in my lap with a cup of hot tea and just sit and worry about nothing, not unlike a cat, I suppose, but without all the creepy insidiousness that comes with a cat.

We had a ship's cat. She spent all her spare time torturing the dogs, marking their lodgings whilst they were chained up and waking them up by batting their noses for no particular reason at all. But when the time came to decamp to the ice, she left, and we haven't seen her since. The dogs seem lonelier for her having left, or maybe they miss her contrariness, or maybe they want for something else to pay attention to. If I just walked off into the landscape, would the men miss me for the same reasons the dogs miss our cat?

In any case, so deep was I in imagining a warm quokka curled up cozily in my lap that I was loathe to leave, and even was tempted to pretend I was sleeping, which was easy enough to do, given the gentle light and the late afternoon time—no matter where you are, late afternoon is a fine time for a nap. But Thomas's voice was too strident for me to ignore, and I called out. He bent into the tent.

"Ah, there you are. Come, I have a job for you."

I dog-eared "quokka" in the encyclopaedia and slid out

of my sleeping bag, trying not to get reindeer hairs all over me. They are short and sharp and most uncomfortable in one's cleavage. It's a pointless exercise, of course, and when one inevitably works its way through your coveralls, your sweater, your woolens, you'll have a terrible time finding it.

I began to pull on my boots. "Is there news? Another penguin colony, maybe? What'd The Boss say?"

Thomas blinked. "I need you to assume my duties as quartermaster."

I paused, one boot half on. "I'm sorry?"

Thomas stepped backward, giving me room to exit the tent. "Come, Clara, we need to move. I need to show you where the stores are and how they're arranged; I have yet other tasks to get to. You have your notebook? Good. Pencil? Good. Come now; let's go."

"Thomas, what happened?" Once again, I struggled to catch him. "What did The Boss say? Did you talk to him?"

"I did," Thomas said. "I've been relieved of my duties as quartermaster. And instead of that job, I am to shoot the dogs."

I reeled. "What?"

Thomas quirked a sad smile at me. "I am to shoot the dogs," he said in the exact same tone, as if attempting to reconcile himself to the statement.

I didn't blame him; I couldn't reconcile it myself. "Shoot the dogs . . . But why?"

"A kind of punishment, I dare say, wouldn't you?"

I dared say. But it also didn't make much sense at all. I channeled Mrs. Pankhurst, who never liked to react without all the information she needed. "What was the reason he gave you?"

"He said that there were multiple measures one could take to ensure we had enough to eat."

". . . Oh."

I turned on my heel. Thomas called after me. "Where are you going, Clara? We need to teach you to count stock!"

I waved at him over my shoulder. "I'm going to talk to The Boss, Thomas. This can't be the best solution."

"No, Clara, wait—"

I ignored him. I hoped he wouldn't follow me; his presence would only make things worse.

Stern, the second-in-command, was slouched in front of the tent he shared with The Boss, working on some maps with Billings when I got there. I lifted my chin at him, trying to portray confidence I didn't quite feel.

When your body is being ruled by anger, it can fool you into doing all sorts of things. I think this is probably akin to what Emily was feeling when she tried to hang one of our Votes for Women flags on a fast-flying racehorse. Emily got trampled for her pains. All I could think about was how stupid it was to shoot man's best friend by way of trying to make a team feel better.

"He in?"

Stern nodded. "But I wouldn't—"

I slipped around him. "Excuse me." I flapped open the tent. The difference in light was stark, and I couldn't see for a moment.

"Boss," I called, and blinked some more. There wasn't anyone standing or sitting anywhere.

"Yes, what is it?" The voice came from somewhere down by my feet, and I crouched—The Boss was having one of his attacks of sciatica, and he was laid flat on his back, a balled-up pair of socks tucked under one side of his spine for relief. He grunted and sat up. "Oh, it's you." He sighed.

"Yes, it's me. Boss, about the dogs . . ."

"What, Milton-Jones told you, did he?"

The Boss didn't seem pleased, but I pressed on. There were more important things here at stake.

"He told me you believed shooting the dogs to be an avenue toward relieving our low food stocks."

The Boss laid back down again. "I see."

I had a terrible sinking feeling that Thomas wasn't meant to tell me this, either.

I plowed on. "Anyway, I'm very sorry you're not feeling well, but I'd like for you to consider that the dogs' presence is critical to our well-being, especially now that we are to be at Camp Patience for some time."

"Oh? Why do you say that?"

"Camp Patience is to be our home for some time, is it not?"

"It does seem that way."

I chose to ignore the dryness of The Boss's tone. I don't have much patience with sarcasm.

"Then let me suggest that our dogs have been part of our home since we launched *The Resolute*, and to kill them off would be a matter of grave depression for the crew."

"And I suggest you leave it. I've already given Milton-Jones the order."

I set my teeth. *Leave it, Clara.* "No, sir, I will not leave it. Please consider it."

Silence. The Boss breathed in and out, painfully. "And what would you have me do about our lack of fresh meat?"

"We hunt; we search more broadly for meat."

"Hunting requires energy, Clara. Resources. And we cannot depend on the appearance of more wildlife."

"We could not count on the appearance of a lead, either, could we?" The moment I said it, I wanted to take it back. The sinking of *The Resolute* is still all too fresh in our minds.

The Boss, after a beat, seemed to choose to ignore my comment. "It will be easier to both keep an eye out for fresh meat *and* shoot the dogs." He paused. "You do understand, don't you, that shooting the dogs rids us of our immediate need?"

I swallowed. I had not considered this "upside" to the dogs' demises. I have never eaten dog meat, and I could not imagine—

I swallowed again. "I . . ."

The Boss sat up again, grunting painfully over his sciatica. "Yes, that's what I thought. Clara, you're merely delaying the inevitable. The dogs *will* have to be shot at some point. We cannot take them with us in the lifeboats to Paulet when the leads open up. And Milton-Jones is correct: we must make a decision now. Which I have done."

I waited. He wasn't going to admit that perhaps if we had been hunting all along, or actively looking to hunt, rather than wasting time packing and unpacking lifeboats and barely dragging them a mile and a half across inhospitable-to-dragging territory, we might not even be having this conversation.

"Go on, Clara. This is the best course of action."

I couldn't think of anything else to say. "Yes, sir."

"If it helps any, you may encourage Milton-Jones to seek out more of the crew to help him divide the task. It does seem unduly cruel to have to shoot thirty dogs by yourself." This last he said with very little emotion whatsoever.

"Thirty-seven, sir," I said firmly, although I wavered on my feet. "Lucy has had her own pups finally."

He nodded. "Thirty-seven, then."

I must think that perhaps The Boss is distracted by pain from his sciatica; otherwise, how could he sound so dispassionate? I turned my back on him and practically ran out of the tent.

Crying in the Antarctic is one of the stupidest things

one can do—the tears freeze almost immediately, and then your cheeks are covered in a sheet of fine, salty rime.

This is a good place for me to tell you about **emotions** on the ice. Oh, you may scoff, and if you are anything like me, you will scoff hard—you will have spent your entire life trying to buck the image of women being soft, wailing creatures of love, candy floss, and wistfulness; reactionary, willing receptacles of whatever one chooses to throw at us. And so, you will have practiced not letting your emotions get any of you, much less the better of you. At times, the vast realm of possibility I see in the landscape becomes a void to shout into. The extremity of the temperatures, which seem like opportunities to underscore the very poles of your will, become sharp tests of your hardiness instead.

Most times, it's okay. But other times, sensations like nostalgia and regret do consume you.

Everything on the ice is bigger than it is on land.

Thomas and I Go on an Adventure

Later, when I flip through the pages of this diary, I will see this heading—Thomas and I Go on an Adventure—and I will perhaps not be overly saddened by the memory of what we had to do today.

We told all the men we were putting the dogs down, so they might come to say goodbye first if they wanted. Nearly all of them turned down the opportunity, and with good reason—dogs are such sensitive creatures, and not a single man we spoke to could keep his pain from showing when he heard what was to happen. Surrounding them with a bunch of men who were upset would only serve to upset the dogs in turn, surely.

Even Hotchkiss was affected, although his reaction was more in line with what we know of him. He stared wildly all around him and began shouting at Thomas: "This is all your fault, Milton-Jones! I just know it. If it weren't for your meddling, and your stupid, poufty, pre-cise *bookkeeping* . . ." He lunged suddenly at Thomas, and if Thomas hadn't stepped back quickly he'd have been punched. Mahoney dragged Hotchkiss away, although he was still yelling and flailing his arms about.

"Sad," said Thomas.

When we'd finally found the weapons we needed from the armory and gone back to where the kennels were, we found Mahoney sat with Lucy, whose pups he'd helped birth, in his lap, muttering into her great ruff. The dog stared into the mid-distance, as if she already had other cares.

"Mahoney," Thomas said, low, and Mahoney looked up at us, eyes rimmed red.

"Good dogs, they are," he said. He stood up, pushing Lucy off his lap. She lumbered off in the direction of her kennel. Mahoney held his hand out for a pistol. "Give one here," he said. "This needs to go quickly, before the dogs catch on." Thomas and I looked at each other. Mahoney flexed his fingers. "Come on, now." Thomas handed him a Colt 1911 pistol and went back to the armory for a third.

Mahoney discharged the magazine and peered at it. He glanced at me. "You know how to work one of these?"

"I can work a rifle very well," I said.

"Right," he said. "If you can work a rifle, you can work this." He handed it over to me, pointing out how to load the magazine, how to reload it.

I hefted the thing in my hand. It was heavy for something so short, misbalanced in my hand, almost.

Mahoney was still talking. "When Milton-Jones gets

back, we'll each take a pair and work through them, quick as we can. Clear?"

I blinked. "Yes," I said. Part of me felt as if I were above, watching what was going on. It was a terrible sensation.

I nodded again, trying to connect my thoughts to my physical body.

"Clara," said Mahoney. "Look at me."

I turned my head, feeling like I was moving through molasses.

"Good," Mahoney said. "Listen. Take two dogs at a time. Stake their leads well into the ground. Press the gun close to the dog's head. Fire away from the direction of the other dog. The bullet may go through, and you don't want him startling and bolting, or getting winged. Then do the same with the other. Above all, be quick. All right?" He watched me for a moment.

No, of course it wasn't all right. It was all wrong.

I nodded.

"Don't look," Mahoney said.

⁓

Mama once told me that I cannot voice a memory properly if I let it go for too long before I write about it. I need to see it for what it did to me in that moment, she said. "You must not delude yourself, not now nor in later years," she said. "Memory is a trickster."

But I cannot bear to have this terrible event painted in stark black and white. I cannot see how the details of this day will do anything but serve to remind me of the sacrifices we made of others' lives for the sake of this expedition.

I will take Mahoney's advice here: I will not look back at what I have had to do—what we all had to do. When I came back for more ammunition, Chutney was there, pipe sending tendrils of smoke into the air. "Here, lass, give 'er here," he said, taking the pistol from my hands. "You go on now, you've done enough. Go," he said again when I didn't budge.

"Thomas? Mahoney?"

Chutney nodded. "Don't worry, others'll be along."

Sure enough, as I trudged my way back to the tents, I passed Blick and Wilson, Figgy, and finally, The Boss himself, moving slowly, limping.

He nodded at me, but I couldn't look at him for very long.

I am going straight to bed. Part of me wants to dream of nothing but puppies; part of me wants oblivion. And the last part of me is fully aware that we have reached some point of no return.

Still feeling absolutely gutted about the dogs. Camp was subdued when I woke up this morning; even though I had once imagined a camp without dog noises, I had never hoped it would happen and never thought it would come to pass. I didn't anticipate the somber mood of my crewmates and their attached quiet.

In some ways, there was some solace to be had in our communal misery, and The Boss, to his credit, did not try to play the jolly, cheer-em-up commander or anything even remotely close to it.

My sleep was thankfully dreamless, but I awoke to hear Per sniffling miserably, so I shuffled my sleeping bag close to his and lay there with him, back to back, until I could feel his crying start to quiet. Sometimes a little human warmth does wonders.

I remember when I had nightmares, Mama would get into bed with me and hold me.

Obviously, I cannot do such a thing here, but I hope Per was able to gain some comfort from my presence.

A good many of us ate our breakfasts silently. I, for one,

wanted to go right back to bed, but the day will be doubly busy today: I need to learn Thomas's method of stocktaking and possibly develop my own, and The Boss has asked some of us to drill packing and unpacking and repacking the lifeboats, so we can be ready to go the moment a lead opens up. This means striking camp every single day until we launch. How tedious.

Later

Stocktaking is an odd oasis of calm amidst all the other things one must consider in the Antarctic. Counting items will always be just that—counting. Whereas even the most basic things—washing up, going to the toilet, eating, sneezing, sleeping—all of these are different in the Antarctic, or even on a boat. It feels good to be competent again at something.

I thought Thomas might be sad to give up stocktaking, but he tells me Wilson has asked for his help on some of the more exacting experiments involving seawater, so I suppose there's something to be said for that.

Total disaster: the men are refusing to eat the dog meat. I'm not sure what The Boss thought would happen, but he cannot force us to eat it, and Cook has also balked at butchering our friends, and so we are set to go farther abroad for a hunt tomorrow. One thought is, The Boss has not much stomach for eating our dogs, either.

Our friends will be buried in the ice. Some part of me knows that if things get really dire, we will dig them up and eat them. This thought fills me with infinite sadness, whether for our current state of doglessness or the idea of a future state so desperate we'd eat them, I do not know.

I am on a hunting team with Thomas, Hotchkiss, Keane, and a few other men. I am too tired to argue over the makeup of this team, even though Hotchkiss is being openly rotten to Thomas about shooting the dogs, which he sees as all Thomas's fault for having told The Boss we were low on fresh meat.

The things he's said! "Wish it were you we had to put down," was one absolute ruby. He never says these things properly out loud, just in passing. When he crosses Thomas on the ice, he mimes putting a gun to his own head and pulling the trigger. He's started calling Thomas "Old Mutt" just to drive home the point.

I always can tell Thomas has had an encounter with Hotchkiss by the way his mustache droops. It's utterly cruel.

And that's on top of the way Hotchkiss is behaving with me. Before, on the ship, he would merely wink whenever he saw me; now he outright leers, looking me up and down with his pig eyes, smiling with those thin, fishy lips of his. It's downright off-putting. I must find a way to make it stop.

At dinner, Captain Phillips came to tell me The Boss wanted to see me. We haven't really spoken since that whole thing with the dogs.

He was flat on his back again. The last two nights have been really cold. "Damn close to mutinous behavior, Clara," he said. He sounded uncomfortable; his face looked pinched, although from pain or annoyance I couldn't tell.

I kept quiet.

"Your show of support for Milton-Jones, I mean." He propped himself on one elbow, wincing. "When I give an order, I expect it to be followed to the letter."

"I know, Boss, but—"

"Ketterling-Dunbar!" The Boss's tone carried some weight of threat to it, but I couldn't really see what else could happen to me that might be so awful as the last few days have been.

"Sir!" I talked fast. "No one deserves that kind of weight on his soul."

Silence from The Boss, but he studied me at length. I struggled to get my breathing under control. Panting never did anyone any good, a lesson one learns when one has to wear corsets.

Finally, he said, sounding utterly exhausted, "You *think* you know the weight we bear on our backs, but the picture is much bigger than you think it. You cannot see it as I see it. You must learn to trust me on this count. If not me, then to trust in the greater intuition of a team of seasoned men, for whom this is a routine exercise, no matter how extreme it may seem."

Oh! Is there ever anything more infuriating than being told one is not as experienced as one thinks! I stood still for a moment, and then asked to be excused.

He sighed, deep and painful, and eased himself back down. He pointed at the tent door. "I do not wish to fight you, Clara. You must fall in line. Please. For the crew."

Oh! How I wanted to cast my eyes to the heavens, but that would have accomplished absolutely nothing. I set my lips, not that he could see me in the dim light of his tent, and left as quietly as I could, although I was raging on the inside. The urge to go rail at something was strong.

12 December

The **nighttime** in Antarctica is both a wonder and a bother. In the Antarctic summertime, the daylight is around nearly twenty-four hours. Keane says it always takes a few days for the crew to not want to stay up all night and experience the bizarreness of a midnight sun, but I have never believed the resulting sleep-hangover is worth it: whenever I've stayed up all night, I go about all the next day in a kind of sunlit fog. It's too disorienting for me to be useful.

Several odd things, anyway, have already happened thus far in the middle of a summer night—dogs, when we had them, kicking up a fuss for no reason, the telltale splash and burble of a killer whale pressing its nose through a thin spot of ice—that I already know the odd disconnect that happens in your head when these things happen at one in the morning and you can still *see*. Last night was by far the worst. I was on watch with Wilson, who was feeling contemplative. He spent a lot of time asking open-ended questions that I didn't care to answer. Why, for instance, is everything we put on toast so violently processed? It is either sliced, or mashed, or macerated, or boiled to within an inch of its life, he said.

I was distracting myself with a survey through the telescope when I saw a significantly sized wave headed toward our floe.

I shouted, "*Wave!*" and started running back to camp, to help with the protocol we'd prepared for such an event: everyone to the lifeboats, as quickly as possible after head count; a good-sized wave could mean a crack in the floe, which could both spell disaster and open up a number of leads.

I shouted as loudly as I could, calling back over my shoulder to Wilson and forward to camp. "WAVE! *WAVE!*" Wilson followed on my heels.

The men must have heard us, because they were out of their tents quickly and all headed for the lifeboats, all except for those in tent number eight. That crew was standing around, looking perplexedly at their tent, and I noticed the head count was off—who was missing?

The wave had hit the floe by then, opposite to where we'd lost *The Resolute* and near where the dogs' snow kennels had been, and I think we all suffered a little vertigo watching the edge of our floe tilt crazily and feeling the significant shift under our feet. It was as if one were slowly being tipped upward at a most gentlemanly pace, enough to make one feel disoriented, unmoored, but not quite violently ill.

A sick crack sounded from the floe beneath tent eight.

Billings and McNish were out already; more tentmates finally came spilling out, arms pinwheeling, trying to catch their balance, but MacTavish was still missing. A surprised bark came from inside the tent and a splash, and then, before our eyes, the tent began to stretch and yaw; the two halves of the floe now each warring for their side of the tent, stretching the fabric and torquing the hoops keeping it all together.

Next to me, Givens groaned—it was he who'd created the hoop design, and now I could see he'd hoped it wouldn't be the death of MacTavish—the floe had split cleanly, right beneath number eight, and the strength of the hoops could very well help the two halves to snap back together again at any moment. MacTavish could easily be crushed.

What happened next is, to my memory, like a caricature of heroism. Rapid steps from behind me and Givens, and then, The Boss's familiar figure shot across the ice and into the open flap of the tent before anyone could move. "No!" someone yelled, and someone else shushed him just as quickly.

We heard The Boss shout from inside the tent, and we all stood stock still and watched like a group of useless schoolchildren as the tent bobbed and undulated. The pegs and the hoops still held the two halves together. Givens sank to his knees. "Please, please, please pop," he muttered. I dropped down next to him, gripping his shoulders.

A loud clap sounded and we all jumped—the floe

had come together again. A split second later, MacTavish crashed out of the tent, nearly taking a hoop with him, trailing water, looking like an inept seal. Billings ran to him and dragged him toward us.

No Boss. The floe rocked again, and the tent pegs finally sheared out of the part of the floe we were standing on. We all watched, horrified, as the new floe slowly started to pull away, dragging with it the tent, now only moored on one side. Under the sagging fabric, a shape heaved, and then, out of a loose flap, The Boss appeared. The sheared-off new floe had only just started to drift away, but already The Boss looked so small.

Our entire crew groaned. Wilson started to run in the direction of the armory. "Harpoons! Fishing hooks!" he yelled as he ran, but the armory was surely too far away. A few men ran with him. I knelt still, rooted to the spot, feeling useless and ill. Next to me, Givens threw up.

The Boss retreated a few steps from the edge of the floe and stood there for a second, breathing hard, and I think we all realized at the same time what he would attempt, because we all went dead silent, except for Hotchkiss who, unbelievably, was moaning about being cold. Some of the crew had wrapped MacTavish in a sleeping bag from another tent. I glanced at him, shivering, his lips going obviously blue even in the strange ever-twilight of an Antarctic night, and something Mama had taught me tickled at my brain, but I ignored it.

The Boss's shoulders rose and fell as he took one more mighty breath, gathering his strength, and then he took a running start and leapt for our floe.

His weight and speed made the floe slip backward across the water, putting him at an immediate disadvantage. We were probably only five feet apart by then, but with The Boss's sciatica acting up, we all worried, and for good reason. The Boss pinwheeled through the air and crashed into the lip of our floe with his chest. He scrabbled madly for a split second and slid right off, into the water.

"*Shit!*" Keane bolted past me and reached over the edge, grabbing The Boss's coveralls just before he slipped under. One mighty jerk and they were both flat on the ice, safe on our floe, as the sheared-off part floated off alarmingly fast, taking the tent and the part of camp with the dog kennels on it. Keane was back on his feet in a second, dragging the wet Boss back toward us and into the warmth of human company.

"Quick, quick!" Stern was yelling now. "Keane, Billings, get MacTavish and The Boss into tent one. Everyone else, go empty your tents. Go get your sleeping bags. Bring me some brandy, Cook!" Keane and Billings fireman-carried the two men into the tent, and the rest of us watched from the flap.

"I'll go!" shouted Hotchkiss and a mean part of my brain went, *Of course he would go for the liquor.*

My memory jogged, uneasy. It took until Hotchkiss had

come back with the brandy to spit out something useful. He had moved past me, uncorking the bottle as he went, before I remembered.

"No!" I yelled. "It'll make them worse; *don't!*" I shoved my way into the tent and grabbed the brandy from Hotchkiss's hands. "Someone go get some spare clothing. Cook, please go get the stove going; they need to drink some warm water. Don't worry about making tea; just make it warm enough to increase their body temperature a little bit." I shoved the brandy back into Hotchkiss's hands. "Here. Sorry about that. Put it away. It'll make everything worse."

MacTavish's skin was waxy, pale, and he was shaking hard. The Boss didn't look much better. I turned to Mahoney. "We need to get their clothing off them."

The men murmured. Hotchkiss laughed unpleasantly. "Whatever does she want their clothes off for? This isn't the place for a slap and tickle."

I ignored him. "Mahoney, Chutney, anyone, please help. Their wet clothes will make them worse. And the brandy only makes one *feel* warm, because it sends all the blood to your extremities. Please."

Hotchkiss tried to push past me. "What do you know about anything?" He started to tip the bottle into The Boss's mouth, and The Boss didn't look like he was going to protest anytime soon.

"No!" I slapped at Hotchkiss's hand, and the brandy

bottle flew out of it, landing far away on its side. Hotchkiss glared at me.

Mahoney shouldered Hotchkiss out of the way then, shaking out an extra pair of woolens. I knelt to pull off MacTavish's socks, but Mahoney stopped me. "Come on, Clara," he said. "A little dignity for the men, eh?"

"What's a little dignity compared to life?" I snapped, but I was already feeling a little bashful now that everyone was back together and out of the water, and I backed out and away from the tent. Hotchkiss was still glaring, but I didn't care.

"Clara." Cook was behind me with two tin cups of gently steaming water.

"Thomas!" I called in through the flap. "Make them drink this, please!" Someone's hands reached through.

Hotchkiss's voice, again. "Taking orders from a woman now, are we?"

No one replied to him. Plenty of murmuring.

I paced outside, hoping I'd remembered right. All I knew was how much better I felt when Mama had treated me the same way after I'd fallen into the pond while ice-skating one year. The local doctor had been impressed by her when he'd finally come to see me.

"Where'd you learn that, madam?" he asked.

"I enjoy the outdoors," Mama had said, and left it at that.

Tent eight on its new home was out of sight by now. I

pictured it, trailing its fabric and its remaining two hoops like a mermaid tail. Next to me, the men who'd been bereft of their home and some of their possessions started to grizzle. I shook myself and pulled out my notebook, reviewing the protocol: head count, look for leads, load boats. "Well, no one's going anywhere just yet," I said. "Where's Stern?" No one knew.

I called out, trying to quell the idea that I should *leave it* to someone else. "Stern!"

"Ketterling-Dunbar, what do you want?" His voice came across the ice.

"Er, sir," I said, feeling less sure now, "are we looking for a possible exit?"

Stern was quick to snap at me. "And just what do you think I was doing, having a cuppa?"

I stepped back. "No, sir. Sorry. Er . . ."

He glared at me. "We're staying put for now, until everyone gets warm again," he said, and stalked away, calling back over his shoulder, "It's colder on the water."

I was glad Hotchkiss had gone away somewhere, although McNish, Billings, and Roland were still standing next to me. "Never mind, Clara," said McNish then, patting my shoulder kindly. "We all get a little excited when something like this happens."

I blushed and buried my nose in my notebook again, looking for something to do. The answer came in the stock count.

"According to the latest stock count," I said, "we should have enough to replenish what you lost, depending on what floated away." I snapped my notebook shut. "Let's go have a look, see what you've lost?"

The men walked with me to the edge of the floe where some sparse belongings lay, looking forlorn.

I picked up volume *M* of the Encyclopaedia Britannica. "Well, there's this," I said.

The men grinned at me. I opened my notebook and made a list of what they had lost.

"Why don't you all go sort out where you'll be sleeping? I'll take a sledge and gather what I can from the Dump Pile."

The men made vague acquiescing noises, and I went to go find a sledge. I called to Thomas as I passed—I wanted him to check my stock work after this run.

He opened the tent flap and gamely came with.

"All right in there?" I asked.

"Better. The color's returned to their faces, and Mac-Tavish's teeth have stopped chattering." He glanced at me. "He says you were right to do what you did."

I nodded, swallowing around the lump of relief in my throat.

It was a half mile to the Dump Pile, even though we'd lost a chunk of our floe, and now that all the men were safe, I caught myself thinking that it was a damned good thing that we hadn't lost the Dump itself in the wave. I steadfastly refused to think about what it would be like if Hotchkiss had been the one to be sandwiched between shuddering pieces of ice.

I shook my head to get rid of the uncharitable thought and elbowed Thomas. "Some night, eh?"

Thomas nodded. "Maybe now we'll be forced to make a move of some sort."

I glanced at him. His glasses glinted in the weak light, and I couldn't be sure if he was winking. He'd sounded almost giddy. "Really?"

"Oh, I was just thinking that something needs to happen. We feel a little complacent to me."

I snorted. "What, like on top of not knowing we needed to shore up our fresh meat supply?"

"Sure, that. We should still be hunting all the time—the few penguins we got yesterday will only last a short while. And I think some of the men are just beginning to feel like we could stay on top of this stable old floe forever and all would be fine, as if a touring vessel will come by with dancing ladies and glasses of champagne and just . . . find us." He shook his head. "Sorry about the dancing ladies."

I waved it off. "But why *aren't* we hunting all the time? It's not like we can't store it everywhere!" I flapped my arm at the expanse of ice around us.

Thomas lifted his mustache, like a shrug. "The Boss has his methods."

We walked on for a while more in silence, the empty sled bouncing and skittering over the ice behind us.

"Well," I said eventually, "What would you have us do? If we hunt a lot and store up a lot of meat, we can't possibly take it all with us when we have to launch the boats."

Thomas nodded. "That's correct. But we'll be well fed and healthy, and if we don't launch, there won't be any forward momentum, and we really could just stay here forever." Thomas leveled a mitten at me. "*That* is the thing I worry about the most. The answer is to both hunt *and* prepare for an imminent launch. Any kind of movement is good."

I absolutely goggled at him. "You don't really think The Boss would let us stay here for too long."

The mustache went up and down again. "Probably not for too long. But maybe long enough to make a difference." He turned to me. "The thing you need to know is that The Boss really only wants to keep everyone happy. He absolutely hates to think that public opinion is against him. It's why the men love him, why he's a great leader. It drives most of his choices."

"I . . . I thought he wanted to discover new lands. God and King and country, and all that."

Thomas shook his head and walked on for a bit longer before he answered. "The Boss wants to be recognized. Discovering new lands gets him there. Planting an English flag in a new fashion, in an unexplored place, will earn him that recognition. But he'd rather do it with everyone behind him, so that posterity is kind to him." Thomas glanced at me. "The Boss is shrewd that way. No one's louder than an unhappy crewman. He wants to make sure no one feels sad or lonely or left out."

I couldn't help myself. "Well then, why in the hell did he pick *me* for this expedition? Who else would stick out more than a woman, feel more left out?" I couldn't say the words "sad" or "lonely."

Thomas grinned at me. His teeth glinted in the low light. "Young women apply for every expedition, you know," he said. "The Boss told me early on he wanted to give someone the chance to explore, someone who wouldn't otherwise ever have the chance, but she had to be the right one. Stern and I counseled against it, but he wouldn't change his mind.

"He'd seen fifteen young ladies—women, sorry—by the time you came along. He'd about given up. But he said you seemed driven."

I remembered how frustrated I'd been the day I'd applied, how I truly felt like I'd never find a place for myself if I was out of step with even the British suffrage movement.

"And," Thomas went on, "you're Canadian."

I snorted. "What's that got to do with anything?"

"Well, the women there—you're true frontierswomen, aren't you? Canada's rough country. I hear the bears there are massive, and the tundra there so broad, you can see forever without even a tree interrupting your line of sight!"

I swallowed, feeling guilty even as a sinking feeling consumed me. Our Bucks County estate and our Philadelphia home, even the scrappy bit of land in the Delaware Water Gap Mama and I camped on, was about as far away from the tundra as you could get. There were trees *everywhere*, a good number of them in deliberately planted, carefully planned copses, just so the human eye could be pleased.

We'd encountered our share of black bears in the woods, it's true. But the few times we had, we'd actually fished peacefully and respectfully far downstream of them for a few minutes before they ambled off in search of berries and grubs.

I changed the subject. "What would you like to see happen in the next few weeks?"

Thomas's mustache bobbed. "In the short term, it's most important we hunt. It's a shame no one could choke down the dog meat, isn't it?"

I wrinkled my nose. "No, that wasn't the outcome, was it?" I tried to stay neutral, thinking about it while we maneuvered the sledge over a particularly bad ice ridge. Thomas gestured at it.

"That's a sign we should get moving, too, and maybe the wave as well. We'd have to ask Wilson, but new ridges and waves are signs of weather and temperature changes, aren't they?" The pile had appeared on the horizon. "Ah, here we are."

I headed for the part of the pile where I'd arranged all the soft goods and burrowed for extra socks and sleeping bags. I handed my notebook to Thomas. "Here, I've rearranged things a little from your system, so could you just read off to me what they lost, and I'll see if I can't quickly find it?"

I could indeed find it. I confess to being very smug by the time we'd finished working through the list. In twenty short minutes we'd ticked off everything on it, except for one set of fork and knife.

Thomas lashed our bundle to the sled and nodded approvingly. "The teacher becomes the student," he said gravely, and I stifled a giggle, feeling like it was truly a job well done.

Cook's bell has rung just now. Biscuits and pemmican, stretched-thin penguin gravy made from those leathery pink feet. No surprise at all.

13 December

MacTavish and The Boss are fully recovered. The shock of cold may have even done The Boss's sciatica a little good. He seems to be moving around more easily, anyway.

I'm glad. I may have entertained the idea of what life would be like without Hotchkiss, but I would have never been able to bear the thought of a life on the ice without MacTavish. He told me his father had passed on early, and that between his four older sisters and his mother, their farm kept on going—and thrived. Life on a Scottish farm, he said wryly, seemed to have a lot of tasks women could do.

I think MacTavish would have greatly enjoyed witnessing the days of my first association with the WSPU.

The possibility of leads opened up by our floe cracking has gone away—the past few days have been cold enough that everything seems to have seized again, especially in the direction we need to go.

Our extended forays for fresh meat have gotten us nowhere.

20 December

If you are reading this and call yourself a suffragist, you will already know about Alice Paul's parade in Washington. You will also recall the excitement around it for all of us, how much we anticipated a nationwide show for all to see, how we might finally be able to demonstrate the power of women. Thousands had come to see us, and all along the parade route were lined policemen, ready to help if things went awry.

The first few blocks went wonderfully. A more proud, high-spirited group of women you never did see, our Votes for Women sashes strapped across our chests, the white of our dresses almost blinding to see in the gray early spring light. But then the woman next to me, Alethea, gasped and lurched and clutched her ear, collapsing against me, and I saw with horror that she was bleeding from her head. I never found out what hit her, for very soon after that the jeers and catcalls seemed to breach the wall of our joy: They came upon us as if in a wave, crushing our fragile hope. Where once there was space for a future, there was suddenly fear, for the voices coming from the crowd lining the parade route were suddenly loud. Accusatory.

The men behind the voices embodied all the opinions we'd read before in the newspaper—that we who wanted the vote were a shame to womanhood, were wanting for a good smack about, or worse—and then came the physical attacks. All around me, women were clutching their arms or their heads or shielding themselves from rocks or rotten vegetables or blows from the men themselves. I felt in the eye of a storm—somehow, not a single thrown object had reached me, and I was too literally in the center of our group of women to be within arm's reach of the crowd, but they were getting closer.

Alethea gripped my wrist hard, and I realized that it was not wholly Alethea who was bearing down on my wrist so tightly, but that she was being pulled bodily from me by two men whose mouths were red and open in fury. The need to annihilate us seemed obvious.

Alethea was dragged away from me, even as I redoubled her grip on my wrist by grabbing onto her with both my hands. I only remember seeing her face, gone pale with primal fear, being sucked into the fray, while I was pressed along by the throng of terrified suffragists behind us.

When I screamed for the policemen who were lining the route to *do something*, they sneered. Some of them laughed outright. Others turned their backs on us.

By the time we reached the end of the parade route, we were a straggling, miserable line of women. Our white dresses were streaked with mud and blood. We had come the way of the route alone, without the protection the presence of the officers belied.

I saw Alethea later, in the hospital. She'd lost her hearing in one ear, been concussed, and left on the side of the road while I was swept along by the crush of bodies. Hours after the parade, a passerby took her to the hospital, and there were at least a dozen more of our sisters who had been injured to the point of hospitalization.

It wasn't until weeks after that we found out about the travesty involving Ida B. Wells and her relegation to the very back of the parade.

I did not expect for some within the leadership of the American suffragists to call this parade a success. I could not have predicted a more contrary reaction from the police. I could not have expected to feel so betrayed.

Nor did I expect, once I left, to feel this way again.

⁓

After a week of quiet, Hotchkiss got too close a few hours ago. I kneed him in the groin, kicked him as he lay there, writhing, and then kicked him again for good measure. They say I might have broken his hands.

And then they sent me and my diary off to think about what I had done, I guess, in a tent all by myself.

I know what I've done. "We need to figure out what to do with this," The Boss said. I don't really see what there is to figure out. I was attacked. None of this is my fault, and I must keep on trying to remember this.

I am so lonely. There is no appropriate way to guide you, dear reader, through this, no appropriate subject matter or category for this. We are in the wilds of human behavior and at the limits of my experience, anyway.

Thomas has just popped his head in. He brought supper. I didn't realize so much time had passed. He shouldered open the flap, his back end still hanging out of the tent, as if coming all the way in would express some solidarity he was not yet equipped to demonstrate.

"Come here, Clara," he said, "and bring your plate and cup." He swapped his dinner for my utensils. Biscuits. Gravy. Tinned pears. Hot Trumilk.

"All right?" he said loosely, scanning me, almost, checking for . . . I don't know what, signs of visible damage? There was a split second during which I worried he wouldn't meet my eyes, and the relief I felt when he finally did was knee wobbling.

He jerked his head in a half nod. "You write this down, Clara. Whatever happened, you must write it down as soon as you can. You must not forget."

He sounded so serious. He's right, of course. Maybe if I had written down what happened to us during the march, I would not be so at loose ends now.

There are lots of reasons to write things down. Will I write it down because I'll need to defend myself later, in some kind of at-sea, on-ice court? Or maybe he just thinks I should write it down because it will shape who I am tomorrow, the next day, the next. Or perhaps he is afraid, as I am, that when the time comes for our peers to judge us, I will be too easily swayed by a jury of my crewmates, their collective need for an easy outcome and their jaundiced view of how they believe it has mostly likely happened.

Thomas put his hand out, hovering it in the air. I wanted so badly for him to come near, for him to hold me the way Mama would have held me. To come all the way in, to show me he was my friend. But I knew he wouldn't. In the end, he just rested his hand on my shoulder for a second and left, calling out, "Eat it all," as he disappeared.

I still hadn't said a single word to him. I will write this down.

It happened right before lunch. Six hours or so ago now, then, since it's suppertime. Nice enough to be sitting outside, actually, as opposed to having to eat huddled in our tents. Sunny. Still cold. Thomas breaks the nib of his pencil; my spoon's fallen out of my pocket or something and I can't find it, so I tell him I need to go back to my tent anyway, since I'm pretty sure my spoon is lying in my sleeping bag somewhere, and I'll pick up an extra pencil for him.

Nothing seems to make any sense. My spoon's never fallen out of my pocket before. And how come Thomas has neither an extra pencil nor pocketknife on him, for sharpening his broken pencil? We always have our pocketknives on us!

I head back to our tent, head down, looking for my spoon along the way, just in case I've dropped it somewhere on the well-trod route between tent and "dining room."

I didn't find my spoon along the way, and I'm feeling a little panicked by now, actually, because I already know the Dump is completely out of spoons. I'm thinking that maybe I really have lost the thing and wondering if it's going to be possible for me to eat all of my meals with my fingers, or maybe I'll just have to wait until Thomas or Blackburn or someone else is done with theirs before I get started on mine, forever and forever, or at least until we get off this floe.

I straight-arm the flap of our tent open and go in. I'm feeling around in my sleeping bag on my hands and knees when suddenly the flap opens again—I remember admiring how buttery gold the sunlight looked passing through the tent's canvas, and how annoyed I was at the sudden intrusion.

I think it's Thomas, and I'm about to say to him, "I *said* I'd only be a minute!" and I'm leaned way forward, patting my sleeping area, looking for my spoon.

And anyway, it hardly matters, because then Hotchkiss is on me. I know it's him because of the way he smells. And I think part of my brain always knew this day was coming. My brain, however, did not pass the message on to my physical body, and I know I lay still for a moment, which was a mistake, because it gave him ever more purchase.

In the meantime, in that moment, I was thinking that I had forgotten what Mrs. Garrud told us to do if we were attacked from behind, and we never really practiced it—even the policemen who were so vehemently against suffrage wouldn't attack us from behind. Most people, I like to think, have a code of honor.

In every case, she did not tell us what to do if we were attacked from behind with our rears in the air, bent forward on slippery reindeer hair, our arms akimbo from scrabbling for an eating utensil.

Hotchkiss doesn't say a thing, barely even grunts. He's behind me, and then he's kicked my legs out from underneath me, and he's just on me, grinding into my rear. One hundred ninety pounds of lanky, randy, unwashed sailor, all confidence and swagger and years of experience taking what you wanted, puts a girl at a disadvantage.

It was like the time I got trapped under the sail of the little sailboat we kept on the river. We'd capsized; it wasn't a thing we hadn't done before, but this time was different. I popped out of the water, fully expecting to be able to breathe, and met a face full of heavy sail and not quite enough headroom. My nose could be above water if I tilted my head, but not my whole head.

Mama told me later she could see the sad little bump where my head hit the sail. She swam under it too and popped up next to me, pushing the sail off my head so I could take a breath.

"Ready?" she'd said, after I'd gulped some air. I remember her, all green eyes and water trickling from her hair into her face, grinning at me, showing me it would be fine.

"Ready," I said, and she took my hand and we swam down a little ways and out from under the sail, and still holding hands, floated on our backs for a time, faces turned to the open air, closing our eyes to the bright sunlight and seeing the starbursts against our eyelids, feeling the gentle current of the river against our bodies. Slowly, I forgot my temporary panic.

Hotchkiss's whole body covers mine, a deadweight, heavier than the sail, heavier than I thought a man would be. His weight seems to spread, if possible, like he's oozing over my sides, all my limbs, and I can't find a way out from underneath him no matter how far I reach my arms and legs and fingers. My face is pressed into reindeer hair, and I am wondering if this is what a reindeer actually smells like when it's wet, like when it's just come out from a swim in the river.

We are *sticking* to each other, somehow.

I buck, but that just seems to make him more excited, and he begins to pant. I stop.

I am still not really making a sound, and neither is he: we are just breathing. Hotchkiss groans, and it's this noise of desire that makes something in my head switch on.

I tilt my head, just like I did under the sailboat sail, so I can breathe better. I'm trying to get on my knees, but nothing is working.

Hotchkiss is using his chin to winnow a window of bare skin under my sweater at the nape of my neck. I could feel his teeth as he reached it, and then his tongue as he licked and then nipped at me, like an animal might if it were rutting.

Even through my coveralls and my woolens I could feel the stiffness between his legs. I went limp, and stupid.

Hotchkiss still wasn't saying anything, and I don't know why I didn't scream. Call it a strange paralysis. All my energy was going toward trying to remember what I'd been taught, but nothing I'd learned from the suffragists had prepared me for this. For ire, for vitriol, for rage from men, yes—but not for this odd mixture of rage and sexual desire.

Hotchkiss swiveled his hips quickly and moved his hands from my shoulders down to my chest, looking for the buttons of my coveralls.

The intimacy was galling, and yet, I remember thinking it might be the only thing that would save me.

I rolled over, aiming for languid as my brain was screaming for physical, violent reaction.

I think I actually was holding my breath, as if the artificially induced panic would give me the strength I needed to survive whatever was about to happen. His breath caught with excitement, and I fought the gag reflex. I forced myself to press closer, even closer. I looped my arms around him, finally facing him on my back now, seeing his tongue peeking out from his chapped lips. I opened my eyes wide for a second, wanting to take in everything, everything, never, ever forget, and then remembered in time to drop my eyelids, pretending to be sleepy with arousal.

I held him tight against me for a moment, looking for purchase as he started to breathe rapidly with excitement, growing ever stiffer against my groin.

I couldn't decide which to be most disgusted by: the intimate, fetid breath coming from him; the obscenely pink tongue; the obvious excitement.

He groaned again. "Ah, Clara, I *knew* it."

Ah, Clara, I knew it. This I'll never be able to forget. Even writing it down, recalling it, I go light headed, nauseated, the meal Thomas brought me rising in my throat.

But write it down, Mama said, Thomas said, and so I'll tell you, diary.

I spread my legs and scooted down a notch, scissoring his legs and freeing my hips from below his. Hotchkiss's breath hitched, and I finally *saw* him, registered the notch of tenderness that appeared between his eyebrows as he told himself I wanted him as much as he wanted to take me, and then I contracted every muscle in my right leg and jerked it upwards, deep into his crotch, and Hotchkiss howled, right into my ear.

He rolled off me, screaming. My ears rang with the sound, celebrating like bells had taken up residence in my head. I got up and stood over him, swung my leg as far back as it would go, and kicked him again as he was clutching himself so that I heard the satisfying crunch of maybe having broken his fingers, too.

I yelled, finally. Victorious. I picture myself now, standing above him, everything I had been told by the suffragists ringing in my ear. Equality, equality, equality, even as Hotchkiss lay writhing at my feet. I stood there, with my hands on my hips, like I was the strongest woman in their world, like I was Emmeline Pankhurst herself. Pankhurst, standing in a tent, flat Antarctic light filtering through canvas. Pankhurst, throwing rocks into shop windows. Pankhurst, refusing to eat while she sat in a prison cell.

Emily, dashing forward into the path of a racing horse, just for the opportunity to wave our flag for the world to see.

At that minute, I believe I called on every memory I ever had of every suffragist I'd met. I don't know if it did me any good. I know I howled, threw my head back and screamed.

Hotchkiss was shrieking, over and over, and I wanted to tell him to shut up, you sniveling little bitch. I kicked him again—crunch, shriek, joy—but by then the rest of them had come, and a lot of activity was happening around me.

There was a quick difference in light—first, sharp blue Antarctic light, then shadows as the men crowded in around me. I remember the air too, changing as a brisk breeze swung in with the others, sweeping Hotchkiss's smell from my nostrils.

"What's the—"

"Are you—"

"Who's—"

"Ketterling-Dunbar!!" The Boss's voice is always deeper than anyone else's. He gripped my shoulder.

"Sir! That hurts! Please stop." I tried to shake him off.

"No!" He doubled his grip, shoulder and wrist now, and pulled me forcibly from the tent.

I blinked in the blue light, feeling disoriented, gleeful, giddy. Lightheaded.

"Everyone, get back to lunch!" The Boss shouted. The men muttered and slowly trickled away. The Boss tightened his grip on my wrist and pulled me to the side of the tent door.

"Did you see what happened there? Hotchkiss is down! I put him *down*!" Distantly, I was aware that I was shrieking myself and hopping a little. I pictured sparks of electricity flying from my fingertips, from my toes. No one could come near me for these sparks; no one.

The Boss put both hands on my shoulders, repressive. I tried to shake him off, but he wasn't having it. "Clara. Clara, Clara, Clara, Clara," he said.

"What? *What?*" I said. "Did you see? I beat him. I *beat* him." I giggled. "Up and down and between the legs."

Still drunk on power, maybe.

"Clara, *stop it!*" The Boss could roar when he wanted to. I stopped hopping, but my lower eyelids jumped, and I could hardly look at him straight.

"Hello, there. Hello, hello." Part of me was shouting

that this was not the conversation I wanted to be having with The Boss. The bulk of me didn't care.

The Boss grabbed my head in both hands and stared at me. I blinked. He called over his shoulder for MacTavish and then turned back to me. "Did he hurt you? Hit you in the head? Look at me."

"No. No, no, no." I tried to free myself, but he had too good a grip.

"Clara, what did you *do*?"

"Are you looking for MacTavish? He's in there with the person who tried to *rape* me."

Saying the words out loud was sobering.

Silence. "Did he say he wanted to do that?"

I glanced sharply at him, and it was he who backed away. "Sir?"

"Is that what he said he was doing?"

Blood rushed straight to my head. My ears began to ring. "Sir, you cannot be *serious*."

"I am. We need to know."

I swallowed, buying myself time before I found the words. "You only need to know what I experienced and what I believe happened. I deserve that much."

The Boss shook his head, sadly, and I thought maybe I had convinced him.

"You may have broken his hands," he said then, and I goggled, all the fizz gone from my mood. I was sober again with those words.

"Sir, he was *on* me."

The Boss went very still again, looking like he was thinking. I didn't see what there was to think about.

"He was *on me*," I said again, just in case he hadn't heard me. He shook his head again, and I took a giant breath and let it out again through my nose, trying to stop the anger from rising up in my chest. "Why are you shaking your head? Sir, do you not believe me?"

"I believe you," he said then. "But. But Clara, that doesn't change the fact that you may have really hurt him. You must account for that."

I backed far away then, out of his reach. "Sir, *he* attacked *me*." I shook my head. "You know what? Fuck your accounting, and fuck all your rules and what you believe. You figure out what you want to do, and then you just tell me what you want me to do."

The fire and sparks in my belly had grown cold. My very womb felt as if it had shriveled to stone, a chunk of Antarctic ice, perhaps. I wonder if this is what Mama felt each time Papa came home.

The Boss beetled his brows. Never had he looked more primeval, like the kind of man we are supposed to have left behind many eons ago. Hunt. Eat. Copulate.

I kept backing away, even as The Boss came toward me again. "We'll be a man down now."

"Hotchkiss," I said evenly, "was not a man. He was less a man than the lowliest man I have ever known. You keep that in mind. You hired him. This is what has come to pass."

I stopped backing away. "Do you know what, sir, just do what you need to do. I'm going to the Dump Pile to take stock." I shook my head. "No. I'm going to finish my lunch."

"Clara, no. I'm afraid I can't let you do that."

I gritted my teeth, hard. "Sir?"

Behind him, I could see Blackburn and Mahoney and Thomas dragging Hotchkiss out on a sleeping bag, still keening and moaning and hands raised in the air in supplication. *That better not be my bag*, I thought to myself.

The Boss glanced over his shoulder. "Put him in tent three," he said. He turned back to me. "Clara, I need you back in the tent. Stay there until you're called. Someone will bring in your evening meal."

What? I stood there stunned, like, I read somewhere, a poleaxed giraffe. The Boss turned and guided me back into the tent. Before he left, he did a classic double take.

"Oh, and, erm—I do hope you are all intact."

I started laughing then and couldn't stop. The Boss shouldered open the tent flap and left.

I've been here ever since, sitting in the ever-unchanging Antarctic light.

What would Pankhurst do?

Hell, what would *Mama* do?

Later

Thomas just popped in again with another ration. Damn hoosh.

"They want you to stay here overnight until they sort things out," he said.

"What the fuck does that mean?" Even before Thomas came by I was already close to yelling, if only to just let off some steam, and swearing seemed appropriate, frankly. "Can I at least go to the fucking loo?"

Thomas winced. I didn't care. His sensitivities could go fuck themselves. He patted the air with his hands, looking ineffectual, and I refrained from telling him just what I thought of his patting the air when my very freedom—and the fact that someone had tried to rape me—was being discussed as if it weren't real, cold fact.

"Clara, don't you even care how Hotchkiss is?"

"No, I don't! Why the fuck would I care?" I have never sworn so much in my life, and now I'm wondering why the hell not; it did wonders for my mental state, to hear my anger released in appropriate fashion.

Thomas cast a quick glance over his shoulder. "Shh. Shh, Clara. People will *hear* you." Oh, I was livid then, if I wasn't before. "People will hear me? People will hear me? People should have been here to see the way he laid on top of me, trying to get into my pants! People would have heard something then!"

Thomas looked contrite then and slid more of his body into the tent. This only served to make me angrier; it was like he was worried people thought something untoward would be going on if he was all the way in a tent with me.

"Clara, I'm sorry. But no one was here, so we need to play the hand we're dealt, don't we?"

"What the hell does *that* mean?" I had gone from being just plain angry to being angry *and* confused. Once, Papa sent me and Mama word that he'd be home one week, only to have that week go by and another missive follow saying it'd be *that* week instead. Two weeks later, he finally arrived as if nothing were wrong, not even bothering with an excuse, while we waited like the good family we were. This was like that—being on tenterhooks of the most unpleasant variety while a group of persons unseen decide your fate, and the rest of the world goes on, trying its damnedest to pretend that nothing has happened at all.

Thomas cleared his throat again. I wanted to tell him to eat a lozenge. "It means no one was there to see you, you look fine, you're in literal fighting shape, and Hotchkiss is in a lot of pain and might die."

I digested this. And then, to my absolute fury, I started to cry.

Thomas ducked all the way into the tent then and wrapped his arms around me. "Oh, no. Don't do that."

I pushed him away, and pushed him again and again until he was out of the tent door.

I shouted, all manner of angry noises, until I finally arrived at exactly what I wanted to say. "Get *away* from me. Get *away*."

Thomas darted that look over his shoulder again. "Clara?"

"Get the *fuck* away from me!"

He backed up then. "Stay well, Clara," he said, sounding low and foreboding. "You need to stay well."

I have no desire at the moment to parse what this means. I pushed open the tent flap behind him and threw the by-then cold hoosh out after him.

If only. If *only* Emily, Gwendoline, and the others were here with me. I wouldn't feel so alone right now. I'd be with women who understood.

I've never missed Gwendoline more than I do right now. Even in our greatest disagreement, she had wise counsel. Another perspective. How I wish she could show me how to see this differently now.

Middle of the night. I can't sleep.

MacTavish came to visit before lights out.

I almost couldn't look at him. All I could think of was him treating Hotchkiss; looking after his hands, his health; making comforting noises through the Scottish burr in his throat. It felt like he was taking sides. Even if he wasn't. Even if he was doing his duty as ship's surgeon.

I was really angry by the time he came to me.

He rapped at one of the hoops on the tent before he came in.

"The door is open," I said, dryly.

MacTavish came in, quirking a corner of his lip upward, bearing a new plate of food. I was starving by then: fighting off an untoward bodily assault makes one hungry. I turned my head away and refused to even look at the food.

"Well, that's better than the reception Thomas got, isn't it?" MacTavish said.

"*Well*, you haven't yet accused me of lying."

He pulled over a crate to sit on. "No one could look at the damage you caused Hotchkiss and think you were doing anything but warding off an attack," he said.

I turned to look at him. "Is he in a lot of pain?"

MacTavish nodded, and I ducked my head to keep my smile from reaching the room. He let a beat go by, and then, "No one blames you for being a little bit gleeful," he said. "Do you want to know what's happening with him?"

I shrugged. The society ladies would have a fit if they saw me today: slouched in my pants, sitting on the floor, legs wide open, shrugging. I scratched my head under my cap for good measure and picked my nails. I didn't know who I was spiting at that point.

MacTavish took my silence for curiosity. He flipped open his notebook. "I'll spare you the details," he said. "Suffice to say that you've broken both his hands and one of his left wrist bones; his testicles should heal with time."

I snorted.

"One of the bones in his left hand has broken through the skin, so if it doesn't heal correctly there is an increased risk of infection and worse."

"Will it hurt?"

"Aye." He shut his notebook. "We'll be a man down now, so we'll have to work to pick up the slack. Well." He glanced around at the tent, my erstwhile prison. "Two men down, for now, until you come back."

"Until they make whatever decision they're going to make and let me do my job, you mean."

"Aye, that."

"MacTavish, how long am I going to be in here for?"

"I don't know. I do know this, though. You've created a split in the crew. A good number of men are taking sides, and it's feeling a little fractious out there now."

I stared. "Come, now."

MacTavish shook his head. "Well, the men were already on edge, you see. Out of meat, and all that. We really needed everyone to get along. And when you—when Hotchkiss—" He waved uselessly. "Suffice to say everyone is a little confused."

"Confused!" I spat. "*He* attacked *me*. Why can no one remember this?"

"Aye," said MacTavish, sadly. "But some of them say you should have expected this, if you were going to sign on as the only woman."

I stared, but MacTavish didn't elaborate. Nor did he need to; I'd heard enough similar arguments shouted at us suffragists as we were carted away to jail, and even when poor Emily died. They said she did it on purpose. That she had a death wish. No one seemed to want to hear that she wanted, probably more than anyone, to live, to live a life equal.

"And others?" I asked, finally.

"The others—we—know that Hotchkiss was going to cause trouble even if there were no women on board. He's . . . not a pleasant man."

MacTavish left soon after that. "You ride this out, Clara. You take care of yourself as best you can."

I bit back the words I wanted to say: "Will you tell them I've done nothing wrong? Will you tell them you believe me? Will you stand up for me?" But I couldn't say those words, could I? I couldn't ask a man to defend me, when I should be damn well ready to defend myself, *by* myself.

No. It was better to stay silent.

And still, I won't eat.

When I first arrived in London, Mrs. Pankhurst had just been released from prison—again. Meeting her in person at the WSPU's offices, after she had been on hunger strike, was like meeting an icon—but it was also like getting punched. Pankhurst was wan, drained, her pallor very bad from being force-fed through her nose. Meeting my hero—seeing her so weak and yet soldiering on—surpassed the parade in Washington as the single most impactful experience in my life thus far, signaling as it did a sea change in the way I viewed the battle for women's voting rights. Seeing her moving from desk to desk, leaning on a sister suffragist for help, was what I imagine getting new spectacles must be like: I suddenly saw that, no matter how strong our movement, no matter how strong our individual women, the men who run the systems will always want us to bend. They will want us to bend until there is no more play left in our spines.

My own miniature hunger strike has done me no good whatsoever. It is midmorning, and still no one has come to any idea of what must be done. I suppose I should be grateful that Wilson would never deign to have one of his scientific tubes used for force-feeding.

Even the mighty Pankhurst was diminished by an instrument of man and the women who held her down as she was force-fed through her nose—however am *I* to overcome, when I am by myself, without the bosom of my sister suffragists from which to draw strength, without their constant chattering in my ear to remind me of the greater cause?

No. I know what I must do now. I see only one way forward—if I cannot change the way the men want to see me, I must act counter to my every better instinct.

I must bite my tongue and pretend that I am in the wrong and try and get along.

I must pretend I am *sorry*.

Is this truly the only way? How I *wish* someone were here to talk to about this! Last night in this big, big tent was the loneliest I have been in a very long time. Without the other bodies near me, the tent seems cavernous, empty, echoey. I didn't ever think I'd miss the snoring, snuffling sounds of my tentmates, but I do. Oh, how I do.

I woke up multiple times last night, from sheer quiet.

Later

Visits from Per and Blackburn. If I'd had younger brothers, I'd want them to be like these boys. They pushed and shoved each other through the tent flap, and stopped right at the threshold, shifting their feet.

"Cook says it's time for lunch," said Blackburn, sounding cheery. "He says you should come get it before anyone else gets all the hot food."

I cast a sidelong glance at him. "Did he?" I shook my head. "I won't eat, not until someone admits they did wrong by me."

The boys goggled. "Why not?"

"They need to make it very clear to everyone that Hotchkiss was wrong."

Blackburn guffawed. "*Everyone* knows he was wrong! A woman doesn't just kick a man like that for no reason, now does she?"

I shook my head. "No, she doesn't. But it's important that this is *said*, don't you agree?"

Big nods, but more foot shuffling. "But, er, Hotchkiss won't be at lunch, like, so . . ."

I waited. "Well, so what?" I said, feeling cross. It is as if no one understands what *principles* are.

"Well, like," Per said, sounding like he was picking up where Blackburn left off, "if he isn't there, and folks know you did the right thing, isn't that all that really matters?"

"Ugh! No! It's more than that!"

Both boys put on skeptical faces. "*Is* it, though?" added Blackburn, as if I needed further proof of their doubt.

I peered at them. "Got something else to say to me?"

They shook their heads.

"What is it, you two? I'm tired and pretty angry, so

you're better off just saying out loud what you're thinking."

Per shifted some and then jerked his head up and, almost defiantly, said, "I told 'em all you'd beat him one day. I did. I told them and told them and it finally happened. I'm only sorry it happened the way it did, Miss Clara."

"Yes. Well."

"Back in Liverpool we'd have made sure he weren't near any birds," Per said, looking furious.

Silence for a moment.

"Only," said Blackburn, "MacTavish says you aren't eating any, and he says it'd be good if you came out for lunch, so we were sent in to see if you'd come eat if you knew Hotchkiss were still laid up."

I sighed. "That's not really the point." They waited. I flapped my hand at them. "Go get lunch yourself. Maybe I'll see you later."

"But Cook said . . ."

I shook my head. "I need to see what The Boss says. I want to know what he thinks. Go. I'll see you later."

The boys backed out of the tent, looking doubtful, but I was tired and hungry and didn't want to explain anymore.

No one seems to understand what is at stake here.

Later

It is senseless to pretend that a person can be alone after living in such close quarters with twenty-seven other people. It is folly to tell oneself that one can get by just fine by oneself. One would literally *die* out here, and no one would know until one thought things were *too* quiet over in this tent, and then it might be too late.

I spent a lot of time pacing around the tent. I did some calisthenics and reviewed, over and over again, the things that had brought me to this sad point. Leaving the American suffragists. Leaving Mama. Signing on to the WSPU. Hearing that we were going to halt all our activities for the sake of the war effort, and my crushing disappointment, and my huge row with Gwendoline not long after. Seeing that notice in the newspaper about The Boss's expedition. The way I knew, without a doubt, that this would be the place I'd finally be seen as a *person*, instead of a mere gender.

I thought about the last time I'd talked to Papa, six months before he died. The way we'd sat on either side of the dining room table, me picking at my toast, his slurping at his coffee between long stretches of reading the news-paper. Mama, next to me, was staring off into the land-scape. Still youthful, still hopeful, wanting to dissipate the ennui in the room, I said to him, "Papa, do you want to know what my governess is teaching me?"

He grunted. Next to me, Mama *sharpened*, sat up a little straighter.

I took this as a good sign, even as Mama laid her hand on my leg. "Clara," she said, low.

"Spanish!" I said, chirruping in eagerness.

My father slowly lowered the newspaper until he met my gaze. "Whyever is she teaching you Spanish? Matty?"

Mama seemed to sink a little. "I just . . . I just thought maybe it would be useful."

Papa snorted. "Whatever for? Is it likely to be useful in marrying her off?"

Mama nodded, but I was perplexed. I'd never heard her say this. She'd said it was so I could read ever more books. Next week, my governess had said, she'd bring some Spanish picture books. I started to tell Papa about them, but Mama's hand on my leg was insistent.

"Yes," she said then. "She is very likely to be more attractive to suitors."

"Well, I suppose that's all right, then," Papa said, and I lost all desire to speak again to my father after that, all desire to understand why he was the way he was, how he saw the world.

The Boss's original route home for us took us through Argentina. If we ever get there, my Spanish will come in very useful indeed.

I've put myself here, haven't I? I've no one to blame but myself, not The Boss, not Thomas's missing pencil, not even that sorry excuse for a human, Hotchkiss.

Still Later

(Will this day never end?)

The crew was split, as MacTavish had said they'd be. I got some glares and some hearty welcomes when I went out there, but the hearty welcomes stopped just short of slapping me on the back and cheering for what a good job I'd done putting a bad man in his place.

The Boss was sat with Captain Phillips, Billings, Higgins, and Amos, our ship's carpenter, having what looked like a serious discussion with some maps and diagrams and things. He noticed my arrival and only nodded at me, a quick up-and-down jerk of the head.

I nodded back, but inside I was screaming—was he waiting for me to come up with the right thing to do? Apparently coming to lunch like nothing had happened was the right thing to do?

Their nonchalance at my appearance was in direct contrast to my roiling guts. There is no one to tell about how I fought with myself before going out there, no one to witness how the gooseflesh rose on my arm at the thought of caving to what was the only way out of this situation. It was equally galling to witness the conviction with which my allies approached me, the way they brought me back into their midst and surrounded me with their protection.

And yet—the suffragist in me is appalled at how safe I feel with these men around me.

The suffragist in me is also wondering—if it had been a man who had stopped another man from attacking a woman, what would have happened to each of them?

I stopped in to see Cook just now, to thank him for encouraging the boys to come visit me. He grunted and scraped some biscuit dough into a bowl. "T'ain't right, what 'appened to yeh," he said.

I laughed, feeling bitter. "Cook, you weren't even there!"

He leveraged the spoon at me. "I know young lads, Clara. I've seen all kinds. And I knew from the very start that young Hotchkiss was goin' teh be no benefit at all to this crew."

"I—"

Cook stepped closer and shook his head at me. "All of which is ter say, Miss Clara, I'm right sorry this happened to yeh."

"Oh!" Those damned tears sprang up again. Cook offered me the edge of a filthy kitchen towel. I shook my head and wiped my nose on the sleeve of my equally filthy sweater.

"You seen Hotchkiss yet?"

I shook my head. "I'm about to go see him, though."

Cook barked in protest. "Whatcher wanna do that fer?"

"Well . . . erm . . ." I chewed my lip "I think the thing to do is apologize." More gooseflesh, more internal cringing. Could that possibly be the right answer?

Cook stopped scraping and pointed his spoon at me. "No, miss. No. You shan't do that."

"I just don't see any other way," I said, even as I flushed with relief. Cook was giving me an out of sorts. And yet—"I have to do something to prove to the men that this can all be behind us, and if apologizing is what it takes . . ."

"No, miss. He'll take that as a sign of weakness, and you are not weak."

Silence. Cook finished scraping and shoved the bowl into Givens's makeshift oven. The lid clanged.

"Deeds, not words; isn't that what your Mrs. Pankhurst always says?"

I nodded slowly. I hadn't thought Cook would follow women's suffrage movements.

"I tell you what you do." Cook handed the spoon to me. "Drop that in the dishwashing pile, there's a good girl.

"I tell what you do," he said again, "yeh go in and yeh see Hotchkiss, like. Yeh just glance in to see that he's still laid up, impossible teh do anythin', like, with his paws all broken and things—" Cook held his hands up to his chest, like a crab with addled claws, and I stifled a laugh. "And then yeh just go on, easy as spring coming, like nuffink new is happening."

I stared. "I don't get it, Cook."

He held up a finger. "Neither will Hotchkiss," he said. "You pop yer head in, cool as anything, and you just nod. He'll take it for an apology, and you never have to open yer mouth once." He patted my arm. "Trust me. People see what they want ta see, you hear me?"

Hmmmm.

"Deeds, not words," he said again, nodding firmly.

I didn't see the point in telling him that this is not *exactly* what Mrs. Pankhurst meant.

Later

I went to see Hotchkiss. MacTavish was in there too. Part of me rejoiced to see Hotchkiss, lying on his back, hands still useless, wrapped in white bandages and up in the air, an oddly accurate double of Cook's mockery of him.

"What the hell are you doing here?" Hotchkiss spat at me, before I could even open my mouth. Good thing, too—I'd spent a few minutes standing just outside the infirmary tent, trying to put together the words I wanted to say to him now that I'd made up my mind to see him. I still didn't know what to say, so some part of me was glad he was filling the space, as usual.

But then Hotchkiss opened his mouth again. "Are you deaf and dumb on top of being useless? I said, what d'you want?"

I don't know what happened the minute I heard those words; I only know that my blood cooled considerably. I stopped breathing for a moment, because it was then and there that I understood why Mama had stayed with Papa all those years. Why it was she wouldn't *fight*.

I was doing what she had done all that time: Appeased. Bided some time. Waited for the right moment, until, for her, the moment had come too late. But for me . . .

Hotchkiss spoke again. "Well?"

MacTavish lifted his eyebrows and moved toward Hotchkiss, but I shook my head ever so slightly and said, "Just seeing how you are."

"You know damn well how I am, you miserable bitch."

I heard the words as if from a great distance. It was as if I'd finally realized just how useless he really was, just how little he meant.

MacTavish laid his hand on Hotchkiss's shoulder. "Hotchkiss, you need to keep your blood pressure down and stay calm," he said. He wrinkled his brow at me, unsure.

"You sound strong and healthy," I said, feeling deliciously duplicitous.

Confused silence from Hotchkiss.

"Glad to see you're on the mend," I added.

"Clara . . ." MacTavish's tone was cautious, but his eyebrows were bobbing in what might be amusement.

From Hotchkiss, then, a half-hearted, automatic, and nonsensical, "Hah!"

"I'm going," I said. "Just checking in."

I don't quite know how I feel after that. Some of me feels vindicated. Some of me feels as if I've gotten away with something, but I don't know what that is yet.

Later

Blackburn came bouncing up to me as I was on my way back from breakfast, reminding me of the puppies we'd had to shoot just before lunch. "Clara," he called, nice and clear, as if he were proud to be overheard talking to me, "I heard what you did."

"What did you hear I did?"

He stopped short. "Oh, you know. Going in to see Hotchkiss. Apologizing, right?"

I shrugged. "If that's what you heard."

Awkward silence. "You don't seem to be very happy about it."

"It is what it is."

Another awkward silence, but he fell into line next to me. "I don't think you need to be sorry for what you did."

"Oh, I'm not."

"Oh." Blackburn seemed to brighten a little more. "I see."

I couldn't help myself. I turned on him. "Do you, though? Do you really see?"

He met me, glare for glare. "No one liked the way he treated you, Clara, least of all me and Per! What we wouldn't have given to see you kickin' at him like yeh did!"

I stared at him. "Well, you almost did. You were one of those to help him out of the tent, remember?"

He slumped. "I know. But if it helps any, I was on my way to help you. I was the first to hear you shout!"

I snorted. "Oh? And if you'd have gotten there in time to see? What would you have done? Would you have punched him? Pulled him off me?"

Blackburn thought about this for a moment. Waiting for him to process was infuriating. But now, looking back on it, I'm glad he took the time instead of just giving me some handy "right" answer. "I like to think I would have."

All the fight seemed to go out of me. "I guess that's all I can ask for," I said, and went on walking.

"Wait, I'm meant to tell you that we're back in the tent with you now," Blackburn called after me.

"Bully for me," I said, and kept on walking. The truth

is, some part of me is trying to forget what happened to me, even as I know I need to remember.

Beyond my tentmates moving back in, there's been no real reaction to my visiting Hotchkiss, which is exactly what I think we needed. The men, even the ones who hung out with Hotchkiss, seem to just want to forget it happened, like someone covering up a stain with a piece of furniture. If everything *looks* all right, it must *be* all right.

23 December

The thing about Gwendoline is this: Gwendoline got out. Gwendoline had a fairy-tale turn to her life, the kind that involves a meeting in the most auspicious of manners. The kind in which she, delivering a load of hatboxes to the milliner, exhausted from working a straight day and a half to deliver them on time so she could make just enough to buy more medicine for her mother and food for the two of them, trips over one of those quaint little cobblestones. In which her stack of boxes goes tumbling.

In which a gentleman who is buying a hat for *his* mother runs immediately to help her.

In which he falls ridiculously in love, owing to both her graciousness and her natural carriage of pride, borne of a woman who has worked all her life and appreciates her own strengths and capacities.

In which his family happens to be one of those who believes in their only son's joy. In which, more importantly, they see all the things a young woman can *be*, and not just her foregone station.

In which the mother is already one who is involved

in the suffrage movement, of which her husband knows some, and further, if he is not exactly supportive, does not care.

In which Miss Gwendoline Clark becomes Lady Gwendoline, Countess of Arundel.

After which I meet Gwendoline; after which we become the closest of friends; after which she teaches me so much more than I would have ever known about transcendence of class, and maybe more. Of rearranging your fate. Of fighting for what is rightfully yours.

Of never, ever believing less of yourself than you deserve.

Genuinely, it is too tragic that we could not see eye to eye on Pankhurst's plan for the suffrage movement.

I suppose, when one sees both sides so clearly, one might be blinded by the breadth of the view.

25 December

Christmas Day.

An exhausting day. While The Boss and Cook have clearly spent weeks, if not months, planning for this day, I am still hard pressed to muster the appropriate feelings deep within me.

I cannot deny the *physical* joy I felt upon seeing that The Boss had secretly been asking Cook to keep back some brandy, some chocolate, some jugged hare, even. I cannot say with all honesty that I did not feel some warmth at seeing the beautiful fruitcake Cook had made for us, brown and crusty on the outside, moist with preserved fruits on the inside, and topped with a shining brandy glaze. (I imagine Cook, benevolent in his bonhomie, safe in a warm, steamy kitchen somewhere, and hope he will be able to experience this sometime in the near future.)

And the pantomime program The Boss, Billings, and Givens put together for us *was* charming. Among the three of them they managed imitations of us all, and I think it is this that was the hardest to witness—they tried to cast everyone in the most cheerful light. They even somehow treated Hotchkiss with undeserved tenderness, choosing to focus on his hard work. It's true, Hotchkiss can work, when he's not distracted by putting someone else down. Which is never.

Thomas was portrayed as lovingly fastidious, Figgy as adorably forgetful—but when it came to me, they executed every tired old thing we have already seen—showing me in front of an imaginary mirror, braiding my nonexistent hair whilst prattling on about hunting and horses and camping with my *dear mama*. Billings rigged up a remnant of sailcloth and moaned about how he'd rather be in trousers, all in a high falsetto, while my real voice is very clearly a high tenor.

I had to wonder—do they actually *see* me?

It was Chutney, of all people, who noticed my glum face, although I was trying hard to hide it.

"Clara, more fruitcake?"

Unexpectedly, my eyes filled with tears. I turned away.

"Clara?" Chutney edged a little closer. "Come for a walk?"

By then, The Boss had invited everyone up on our makeshift stage for a little of their own improvisation. Giddy with unexpected brandy, the men were louder than usual, and Figgy was busy singing a new song he'd composed about our beloved sled dogs, complete with a howling, barking chorus. Hotchkiss was crying dramatically from his prone position, and I was gratified to see Chutney roll his eyes.

Yes, a walk was just right.

We walked away from the group, our boots squeaking in the snow and ice. I couldn't help glancing over my shoulders to see if anyone had noticed, maybe half-hoping someone would.

Chutney glanced at me. "Come now, Clara, this isn't like you."

I wheeled on him. "But how would you know, Chutney? Do you know what The Boss did to me while Hotchkiss was getting treated with kid gloves? Do you know what that was like?"

He nodded solemnly. "I know," he said. "I know. Me and some others wondered if he were treatin' you right. We none of us knew how to handle it. But you done all right, didn't you?" This last was said with a sideways hopeful glance.

"That! That!" I pointed, and he jerked reflexively. "That thing you just did. You cannot be sure of me, can you? You don't want to know me, or you think you know all there is to know already. Or some combination of the two! It's not right!" I sat down in the snow. Really I just wanted to lie down and give up.

Chutney sat down next to me.

"Oh, that's not what I meant at all," he said. "What I mean is that you really do seem fine. And that I'm . . . well, I'm proud of you for doing what you did, apologizing, like."

I opened my mouth to protest.

"Now wait. I weren't going to say it was the right fing to do, but it were the *only* fing to do. You can see the difference, can't you?"

"Yeah, but Chutney—that was awful. It was *hard*."

He glanced at me. "Surely not as hard as putting bombs in letter boxes. Or cuttin' electrical wires."

I sat up straight. "I . . ."

"Oh, I know. You thought it were a secret."

"I . . . does *everyone* know?"

"Aye, Clara." He thought for a moment. "In the grand scheme of things, I'm not very sure anyone cares if you was involved in a terrorist group or not. Once we saw you could take care of yerself, that were all that mattered."

I am not sure if this makes me feel any better. What am I, if not a shocking, untoward member of society? If not someone who has been branded a danger to the order?

Chutney sat with me for a moment but ultimately left me alone, probably to have a good think about what I had done wrong. No. That's unfair. But it's what it felt like: being left in the tent by myself all over again.

Merry fuck-all Christmas!!

1 January 1915

A whole new year. The last six days have gone by as if the crew saw our Christmas celebration as a kind of wiping clean of the slate. I don't know how to show them what it feels like to me, so I say nothing.

Hotchkiss is still laid up, but the men don't speak of it to me.

I go in and read the encyclopaedia to him every other day for ten minutes. I don't know what compels me to do this; is it a kind of sick penance?

He turns his face to the tent wall, but I know he's awake.

I am back on the standard work crews and the men don't seem to care one way or another what has gone on in the past.

I have never felt so unseen.

I cannot but think of the WSPU, our whimpering war cry, our desire to loan our considerable power to a society that has done nothing but take advantage of us. "In the black hour that has just struck Europe," wrote Mrs. Pankhurst, "the men are turning to their women and calling on them to take up the work of keeping civilization alive." I will never, ever forget these words. Once again, we have put our needs second. Once again, we run the risk of our work being taken for granted. It's six months since we left on *The Resolute*. Who knows what state women are in by now?

"'Tis our very best chance at proving our worth," said Gwendoline, on the eve of our last conversation together. "We must show them what we are capable of."

We were sat in the WSPU offices, rewriting the next edition of our newsletter to show support for our troops. Taking the teeth out of our movement. "Gwen," I said, "if they haven't seen it before, they won't be able to see it in a literal fog of war. Men just take and take and take, emboldened by the system behind them! They believe it is their *right* to rely on the backs of women, don't you see?"

Gwen had blinked at me then, her great brown eyes looking hampered by her eyelashes. I had the unkind thought that moving into the wealth of landed gentry may have made her daft. "Oh, my dear, dear, Clara," she said then, "however would you know?"

I flushed then, anger and shame flooding my face. "I . . ."

"You've only *ever* fought, haven't you? You've never just barely existed. You've never worked, not had to depend on your earnings. You've not seen anything, really, of the world. You don't actually know how it *works*. What makes it *go*." She sounded bitter, but that couldn't be, could it?

She went on, standing now, tapping some loose sheets of paper into neat piles. "Did you never stop to think that, with the men gone, the women will still have to feed our families? How did you think we would earn money to do that?" When Gwen got angry, her accent slid back into cockney. I hated myself for noticing.

She wouldn't look at me. "You can't be blamed, I suppose," she went on. I don't know if she was looking at me or not. I had my own face turned to the desk, blindly folding the same newsletter over and over again. Shame was flooding me, but I didn't know it as shame then. I only knew it as anger, hot, blinding anger. Fury at being laid so bare.

Gwendoline was still talking, but her voice faded. I had turned my back on her, on the truths she had yet to tell me about myself. I didn't want to hear it.

I gathered my things and left her, navigating the WSPU offices through a fog of tears. The next day, I interviewed with The Boss, on a whim, I thought, but now I know it was something more—hearing about my own cosseted life made me long for something truly life changing, in a world where things didn't change fast enough. I needed something where the *only* option was to fight on.

The thing about **tents** is this: Ours are made and patched from the same thick, sturdy canvas as our sails. On a ship, this fabric looks so fine and majestic, luffing out with wind . . . and if you've ever touched a sail while it's full of sea breeze, you'd be surprised to feel how stiff it is, how permanent seeming.

Sometimes they can seem like pieces of stained glass; the pale color of the canvas nonetheless provides a kind of shade through which the light acquires a gentler, friendlier light: Outside, so bright and near-blue you must squint to see properly. Inside, perfect reading and napping light. Tent fabric is like one of the color filters Higgins drops over his lantern slides to give off a certain mood.

And, even though you can stretch and drape and bend this fabric to your will, there is something homely about our tents; when we enter into it for sleeping and we know that outside the wind is blowing, very soon our bodies warm up the space inside, and the whole endeavor suddenly feels very like one's cozy sitting room, with a few friends over for tea or coffee or a card game.

But really, a tent is just a piece of fabric, draped and stretched over some ingenious bentwood hoops. And the thing about the Antarctic is, a sound coming from one hundred feet away can sound like it is coming from three feet away. It plays tricks on you. Even a whisper can sound so loud.

I heard Thomas coming back from watch in the middle of the night, speaking to someone in low, urgent tones. It's kind of funny how the human brain reacts and takes the body with it. I froze, feeling as if I was about to overhear something I maybe shouldn't be overhearing. But then again, what was I supposed to do? Go barging out of the tent and declare myself? So I just lay there, hoping that the sound of Per's snoring would drown out anything I wasn't supposed to hear.

No such luck. Thomas was talking to The Boss.

"The men are going to need more," he said. "We must make a move. Maybe send out a crew on a boat, attempt a rescue. Maybe just send out a hunting party, insist they return in two weeks' time."

The Boss sounded committed: "I'd rather not, Milton-Jones."

There was a pause, and I could picture Thomas pursing his lips under his mustache. "Sir, we need to plan for the future. What's the harm in sending out a party?"

There was a pause, then a slight squeak. I could picture The Boss turning to look squarely at Thomas, so the message wasn't lost. "The harm is that the men will get the impression that we are in dire straits."

Thomas had stopped walking, but the squeak of snow told me The Boss was moving on. "Sir!" Thomas whisper-shouted. When will people figure out this is nearly louder than shouting itself? The walking noises stopped. Per snored on. "We *are* in dire straits, or we have to at least plan for them. Don't you see? The men mustn't be without fresh meat for long, and it has already been over a week. You almost died of scurvy yourself the last time out!"

Oh, dear.

Stomp-squeaking back across the snow to where Thomas was standing, right about where my head was. I tried to quiet my breath. "Milton-Jones, if I hear you mentioning dire straits to anyone, I'll have you in court martial for mutiny. The men must not feel as if we are in any trouble." Pause. "This is not *that* expedition, so help me God."

There was another awkward pause. I pictured Thomas, working his way up to something.

"Sir, please," he said. "Surely it won't hurt just to send a party out? And in case they see something, they can bring it home." He sounded genuinely upset.

"No. The men are feeling flush after Christmas."

"Sir—"

"*No.*"

"Sir! Court martial won't matter if we never get home

for death." Thomas was sounding desperate, and I really did not want to hear what The Boss had to say to that thinly veiled threat. I couldn't take it anymore. I pretended to sneeze, loudly enough to wake Per out of his sleep, which he did with an even louder snort and a "Hunh? Whazzat? Time for watch?" to boot.

Both men shut up fast, and Per, after sitting up and looking wildly around, went back to sleep.

I didn't though.

We were at the end of watch when I finally spotted it, a smallish blob near one edge of the floe. It must have come up recently; its fur was still sleek from water. Its fat rippled as it shook itself and wriggled into a more comfortable sleeping position. I adjusted the telescope again and squinted hard. From end on, it looked like a crabeater, fat and sweet and just into adulthood. A good amount of meat. I glanced at Chutney, who was yawning hard. For a second I wondered if I should tell him about it, but then I remembered who I was talking about—Chutney, he of the gossip and the joy and the good cheer. He'd never be able to keep a secret, and he wasn't likely to want to step outside the lines.

And anyway, Chutney would never understand how important it was for me to buck the rules, just this once, and bring back a victory, if only for myself. And Hotchkiss and his ilk would only sneer if I had to lean on a man to bring back my kill. No, I'd have to do this one myself.

Chutney was still yawning when we exchanged watch with Wilson and Figgy. He couldn't see to stop for anything more than a passing nod. My heart leapt. Almost time now.

As it was, I'd have to navigate around the watch's line of sight and hope no one spotted me on my way out. I might be lucky and find another seal—they didn't always like to hang out alone on ice floes. That would keep us in fresh meat for a week, maybe.

Chutney saw me to my tent, but I told him I needed to go visit the loo. He sloped off to his own tent, and I took the long way around to the armory.

I pulled two rifles from our stock and hooked up a sled quickly, silently. For a moment I admired myself. I had spotted the seal; I had successfully chosen the right guns and loaded them by myself and even thought to remember to bring extra ammunition. And no one sounded like they were following me—the snow was falling in big, fat flakes for once, instead of the paltry stinging ones, and it seemed to dampen all the noise. And fat flakes would make it harder for watch to see me.

I walked as deliberately and quietly as I could.

Hope is a funny thing. It puts a completely unreliable lens on all your thoughts. I pictured myself, putting a clean kill shot right through the seal's head, like Mama had taught me to. Then I pictured dragging it back to camp on my sled, like some kind of victorious warrior. Never mind that seals can weigh up to one thousand pounds, never mind that I didn't even think about how I was going to load it by myself; I was going to drag the thing in by my bare hands, using its slick pelt as runners if I had to, like some specimen of Roman gladiator.

Hope, stupidity—sometimes they are the same.

In any case, it hardly matters—I was well on my way to where I'd remembered seeing the seal.

I could see it, just barely on the horizon, and I made an attempt to walk more quietly— tiptoeing, practically— before I felt like I was in a good position to shoot it.

My heart lifted: there *were* two of them. This was becoming a reality. I could practically taste the near victory, hear the cheers of the men as I came in with my seals. Or even as I came back to camp, rifles slung casually over my shoulder, to tell them I needed just an extra pair of hands to help me load.

(Reality, it seems, was already intruding on my dream.)

One of the seals made a snuffling noise, and I stopped walking. I needed to get still closer so I could have a good shot. I mentally shook my head—these wouldn't fly away, or startle like grouse or rabbits.

And then the larger seal started growling, and I realized I'd made a mistake. These were not the docile crabeaters I had hoped for. These were the seals Thomas had said always to run from if we ever saw them. The best, he said, would be if they didn't ever see you. These were leopard seals, and from the way the larger one was posturing, it was the mother of the juvenile. But by then, it was too late to run. The mother seal lunged toward me, all evil-intentioned, rippling, slithering muscle. It was like watching an engine start up. One minute it was still; the next, it was moving, growing larger in my line of sight by the split second. Even in the watery midnight Antarctic light, I thought I could see the gleam of its teeth as it roared at me.

I stood there, frozen by sheer incapability to act, which is saying a lot in the subzero of an Antarctic night, and then I finally turned on my heel and started running, the sled jouncing and hustling and in general acting a nuisance. I thought briefly about releasing myself from the traces. But behind me, the thing bellowed again, and I pumped my legs harder, trying to ignore the burn in every muscle and the Antarctic cold shearing its way into my lungs.

Somewhere in the distance, the juvenile wailed for its parent to come back, but I didn't hold out much hope. The thing was gaining on me. I could hear the scrunching of its claws against the snow and ice, even over my labored breathing.

Perhaps it was the cry of the younger seal that jolted me out of my near panic, or perhaps it was the knowledge that the seal would always be faster than I was, even dragging its awkward body over the snow. I was dragging a sled. I had no hope of outrunning it.

Quick as I could, I spun to face the seal. The sled, carried along by momentum, slammed into my shins, and I gasped in pain. Never mind—it would provide a neat sighting platform. I slung both rifles off my shoulder and propped one against the lip of the sled, dropping to my knees. I racked a cartridge into the chamber. Spent a valuable moment with my eyes closed, trying to quiet my breath. Sighted down the barrel—*there*. Still coming, much closer now, in a straight line. Easy prey, I told myself. Not zigzagging; no trees for me to sight around. Pulled the trigger.

The recoil slammed against my shoulder, and I felt a kind of savage nostalgia as the seal bellowed. It had been so long since I'd been hunting. My veins felt as if they were roaring with blood, my ears screaming with the sound of the shot. But no—the thing was still coming. I blinked and racked another cartridge into the barrel. Took a breath. Let it out.

Bang.

I sat up. No. Still coming, looking to my wide eyes as if it were nearly on top of me now. How? The scrunching was closer now but it seemed to be coming from the side of me, and I looked wildly around just before something—a third seal?—charged into me. I closed my eyes and swung out with my fist, just as a voice yelled, "Get *down*!" and then, "Dammit!" as I connected with its head.

I was already down and reeling with confusion, so I just covered my head with my arms, but I could finally see, understand, that it was Thomas, shaking off my punch, scrabbling for the rifle that had been knocked an arm's length away, then kneeling next to me, racking a round in, lifting the rifle to his shoulder, shooting once, twice.

He racked a third cartridge in and shot again, and finally

sat back on his heels on the snow, breathing hard now that he didn't have to steady his hands for the rifle, resting his head on the sled. The echo of the last shot seemed to go on forever, and I knew the other men would have heard it, even the ones that had been dead asleep. I peeked over the sled. Still a way off, two dark shapes slumped on the snow, all that muscle and intention bleeding out.

"Oh, Clara," said Thomas. His eyes drooped. "What were you thinking?" He touched his head and shook it, looking dazed. "Ugh."

I flipped over, tangling myself in the traces and lay flat on my back, feeling defeated. "I only thought to help."

He shook his head again. "No, I mean throwing punches like that. I almost didn't have time to shoot the thing."

"I thought you were another leopard seal coming for me."

"And what, you thought you were going to *punch* it to death?"

I thought I was going to throw up. Adrenaline does that to you. "I don't know. I didn't want to go down without fighting it," I finally said.

"Mm," Thomas said.

I glanced at him. "Where are your eyeglasses?"

Thomas flapped his hand weakly in any general direction. "Somewhere over there. You knocked them off my face."

"You shot the seals without your eyeglasses on?"

He grinned weakly. "No wind, the only thing moving out there, dark target against light background . . ."

I shook my head. "I couldn't even hit them with plenty of time."

"The light plays tricks, especially in falling snow . . ."

"Please just shut up," I said. I couldn't stand to hear him making excuses for me.

Thomas let it go.

"Those weren't the right seals," he said.

"I know that, now." I said. I sat up a little. "Did you have to shoot them both?"

"Yes."

"Why?"

"Many reasons. The young one may not have survived without its mother anyway. And if it had actually learned to hunt, it might have come after us after it saw its mother die. We don't know."

"I'm sorry," I said. Completely inadequate.

"You could have died," said Thomas. "Don't do anything like it again. Always hunt in pairs."

"Yes," I said. "I was just . . ." I petered off. What? I was just what? *Pass the ball, hunt in pairs, don't get caught alone with the Villain* . . . How many more times would I have to have it drilled into me that there was no room for lone wolves on this expedition?

Thomas shook my arm. "Clara?"

"Hm?"

Thomas sighed. "It doesn't matter." He let a beat go by. "Now then." He clapped his hands together and broke the rifle open, motioning for me to do the same. Good marine manners around a gun. "What do you want to tell everyone else?"

"About?"

He waved an arm. "Everything. This."

I thought about this. "Better to just tell the truth, I think."

Thomas glanced at me. "You're certain of that? We can make something up."

"Like what?"

I knew he was just staring at nothing in particular, but I wondered if he was also thinking about those bodies freezing on the ice.

"Let's go collect those seals," he said finally. "It's not the easiest thing to see the difference between seals at a distance, and in driving snow, too," he said, pushing himself off the ice. He held out his hand to me. "Come on, you've already brought a sled. And that is a lot of seal meat."

I finally spotted Thomas's eyeglasses lying on the snow and ran after him with them—he was already walking toward the bodies at great speed. "Listen. We tell the truth, mostly. You went out to hunt. You wanted to surprise the men. I went with you. That's all." He laughed. "The men already think me a little dozy. They won't be surprised I thought this a good idea, not at all. I'll just say we were both sure they were crabeaters. We won't say much else. Things happen here. We can be excused for having enough on our minds that we might mistake one kind of seal for another, can't we?"

We were partway back to the seals. "How did you find me, though?" I asked. "I was so quiet."

Thomas snorted softly. "Not half as quiet as you thought you were," he said. "I followed you out from the armory. I just thought I'd better back you up." I remembered too late that Thomas was prone to insomnia when he wasn't snoring.

"I'm glad you did. Those things . . ."

"They move like lightning, and you never know what they're thinking, really."

I nodded.

My overalert ears picked up more scrunching, and I spun in a mad circle before finally seeing that it was only Higgins and Mahoney, walking toward us with some big grappling hooks as if they were just out for a stroll. "Ahoy there," said Mahoney, sounding dry, and I blushed from sheer embarrassment.

Even though the gig was up, part of me still felt the need to equivocate. "What are you gentlemen doing up and about at this hour?" I said, as if we were just fine, me and Thomas.

Mahoney grinned. "Heard something about a hunt," he said. "Wanted in on it, didn't we?" He nudged Higgins, who grinned and said, "Yep," as if he were only waiting for the chance to join in.

Thomas nodded. "Let's go, then," he said.

"Seal meat tonight, eh?" said Higgins. "I thought we'd be eating hoosh for months on end."

I glanced at Thomas, wondering if he'd reveal his desperate conversation with The Boss. Mahoney snorted. "Not a moment too soon, eh, Milt?"

Thomas nodded. "Not a moment too soon."

I goggled. "You *all* knew?"

Mahoney nodded. "I'd wager most of the men know, at least the ones who're payin' attention," he said.

"But why did no one say anything?"

"We trust The Boss," said Mahoney. "He knows what he's doing. Not," he said, interrupting himself, "that we won't be grateful for this meat. But I wouldn't be surprised if he's got something up his sleeve."

We'd arrived at the seals. Higgins nudged one with his elbow. "Wrong seals, Clara?"

"Wrong seals," I said.

"Happens to the best of us." He bounced on his toes.

I cast Higgins a skeptical look, but all he did was wink at me and lift his upper lip in what might pass for a conspiratorial smile.

Maybe it did happen to everyone, but the stakes seem higher to me, somehow. Like, if it had been Thomas who'd mistaken one seal for another, say, they'd mock him mercilessly and then move on. If it had been The Boss, they'd pretend it never happened. MacTavish? They'd have laughed and said he spent too much time squinting at their weeping rashes to know the difference. But me—on the heels of this thing with Hotchkiss—I don't know if I can even begin to predict the things they'll say about women as a result of this. Women, those silly cows who can't tell one seal from another. Women, who think they can do anything but really can only do with the help of men. Women!!!

Next to Higgins, Mahoney snorted and then double glanced at Thomas. "Oi, Milt, one of them seals run into you with its rocks-for-brains? What's the matter with your eye, like?"

Thomas flapped his hand at me. "Clara happened," he said.

"Say again?" Mahoney goggled.

Higgins positively chortled in glee. "D'you not remember what she did to lovely old Hotchkiss, Mahoney?"

A moment of awkward silence, and then Higgins shrugged. "Shall we load up?"

Maneuvering a floppy deadweight leopard seal onto a sled is a tricky proposition at the best of times. As we grappled with the bodies, they seemed to resist even the grip of the grappling hooks, as if they were determined to not go easily. Up close, the things looked like enormous sleeping puppies, and I couldn't study their faces for too long. But nor could I look at their bodies, shiny vibrant pelts catching the weak light, except for where they sported gaping holes from Thomas's rifle.

We did the juvenile first, and then, what felt like an hour later, the four of us finally got all of the adult onto the sled and secured.

The two made a strange nativity scene, nestled against each other, the four of us a shabby escort.

Thomas and Mahoney harnessed themselves to the sled. I went to loop myself in as well, but Thomas shook his head. "You and Higgins walk alongside, Clara. We need to make sure those bodies don't fall off the sled. It'll be hard to get them back on again."

Here I am again, at the back of a sled, hands on rapidly cooling seal flesh, an escort to an escort. At least Higgins is here with me.

When we got back to camp, there was an odd amount of activity, and not of the type where folks are stumbling around trying to wake themselves up for breakfast. This was . . . more frenetic, like. Purposeful. At first I thought it was because they'd caught wind of our return and were very, very excited to see us. A ticker tape parade type atmosphere was in the air.

My heart lifted.

But then I noticed the crew walking around us, almost, as if we were in their way. They were heads down, or had ten-thousand-yard stares on, and then Figgy came running up to us.

"*There* you are. We've been looking for you!"

"Aye?" Mahoney, laconic as ever.

"We're packing up. It's time to go; we're going to make a run for Elephant Island in the lifeboats! We're leaving tomorrow." Figgy was hopping with energy, almost. He pointed. "Boss is there. He's been asking after you. Where've you been, anyw—oh." Belatedly, he spotted the sled and its cargo. "Corrrrrr," he said. "*That's* interesting." He backed away a few steps and went on to whatever he was doing before he'd caught sight of us.

For my part, I had caught sight of The Boss, and the set of his eyebrows told me he was not impressed. He came toward us, double time, and I found myself shifting to stand in front of the sled as if to hide the cargo, or something futile like it.

"Clara, men," he said.

"Sir," we returned in unison, trying to not betray our confusion.

"I see you've brought some meat. We'll have seal steak tonight before we go," he said, casually. "Er. As you were not here this morning, you should know that I have today announced we will strike camp entirely and leave for Elephant Island tomorrow morning. The captain says a long enough lead has opened up, and Wilson says the weather is likely to hold."

I looked around at the men. They were all nodding. Thomas's eyes were huge behind his glasses. He shook his head at me ever so slightly as I opened my mouth to ask how long this had been the plan for.

I shut my mouth.

"Take the fresh meat over to the galley. Well done, everyone. Gather in an hour for a briefing on our timeline and route, please." He paused, squinting at Thomas. "Milton-Jones, is that the beginnings of a black eye? However did you get that?"

He shrugged and moved on. Thomas winked at me with his good eye, looking momentarily as if he had both eyes closed.

We dragged our cargo over to Cook, who flapped his hands, whether in joy or frustration that this was a glorious pile of meat we wouldn't be able to take with us, no one could tell.

Thomas and I gathered the weapons and stored the sled in near silence, until I couldn't take it anymore.

"Do you think he knew all along? I mean, while you were talking to him about the stock?"

Thomas nodded, overlooking the fact that I'd overheard what was meant to be a confidential conversation. "I do." He laughed ruefully.

"The Boss keeps his cards close to his chest, doesn't he?" I said.

"Well, if that isn't the most obvious statement of the expedition yet," Thomas said.

I shrugged. Thomas was bent out of shape, and who blamed him?

For now, there's stock to be taken, one final time before

we leave this floe forever, it seems. Next, Amos will alter the shape of our lifeboats, raising the gunwales and patching any holes with whatever we can find. It is hard to imagine who would want such Frankensteinian boats once we've done with them; they'll be ruined for any future work.

This expedition seems to be filled with points of no return. Which also ranks as one of the most obvious statements ever.

Later

The plan: Load all three lifeboats; sail directly for Elephant Island. Clean and simple.

Should take us only a few days, wind prevailing.

Hotchkiss is still "convalescing." Some seem to feel he's just trying to scrape out of work, but I have seen the hands, and there is some question of whether or not he'll ever be able to use them again. I cannot feel sorry, especially because there is no question of whether he'll be able to row or not. Equally, there is no question about leaving him behind to be rescued at a later date. We shall have to carry his weight. I can only hope he'll stow his vitriol, even if temporarily. He has no one to blame for this but himself.

According to Keane, Elephant Island is just a big, guano-covered piece of rock.

"But it's land, real land," he said. He sucked on his pipe, looking lost in a dream.

I suppose it would be a kind of dream. Here on our floe, we're never really all that far away from the idea that we might experience another crack. And Thomas is forever looking around for killer whales.

Never mind the minute, eternal sensation of floating. The ice is reasonably thick—eighteen feet in places, I've heard Wilson say—but still, there's always the odd piece you might walk on that'll be disconnected from everything else.

6 January

Just a few minutes here to say we're off in the boats. We've had a bizarre warm wind and parts of the floe seem prone to breaking up beneath our very feet. Already we've had to rush to get the *James Connick* over a crack in the ice and onto our side of the floe before it drifted away. Thomas is seeing killer whales everywhere, and finding a way to load Hotchkiss so that he's not in the way of any rowing is proving to be a strange, unexpected kind of challenge.

We are just minutes away from pushing off for Elephant Island. If these are the last words I write, I wanted to at least mark where we are and what we are doing.

Thomas is calling. Time to push off and go.

10 January

We weren't ever really on the open ocean—there were ice
floes all around and bits of sea mush for the duration of the
trip. Still, I had never experienced anything quite so terrifying as the sentiment of *seeing* what looked like safety, and
yet *feeling* with one's whole body the sensation of being
afloat, adrift. The wind was high the entire time, and adding to the sensation of being adrift was the sensation of
being carried along by an unseen tide in the air.

For the first two days, our three boats were lashed
together by very long pieces of rope. And for the last two
days we lost sight of one another, having long abandoned
being tied together; the ropes had become encrusted with
ice and weighed down, acting as painter ropes and anchors,
steering us in all manner of cattywampus fashion.

Chipping ice off a rope is the very definition of a futile
endeavor. Besides, one was already chipping ice off every
other possible part of the boat, from gunwales to oars, from
bow to stern.

And there were still so many other ways to be in danger;
sometimes, the waves were large enough that being lashed

to each other, one of us at the crest of a wave while the others were in varying troughs, was hardly the best situation.

We took turns rowing and chipping—and urinating over the sides of the boat when we had to. This was the height of embarrassment—where the men were able to whip out their willies for a pee, I had to hang myself over the side of the boat at each opportunity. Too often there was nothing to hold on to, or the boat was far too pitchy, and so we had to engage three of us for me to perform a simple biological task; me to hang my fanny over the edge, and two men to hold on to my hands, lest we encounter a particularly rough set of waves. There is nothing quite like a wet bottom and a wet fanny, crusty from seawater. I heard two of the men in my boat who'd been friendly with Hotch- kiss make absolutely disgusting comments about how use- less I was. Sometimes, it was one of them whose arms I had to depend on to keep me from falling into the water while I went to the bathroom, and I'll never forget the strange terror of wondering if he would see fit to drop me.

I had to constantly remind myself everything would be all right—that I could trust every man on the expedition. But the truth is, once you know you can't trust one of the party, everyone else begins to take on the pallor of the mali- cious, even those you count as friends.

The tension in all the boats was high. More than once, even over the splashing of our oars, you could hear the crew in the other boats shouting at each other for one infraction or another. I heard Per completely lose it with Hotchkiss, screaming out in his high boy's voice, "Yer fakin' it! Clara didn't break nuttin' on yeh! Yeh've always been lazy; yeh canna deny it!"

In my own boat, the discontent was quieter. More of an undercurrent. We had Billings, our expedition's fine navigator, and we did not dare to upset his work too much, and so things were whispered. Or direct glares were made. Or—

The men did not escape infantilism or mortification in the biological area, either—several of them became ill from drinking contaminated water, and they were not only seasick but also all had diarrhea, which also necessitated hanging their bums out over the sea. If it weren't so life threatening, it might be amusing.

Our rations were minuscule, whether because no one wanted to hang their bums out for longer than necessary or because people were too seasick to eat, one cannot really say. We drank our entire rations of water though, every day. And Cook, bless him, managed to get the stove lit at least once a day to boil down chunks of ice for hot beverages, and at least once a day we managed to circle the boats and hand around our tin cups for filling, all twenty-eight of us. However he made it happen one will never be able tell, and even if there comes another day when one must survive entirely on bits of mint cake and dog pemmican, I will always remember the life-giving force of a hot cup of water or weak tea.

Hotchkiss's behavior, apparently, was utterly shameful.

All he had to do was lie in the bottom of the boat, since he couldn't row. But I'm told that he complained bitterly at every bump in the boat, at every unexpected wave. It's a damn miracle no one threw him overboard. I'm told Thomas played the martyr, and warmed Hotchkiss's feet against his own chest: while the rest of us could keep warm by rowing, it is true that Hotchkiss would not have had that benefit. I would be remiss in not mentioning that it feels somewhat like betrayal to know that Thomas looked to Hotchkiss's comfort whilst I was suffering the unkind words and looks of Hotchkiss's friends.

We are here now. Already my vision seems to have expanded, like I am seeing things I've never seen before, or having to relearn everything I thought I knew.

Rocks: their lovely, dark color is an obsession until my eye moves to lighter colored rocks, and then I can only marvel at their incredible variation in size and cracking and crazing and crevices and capacity for shadow. The contrast between the rocks and the snow and ice on the shore here is absolutely shattering. We have been looking at variations of white and blue for so long now that the depth of something like black or gray or brown is near an emotional experience. Birds, landing on their spindly legs, hopping here and there, looking busy and industrious; their feathers gleaming in even the weak gray light. Birds' *nests*, a terrestrial thing if ever I understood what such a thing was, looking alien to my eyes, with their sticks akimbo.

When I was a little girl, Mama used to make a game of hunting for birds' nests. I remember the tiniest ones, the hummingbirds' nests that we would occasionally find in our garden, no bigger than the palm of my little-girl-sized hand, and their miniscule, precious eggs.

The *eggs*. Oh, to have some fried eggs for breakfast. Maybe Cook will indulge us soon, although he has already worked yet more miracles by handing round mugs of hot Trumilk.

When one has not stared at anything but ice and snow for so long, one finds remarkable detail in everything. I couldn't stop looking at the ground, of all things. We hadn't seen ground in such a long time, and to my eye, it was a thing utterly novel in composition and form. I found myself asking such odd questions of myself: What is its makeup? How far down does it go into the Earth's crust? How long has it been here?

Who knew a thing like a boulder could seem so solid, so forever in nature? Who knew that even the smallest outcropping could serve as a solid perch for such a fat bird? And then, after a time, one's eye begins to track upward, far up, to the sheer cliff that borders our cove, in which some of these birds make their nests. It rears straight up like a protective thing, and one cannot quite get oneself to believe that there will be no worrying that this may melt; that it may behave treasonously, disappearing overnight because of having floated away, or causing big waves for having decided to crack off a bit of itself in the middle of the day, forcing us all into a state of near panic as we wait and see if a wave from a shorn-off piece will capsize us in our home. It is a new sentiment, to be so sure of something.

I feel certain that none of us will ever take it for granted again. I wonder if we will ever get tired of reknowing it.

I have not yet mentioned the most exciting feature of the cliff. I think it took us all a moment to figure out what it was; to even register the odd timbre of the sound we were hearing, so long it had been. The sound was a wonderful stream of fresh water, real glacial fresh water that came trickling right out of the cliff face and down into our cove in a generous, forever stream.

We all of us quieted as we one by one understood what we were hearing and seeing. It was a little like the way an audience might pause just before giving thunderous applause at the end of a performance, to let the last tone of music die away in the theater. But then, one of us shouted, "Fresh water!" and we all ran for it. I remember seeing Higgins's woolly head of hair leading the pack, and then it disappeared as he fell face down in a little stream and lapped like a poodle. Some men splashed their faces over and over again with it. Some put their faces in and blew bubbles in it for the sheer novelty of it. Thomas sat at the side of the stream and washed his hands in it, like the raccoons we used to see in Fairmount Park. Mahoney had carried Hotchkiss over and set him down next to the stream and was cupping water into his mouth with his hands.

I did all these things and more. I had to refrain from stripping all my clothes off right then and there, so keen was I to feel fresh water against my skin. All around me, the men gibbered and gabbled at one another, sounding like the ape house at the zoo at feeding time. No one cared what was said; no one cared to remember anything but this moment of communal bliss.

For my part, I remembered suddenly the day Mama told me Papa had died. She had come into my room, moving like a ghost, silent and true. She lowered herself onto my bed, but I was working busily on an encyclopaedia I had started making for myself of creatures to be found in Fairmount Park, and it was some time before I wanted to join her. "Come sit, Clara," she said.

I put some final touches on my rudimentary drawing of a nuthatch and went to her. I was thirteen. She put her arm around me and held me close, talking into my hair. "Papa has left us," she said quietly, but beneath her words there was a strange frisson of energy that I can remember to this day.

I squirmed out from under her embrace. "Well," I said, looking into her eyes and wondering at the odd spark I saw there, "this is nothing unusual, is it, Mama?" Recalling this makes me cringe; children have such smart *mouths* at any age. "I was not aware he had come back to us. How long had he been home for?"

Mama shook her head, closing her eyes for a moment. I wonder now if she was trying to arrange what she was truly feeling into something more appropriate, and when she opened them again, they were glistening with wet. "No, Clara, I mean he's died. We shan't see him again," she said. Her nose reddened and her voice quavered, and I thought at the time that she was expressing sadness, but now I think it was an odd confusion of freedom and something else.

I nestled back into her side. "Oh," I said. "Does this mean we won't have to see him again?" I remember distinctly a shift then, something fundamental in Mama's body, and when I pulled back to look at her again, her mouth was wide open, and she was laughing, soundlessly, tears streaming down her face.

She reached over my head and rang the bell for a maid-servant. When Jane opened the door, she took a single look at my mother and held her hand out to me. "Shall I take Clara out for a turn around the garden, madam?"

Mama nodded. Words failed her, it seemed.

Jane bundled me into a cloak and we worked our way down the stairs quickly, but not quickly enough to avoid hearing Mama slam my door shut and then, a great whooping laugh.

Jane looked at me gravely. "Shock, I should think," she said.

The kind of joy I witnessed and experienced today bests even that day. And yet, as I looked around, I realized that one of the most joyful of our crew was nowhere to be found, and I found him still sitting in one of the lifeboats, too wrecked, it seemed, to even call out for help while we were all stumbling around on land.

I ran back to him, relishing the scrunch of pebbles and sticks under my feet.

"Blackburn, are you not coming? There's fresh water!" I turned back to the waterfall, pointing. "Come quickly now, before the water gets too mucky with everyone's grime."

"Clara, wait."

I turned back to him. "I can't feel my feet," he said.

" . . . Sorry?"

"I can't feel my feet."

I laughed. "Yes! You've been sitting in that boat too long! They've gone numb. You must move them about a little."

He shook his head at me, looking scared.

"Blackburn . . . come. Get out of the boat."

"I can't. I can't stand."

I got into the boat and knelt down to his level, not wanting to look at his feet. "Is it pins and needles?"

He shook his head, looking desperate now. "Clara . . ."

"All right, all right." I put one leg out of the boat to stabilize myself on the ground—*ground*! "Come on, let's get you up." Blackburn reached for me and looped his arm around my shoulders. "Hold on tight to me, all right?" I wrapped his waist with both my arms for a stronger grip and lifted him a little. I could feel the bottom of his ribcage even through our clothing. He was lighter than I thought he'd be. "Come on, come on. Let's see what we—"

It was useless. Blackburn couldn't put any weight on his feet; his legs were like spaghetti. "Clara," he said again, sounding truly panicked now. He began to pant.

I turned over my shoulder and screamed for Keane and MacTavish. I couldn't support Blackburn much longer, and I didn't much feel like dumping him into that boat again. I had to call twice more; the noise from the men over the running water was too loud, although to be fair, some of the men had discovered the birds' nests and were pillaging them for eggs, and the birds were *also* raising a ruckus. Of course they would. Wouldn't you?

Finally, someone heard me; neither MacTavish nor Keane. Two of the seamen came over, and with two of us making a seat with our arms and the third supporting Blackburn's legs so they didn't dangle painfully, we got him farther inland. MacTavish had finally got the idea that someone might need a doctor's help and came running at a clip. I smiled to myself at his eternal efficiency and care for each one of us. I ran for some fresh water in a tin cup, hoping that would cheer up Blackburn, and by the time I got back, MacTavish was working Blackburn's socks and boots off gently.

None of us was expecting to see a good number of the toes spotted with waxy gray or yellow patches.

"Oh," I whispered. Frostbite. He could lose every toe. Later, we'd find out that their boat had shipped a solid six inches of seawater through the entire journey.

MacTavish shot a look at me—*shut up, shut up, shut up*—and I looked wildly around for something to do. The captain and The Boss were walking a little ways away from the men in the stream, herding birds away as they walked. I ran in their direction; I didn't want to see what would happen next.

Later

They were looking for a place to set up camp.

"We can turn the boats over and make some pretty good shelters while we wait for someone to come along," I said, feeling helpful.

Captain Phillips smoked and nodded. The Boss said, "No one will come along. We're out of the way of every whaling route and shipping channel. It'll never happen."

"Um," I said fast, trying to think of something else to say, "we should set them up anyway. Hotchkiss needs a place to rest, and Blackburn—" I started choking up, taking myself entirely by surprise. "Blackburn's feet are really bad, Boss."

The Boss glanced at me. "Aye."

"I think he might lose all of his toes," I said.

"Aye," said The Boss again. "Poor lad."

"So we should find a place to make an infirmary of sorts, no?" I was keen for something to do with my hands. "Please?"

The Boss took his pipe out of his mouth. "No need to beg so, Clara."

I glanced at the lifeboats, lying flank to flank on the rocky shore. We'd need space between them for exits and entries and general health. "I think we'll need a good thirty meters by fifteen meters at least, Boss," I said. "Let me go pace it out. There's a good spot over there."

Silence. The Boss only gazed at me. I got the impression I shouldn't pace anything out just yet. Phillips stalked off in one direction while The Boss took my elbow and steered me in another direction.

"Walk with me, Clara," said The Boss. "We're only going to need space for two boats."

I did the math. "You're going in search of help," I said.

The Boss nodded and pulled on his pipe. I waited.

"We have room for one more on the *Dudley Stanwick*," he said. "I can take you or someone else, but I wanted to give you the choice."

"Give me the . . . but why?"

"I can't make the decision for you. Staying and leaving each carry their own risks. To my mind, they are equally fraught."

I thought about this for a moment. We were nearing the end of the cove as we walked, and unless we wanted to continue our conversation clambering over the sharp boulders that bordered our new home, we were just going to have to turn around again.

The Boss favored walking meetings, but here it was going to be a problem.

"I take it you're not taking Hotchkiss," I said.

He hitched a laugh. "Wouldn't that be an adventure," he said.

"So my choice is to either stay here, with Hotchkiss, and wait for you, or go on to . . . where?"

"South Georgia," he said. "Billings reckons it's eight hundred nautical miles if we make it as straight a shot as possible."

I did some more math. Eight hundred nautical miles was an even nine hundred twenty land miles. The *Dudley Stanwick* was twenty-four feet in length, the *William Jenkins* twenty-six feet in length, like the *James Connick*. Neither of those measurements had anything to do with the other really, but somehow they seemed too deeply tied to each other for me to not think of these facts in tandem. I didn't want to think about how deep the Southern Ocean could get in places—or how big the waves. Or how strange the Antarctic summer storms could be, how unpredictable.

"Just have a think about it," The Boss was saying. "But I need to know as soon as. The weather looks decent for the next few days, so we'll want to launch as quickly as we can. No later than the day after tomorrow, I should think." He smoked and stared out to sea some more. Never would I question again why so many expedition leaders looked as if they were staring into the far distance in their portraits—it is as true to life as one can possibly understand.

"Now that Blackburn's feet are in such danger—we really mustn't wait. He'll need help."

He took out his pocket watch. "Near time for a proper breakfast," he said. "Cook should have the galley up now. Let me know."

"Wait, Boss!" He turned back to me. "Who else is going?" I felt silly, as if I were asking who was attending a party so I could decide if I too wanted to go. Would I have refused to join the suffrage movement if it comprised women I disliked?

"That you're close to?" I blushed. The Boss was more insightful than I gave him credit for. He bent and knocked some tobacco out of his pipe. "Milton-Jones, Per, Blackburn, MacTavish, Givens, and Higgins are all staying here. Keane will be with us, however. Obviously Captain Phillips. And Amos and Burch will round out the crew." I nodded. Our carpenter and an able seaman were obvious choices.

"But wait . . . Stern's not going?" The Boss's second-in-command was his near equal. No big decisions were made without him. I couldn't imagine he'd stay behind.

"No," The Boss said. "I need him here. Muster the men; give them hope every day we're gone." He scrunched away in the shale.

I've been on real land for just a few hours, possibly even

less, and now I am having to contemplate getting back in a boat. I glance back at the men, splashing one another with stream water, lying on the ground, and moaning with pleasure. Givens and Per are making dirt angels, flat on their backs and pinwheeling their arms and legs, one belying his age, the other giving rise to his internal sense of joy. A little distance off, Mahoney is smoking his pipe, picking at his nails; Figgy has got out his banjo (I had not known that piece of equipment had made it on board) and is strumming meaningless, tuneless chords, maybe just seeing what his music sounds like bouncing off the cliff wall.

Chutney is flinging rock after rock into the ocean, shouting, "Ey! There goes another! Many rocks! So many rocks. Throw 'em all day and night! There'd still be more rocks!" and the birds are adding to the noise.

I never want to leave this place. I need to leave this place. I just don't know.

All my friends are here. But Hotchkiss is here, too.

Later

I'm just back from seeing The Boss. "I want to go," I said quickly before I could change my mind.

"I thought you might," he said, not even glancing up from the map he was perusing with Billings. Billings, for his part, merely looked up and nodded once at me, as if my decision had been a foregone conclusion. I ignored him.

"Really?"

The Boss nodded, still not looking at me. "You understand too much now, of what happens when a single disruption occurs in the crew. You see it."

He stopped talking. I wanted to tell him to complete the thought. I wanted to hear him say I had caused an irreparable rift in the crew, and none of us would make it if I stayed behind.

I was with Amos, patching up some weak spots in the *Dudley Stanwick* when Thomas crept up to me. Walking on rocks hasn't made him any less of a stealthy individual. I wonder if this is something you learn in the Marines.

"Can I borrow you for a minute, Clara?"

I glanced at Amos.

"Can you trouble Givens for some more of them oil paints while yer gone, Clara?" He knocked the side of the boat. "Found a few more cracks what need shorin' up."

I nodded. "Walk with me, Thomas."

He fell into step next to me. "I hear you're headed to South Georgia," he said.

I nodded again, not wanting to talk around the sudden lump in my throat. When the list of crew that was going to South Georgia had been announced, very few had been surprised to hear me on it, except for Hotchkiss, who'd yelled, "It should have been me, damn the bitch, it should have been me!" from his litter, and MacTavish had smiled wearily and said, "It's the pain talking, never mind."

"I think you're going to be great," Thomas said now, and slowed to a stop—we were close to where Givens was trying in vain to set up an easel of sorts against a pile of rocks, looking toward the cliff, sea at his back.

"Thank you," I croaked.

"Clara—" Thomas was rooting in his pockets. "Here, I want you to have this."

He pressed something small into my palm, and I opened my hand. It was a good-sized chunk of soap.

He smiled at me. "I've been saving it for when we get off this rock, but you should have it. When you get to South Georgia, you want to be nice and clean, and The Boss will want you to be nice and clean, so take it."

I started crying and could not stop. "Thomas, I—" I tried to hand it back to him.

"No, Clara, you keep it. It's one thing of value I have left, and I really want you to have it." He closed my fingers around the nubbin of soap. I held it to my nose and breathed in deep. Slight whiff of lavender, still. Must be a piece he'd been saving from home, so far away.

I stowed it away in my pocket, next to the chunk of soap I'd been saving myself.

Sometimes, it doesn't quite matter what the truth is. What matters is what people mean.

Good gracious, have forgotten all about poaching more oils from Givens. More tomorrow.

Have spent the bulk of the last twelve hours building up the gunwales and patching holes in the *Dudley Stanwick*. She is the least banged up of all the lifeboats and, luckily for me, the one I know the best, since it was she I ran behind when we attempted our sledge to Paulet Island, she I took shelter in during our water crossing to Elephant Island, over whose sides I hung myself to have a pee.

We are, as they say, intimately acquainted, and now I know every crack and crevice, as Amos, Givens, and I have been carefully going over her every inch to make her as seaworthy as possible. I am even familiar with her patches now—the little precious metal patch we made over a particularly weak spot, and the nails around it, are of especial significance to me, since they are parts we cannibalized from *The Resolute* before she went entirely under. Never mind that the nails are raggedly spaced; such things are hard to make even, when one is shaking from cold.

Everything on the *Dudley Stanwick* has been altered, really—the gunwales are built up even higher than they were for our crossing to Elephant Island; her caulking has been reinforced with seal and bird blood, flour, and Givens's paints; we've sealed up some cracks with pages from the encyclopaedia or with cards from our extra set of playing cards before caulking; Figgy's extra banjo strings have gone into reinforcing the grommets in our sails—it is as if this little boat is the evidence of our time spent together as a crew. Should the worst happen, and our trusty vessel find its way to shore without us, anyone who cared to look would be able to read in its construction the entirety of our efforts together, a summary of the time spent in one another's company.

Ballast is another thing altogether. Because we will only be six in the boat, we're needing to compensate with rocks which will line the bottom of our boat, hopefully evenly. We are trying to find the smoothest, broadest, flattest ones, so that we may at least consider sleeping on them during our projected weeklong journey, but one cannot be too choosy in the interest of comfort when time is of the essence.

To think I was just imagining that I would never be tired of looking at rocks; now I will literally be sleeping with them.

We will carry water, of course, and foodstuffs, but Cook is not making the journey with us. The Boss has tasked Keane with learning everything he can from Cook about lighting a blubber stove on a rocking, rolling sea, for which I was only temporarily grateful; oddly, the slight I experienced at being stuck with a "feminine" task seems to no longer chafe as much as it used to.

Later

Just back from visiting with Blackburn for the last time. There are a few hours yet until we shove off, but I cannot bear to see him again. His eternal hope and joy breaks me—he fights wave after wave of tiredness in order to show it to us when we visit. After we leave—after the crew has seen us off—MacTavish will cut off all the toes on his left foot to save the foot and probably the leg, and I believe his body is harboring his energies. The right foot seems all right, and I think it's better that he was half asleep while I was speaking with him. He hardly seems to know what it is that will happen to him today, or even that we are really leaving him.

"We're going soon, friend." I fought the urge to push some of the messier curls off his forehead.

"Mmm," he said. "Come back soon, Clara, you hear?"

I worked to keep my voice steady. "Yes, we'll come for you very soon."

Blackburn snapped his eyes open. It took an effort, I could see, and he couldn't stop them from almost immediately beginning to close again, but when he spoke, his voice was strong and firm. "The Boss said two weeks for you to get there," he said, holding up his hands and counting off seven days, twice. "And then another week, say, for you to line up a ship and get back." He closed his hands into weak fists and counted off seven again. "I'll be here waiting, and after you've come for us and we've all had a bath, we can all go for a pint in Punta Arenas, won't that be just the thing? A *pint*! Imagine it!"

He held both hands to his eyes then and prized open his eyelids, comically. "I'll be missing some toes. But one can walk on two good feet!"

I blinked hard. Thankfully, he was close to sleeping again. "I can't wait," I said.

All the while, Hotchkiss slept.

I sketched a wave in his direction before leaving the tent; I didn't want to feel like I hadn't bid him goodbye and good riddance, frankly speaking.

The crew had a surprise for us—they had made us a little washroom area complete with rocks by the stream, so we could each have a private wash in turn. I stripped off all my clothes and used my own nub of soap on myself, picturing the welcome we'd receive when we landed square into the center of the whaling village of Stromness. We'd want to be as clean as possible, wouldn't we, even if we were caked in seawater from the boat journey. I'd save Thomas's, I told myself, for when we got to South Georgia, a kind of talisman. The sun was out, and I scrubbed my head as best I could before it got too cold again. Putting on my filthy clothes and hat again was a small tribulation, but everything was changing, and I had long ago stopped expecting any experience to be familiar, or even comforting. That kind of expectation seems to be the purview of a person who hasn't lived.

Cook made omelettes. They were the most delicious I have ever had. The mood was strange, subdued. It seemed as if we had just gotten used to feeling celebratory, having made such a dangerous crossing and survived so many months on ship and on the ice, and now, our family was breaking up, with no real guarantee we'd ever see one another again.

"Whaddya reckon you'll do when you get back, Clara?" It was Chutney, at my elbow.

I shook my head. "Sorry, Chutney, I was miles away."

He nodded, looking thoughtful. "No doubt thinkin' of visitin' yer friends and the like, all the company and the teas and yer mam, I should think." He winked at me.

I was quiet a moment. The truth was, I wasn't sure what I'd do if we made it back to England. I hadn't really thought past what I'd do when we got to South Georgia. Send a telegram to Mama, likely. I doubted I'd go back to the suffrage movement. "What about you?"

Chutney squared his shoulders. "Me an' Figgy and Givens, we made a pact. We're goin' to sign up for the service. Hopin' to be sent off to the front."

"You—you want to go to the war?"

He looked at me strangely. "Well, yeah! Never did sit right wi' me that we were off gallivantin' on a nice ship 'n' all when other abled-bodied men like me were gonna have to go and leave their girls and families to help us win t' war! I mean, wouldn't you go if women could go to fight?"

I thought about this a moment. Too long, it seemed,

for Chutney soon tired of me and went to go see Captain Phillips, to "say a proper goodbye," he said, which consisted of his collecting Figgy and the two singing a bawdy ballad to him, something about navigating around a woman's drawers.

These men—the men who will be left behind. They are brave and true. It sounds like something out of a bad novel, but I'm truly taken by the way they're setting to their task of standing by one another, building a community. Already the two other lifeboats are looking festive and happy—the men have strung up lines for laundry and are even drying kelp on the lines—Cook is wanting to try something new. This will truly be Camp Patience.

They will stay here, on this scrap of rock, while we try and get back to them.

Two of us row at a time in a kind of haphazard round-robin that only The Boss and Captain Phillips are keeping track of. The rest of us just go where we are told: row, rest, or steer. Maybe one of the two of us who are meant to be resting also hold on to Phillips as he is taking sights. Phillips is always either steering or navigating.

Rowing keeps us warm. Stopping is a temporary fool's relief—your muscles thank you for it, but soon enough your skin begins to wonder why you did, for between the water and the sweat you are very quickly freezing. Truly a life of extremes.

As I write, my fingers jostle and skip, from both cold and the movement of the boat. No doubt I will never be able to read these words again.

Phillips's navigation is a thing of heroism and innate talent. So many times we have had to hang on to him as he squints through the clouds or driving rain or sleet, looking for a clear sightline to the stars. He takes six bearings each hour, twice a day. He peers through the sextant and calls, "Mark!" and the one who is not holding on to him writes down the time and measurements. In this way, we navigate the massive emptiness around us.

Chipping ice off the rudder, another regular task, requires two: one to hang over the side of the boat, the other to hold on to her.

Her—yes, always her, because I am the lightest and the smallest and it costs the men the least amount of energy to hold on to me.

Have not had to pee all day but finally went in a jar, which I thought to bring along after the miserable crossing to Elephant Island, and emptied it over the side of the boat. It's too rocky-rolly in the boat to hang myself over the side. The waters out here—really, truly open ocean now—are too rough. Even the men, when they go, need to hold on to something now.

At least I don't have to hang my willy out in the wind and water and ice. Offered my jar to the crew but was scoffed at, as if dangling the willy in the wind were a matter of pride . . . !

We row all day and all night.

We sleep on lumps.

Ice crusted over the sails and boat makes noises canvas and wood should never make: creaking, thumping unhappiness.

Hot hoosh tastes better than ever in our rocking, tumbling new home. My ears are filled with saltwater and fresh water all the time, all at the same time; the wind blows sideways, pushing both rain and waves into every part of me.

I keep my diary stuffed in my woolens now, next to my skin, with a bit of string tying this pencil. I feel it is the only thing keeping me tied remotely to reality, as the world flips and turns around me.

Row, row, row.

Chip, chip, chip.

Pee.

Sleep.

Repeat.

Repeat.

Repeat.

And yet . . . would I give this up? If I could snap my fingers and go right back to civilization as we know it . . . ?

My fingers are near frozen. My breath barely warms before it gets to my lungs, raking a thousand cold fingers down my throat each time I inhale. My memories are filled with the dogs, the penguins, Hotchkiss's assault on me. With every rise and fall of the waves, my stomach lurches; the skin on my face feels scrubbed down to its last layer. Our future is desperately unclear. And yet . . . Surely, this, here, right now, being a part of this crew, is a step toward equity. A small move toward showing all of us—we here in this boat, and, if we make it back, everyone in the world—what a woman can do.

Captain Phillips says progress good. We each row four shifts, two hours at a time. Feels good to be going somewhere, but The Boss says our luck, such as it was, is ending—big, towering storm clouds on the horizon and winds picking up. More noise than ever.

It is some comfort to crowd beneath the makeshift sail cover that keeps what I think is the bulk of the rain out—but how quickly we humans become inured to small comforts! Within minutes, it seems, my body is grousing about crouching under the cover, about the rocks beneath and around our bottoms, about having to sleep cheek-by-jowl and sometimes butt-cheek-by-jowl with my crewmates.

Hard to write. Fingers cramped from rowing and cold, split at the tips even inside my mittens. I remember Thomas and Mama both: write it down.

My turn to row again.

25 January

It seems I have never done anything as long as I have rowed. My shoulders are locked, cramped. Not rowing is not a possibility.

The noise is terrible. How can one be in so much water and still hear so much noise? Isn't underwater always quieter, somehow? My hair is streaming with it, even from underneath my woolen cap; we are soaked every minute. We shout all the time to be heard over the wind and water in our ears. The seawater whips up and over the side of the boat. I fantasize about becoming a mermaid, like the one on the prow of our *Resolute*. Would that I could dive in and help to push our brave little boat, right its course—the captain says we are being pushed sideways, putting paid to all our efforts. How many miles will this add to our nine hundred twenty?

The pain in my shoulders, back, the tiny muscles between my ribs, is terrible. Sometimes I think I should just stop, lie down on the rocks ballasting our boat, or better yet: jump overboard, maybe. No sense in making the men feel guilty for something I'm now happy to do. There'd be more hoosh for them. More water. Less weight.

But more rowing for them, and who'd chip the ice off the rudder?

Fingers cracked, frozen, temporarily bleeding before the blood freezes the cracks shut again. So tired.

29 January

Land.
   Utterly flat from exhaustion.
   Shouting, coming from far, far away.
   Rescue?
   Land?

Nota bene: landing on a dark, shale-riddled beach in the middle of an Antarctic night is very disorienting. Avoid this at all costs. Some things you may suffer are:

- Delusions of rescue.
- Delusions of people other than your crew. Any voices you hear are likely bellowing elephant seals or crying birds or waves on rocks.
- Delusions of the end of a very, very long journey.

Of course, some things you might do to avoid this are:

- Not rowing a dinghy across nine hundred miles of rocking, rolling ocean.
- Not spending all your time with five other people.
- Not landing on the wrong side of a big island, having actually navigated through nine hundred miles of aforesaid ocean.
- Not signing up to cockamamie expeditions.
- Not leaving one's home country.

Oh, never mind.

What happened was this: I passed out after my last turn at the oars, and when I awoke again, the men were shouting, and the rocks in the ballast of our lifeboat were trembling with a million different vibrations from scraping along the shale on the beach of South Georgia Island. In effect, we'd finally managed to find a good place to beach ourselves. The Boss was shoving some hardtack under my nose, telling me to get up and help to secure the boat before it washed away in the surf of the bay.

I did think it odd that The Boss thought shoving hardtack in my face would get me to wake up; it was probably the best thing he could think of, as he was in much pain from sciatica. I stood up to get out of the boat, and Keane caught me just as I was toppling over again; I had an odd impression of having to be lifted out, like a bride over the threshold of her provided-for new home, but that's not what happened in the end. I kicked and scrambled to get my own feet under me, and Keane dropped my legs, landing me with a thump back into it.

Eventually I pulled myself up by my arms, I suppose, which I could not really feel anyhow, and tripped my way over the high gunwales with Keane holding on to my elbow like I was an elderly aunt and he my attentive nephew. How he was still standing, even feeling strong enough for me to lean on, I'll never parse. I just understood that this was the end of a long, long boat journey.

Later

Let me tell you a little something about the **geology** of this island. I know, I know, I said you could read Wilson's diary for such things. But Wilson is left behind on Elephant Island, and I am beginning to despair that our diaries will ever be reunited, and so I will endeavor to spell out the particular shape of this place for you.

First, it is the nearest one will find to civilization. South Georgia Island has whaling stations on it, one of which is Stromness, from which we embarked a lifetime ago.

Second, South Georgia Island is large enough to have a number of different ecological zones on it, from shale beaches to impressive mountain peaks to gentle bays that can sustain life and those whaling stations. As far as I can remember, these bays are shielded from a good amount of weather. Some say, after weeks and months at sea, that coming into these bays is like pulling into a tropical paradise.

Third, you might imagine South Georgia Island a giant sea dragon, with a great ridged back in the form of a massive mountain range. On the northeasterly side of its back are the aforementioned friendly, civilized bays; on its southwesterly side are the aforementioned shale beaches.

I know this and I shall never forget it, because we are on the shale beach side of this great hulking beast, and we must now cross its ridged back, which is said to rise to over nine thousand feet, just as you would expect from an ill-tempered reptile.

This is all conjecture, from Captain Phillips's seasoned eye for measurement: Our map shows a great blank spot where we must cross, since the island is uncharted apart from its exterior. What is not conjecture: Getting back in the *Dudley Stanwick* is not an option; we are short on time, and navigating through the rough surf to get out into sailable waters for the chance at reaching Stromness might well take a few days by itself.

However we shall gain the strength to move on to Stromness, I cannot say as of now. The Boss's sciatica is very bad indeed.

Amos has been throwing up, having strangely taken in more seawater than the rest of us; did he drink it in his sleep whilst he was taking his rest? Sleep with his mouth wide open so that it just dribbled in from the canvas cover? The captain is just too damn tired from navigating all day and night, although he did eventually let go of the reins enough for me to have a crack at it. Goodness knows I'd learned enough from our time together to be halfway decent at the sextant.

Burch looks as if he'd like to sleep for a month but is trying his hardest to stay awake, resulting in his falling asleep whilst sitting up and then jerking awake with a most unusual combination of snorts and odd sayings, things he picked up from his grandfather, say. He also cannot walk— one foot seems to be permanently numb from frostbite, and I for one am a little afraid to help him off with his shoe to see. . . . The memory of Blackburn's foot is too fresh in my mind.

The crew is a shambles.

We have been here for six hours already, hoping people's conditions will improve. The elephant seals lie all around us, having determined that we are too useless to pose any danger. Keane has shot and brought back four young birds—albatrosses—for a meal. The Boss managed to help me light the stove for tea, but he is once again flat on his back.

Our lips were too chapped for us to open our mouths wide for the succulent bird meat, so we ate in tiny bites, like new pups searching for the teat.

The sense of urgency cannot be overstated. I am keenly aware of our crew back on Elephant Island. I recall The Boss estimating three weeks until they could expect to be rescued; we are now at seventeen and a half days, and I've not yet calculated how long it will take us to cross these mountains.

But we cannot hope to cross with most our team immobilized—can we?

Later

One option: Keane and I might set up the crew here with the bulk of the supplies we've brought in the dinghy. I estimate we're twenty miles as the crow flies from Stromness, if we can manage it without getting lost or falling into any terrible crevasses, and if I'm generous about our walking pace, maybe we can manage it in twenty-four hours. With two of us, we would be faster and lighter than if we were dragging around some invalids. And The Boss *must* rest if we are to rescue the men on Elephant Island.

Just been to talk it over with Keane. He said, "Not a bad plan, that."

I absolutely goggled for a few seconds. "Aren't you worried about us making it?"

"Not. Seen you navigate; seen you measure distances. Good as any." Keane wasn't even looking at me; he was busy piling a bunch of rocks into some kind of structure.

"What're you doing?"

He glanced at me. "Makin' a shelter for the crew," he said, and began walking away.

"Wait, Keane, where're you going?"

"Gotta drag the boat up here and flip it onta these rocks. Gonna help?"

I ran to catch up.

"Good plan, that," he said as we were dragging the boat up the beach. "Move faster just the two of us, and The Boss can rest up."

I nodded. We can cover two, three miles an hour at a good clip over rolling terrain; accounting for elevation and altitude and sheer cussedness *and* tiredness, I reckon we can cover a mile an hour at the inside. If we don't stop moving, we can make it in good time. If I navigate perfectly, we should make it in very good time. Might even make Stromness in less than twenty-four hours.

If we allow ourselves a night to rest, we can be back here with a whaler to pick up our crew by the next day.

Later

Keane says I must posit it to The Boss.

There is something appealing about the idea of the Old Hand and the newest of all the crew members embarking on this journey together, but also something terrifying. We are in literally unmapped lands here; with the very basic kit of some rations, each of our compasses, and only a rope to keep track of each other with, we will have to tread carefully indeed.

31 January

Boots absolutely busted all to hell; will be eternally grateful to Amos for remembering, between throwing up, to plant some screws we'd pulled from the Dudley Stanwick into our soles. I've never encountered a more slippery surface, not even ice-skating on the Schuylkill, or maybe it's that when one falls down on the Schuylkill one is within reach of company and warm clothing. Here, one has the option of falling forever down a deep blue crevasse, leaving one's teammate to soldier on by himself if he doesn't go down with you, or endless trudging, if one does not set one's course correctly and becomes lost among the peaks and snows.

The Boss kicked up very little of a fuss when I suggested we go on without them. I'm not sure what I expected, but it wasn't the calm acquiescence we got. He asked me to lay out in detail what our plan was, and then he ran it through with me again.

When we had worked out the potential kinks, the things I had not thought of, he asked for my notebook and pencil.

"You'll need a note from me, Ketterling-Dunbar, for your arrival," he said, and I handed over my book and pencil. He wrote holding the notebook over his head, so severe was his back pain.

> Clara Ketterling-Dunbar and Michael Keane are members of the Antarctic Expedition of 1914. They have set off with my, Douglas Henderson's, express permission to seek rescue. I am with three other members of the crew at King Haakon Bay on South Georgia Island. The remaining members of our expedition are awaiting rescue on Elephant Island. Please provide Ketterling-Dunbar and Keane with the means necessary to complete the safe return of all our crew.
> At King Haakon Bay we have rations enough for six weeks.
> Douglas Henderson
> King Haakon Bay
> 30 January 1915

"Thank you, sir," I said, blinking. The words seemed outsizedly moving, for their brevity.

The Boss peered at me. "All right, there?"

I nodded. "All right. I only . . . I wish you could come with us, sir."

The Boss pushed himself up onto one shoulder, grunting. "And why's that, Ketterling-Dunbar?"

"Er . . . well . . . you're The Boss."

He peered at me. "And?"

"And you . . . well, you've been there all along, leading us."

"I see. Do you not think you can do the job?"

I could feel the flush start creeping up my neck again. "'Course I can!" I said. Even to my ears, it sounded shrill.

"As if you mean it," he said, dryly.

"I do mean it, I do!" Less shrill now. Still, methinks the lady doth protest too much.

He arched an eyebrow and sighed. "Clara, sometimes a boss is at his best when he steps aside and lets someone else lead." He cocked his chin at himself. "I'm in no shape to go anywhere. You know it. It's why you hatched this plan."

"Well, Keane—"

He waved me off and lowered himself back down to his sleeping bag. "Yes, yes, Keane quite agrees, I know, for good reason. But you had already made up your mind anyway, and it is the right decision. Leave me now. Can you and Keane manage to find dinner for us?"

I nodded and backed off. He was snoring before I turned my back.

The next morning, Keane and I settled the crew into their new quarters. We moved our meager supplies and belongings to the little cove of rocks and upturned boat that we'd made for the men, tacking the sail around the gunwales to form a buffer against the wind. The stove we set up just near the door flap so the men could get at it easily; we took one sleeping bag, plus a good length of rope.

We made us all a last fine meal of eggs, young bird, and Bovril made with fresh snowmelt. We each packed a small knapsack with enough rations for two days and said our goodbyes. I set my compass to ENE, pegged a point on the horizon, and off we went, not once looking back. Well, I didn't, anyway. I remembered too clearly what it was like to leave our crew on Elephant Island, how small they looked onshore as they waved us off. . . . To see our crew of four clustered below us as we marched up the rise would have been too much for me, I think.

To call it an arduous walk would be too generous. But I am a good navigator, and even though it has been some time since Mama and I have been out in the woods together, I have not forgotten any of my skills. Navigating in the Antarctic is easier, anyway, than navigating in the Pennsylvania wilderness; in Antarctica the landmarks are big, like mountains or giant outcroppings of ice, nearly impossible to lose track of. There are no trees to get repeatedly into one's line of sight. The danger here is in the sheer sides of the mountains, the rocks, the ice formations. Everything is so large that one must choose a *feature* on them to navigate by, like an outcropping or an odd-shaped rocky crag.

One must be hyperalert, lest one stumble into a crevasse. One is tied to one's crewmate at all times, just in case this should happen. There is an odd kind of sentimentality about this setup—it casts into sharp relief just how dependent on one another we really are in this world. After only a few hours with Keane, I have been wondering at the wisdom of trying to do everything by oneself all the time.

Were we tired? Yes. We were beyond tired, even after two good meals and a good night's sleep. We had been on the water for seventeen days; one does not simply recover overnight. But I felt alert. Eagle-eyed.

What does one think about over twenty-four hours? I know that Keane sang whole songbooks to us from his childhood. He sang me to sleep as I took a much-needed twenty-minute nap. When it was my turn to keep watch while he slept, I walked in slow, deliberate circles, counting to or near as possible to one hundred fifty in multiples of two, and then four, and then six, and then eight. I skipped ten because it would have been too easy. I went to twelve and then fourteen. Then I started all over again in multiples of three, then five, then seven, and nine, and thirteen. Staying awake while my teammate slept was the hardest thing I have *ever* done. I will never forget it.

I would like to say that I thought long and hard about what we would say when we arrived in Stromness, but the truth is, I couldn't see that far ahead. I could only see to the next mile. I counted steps as accurately as I could, hoping to get a good idea of how far we'd gone, marking them off in sets of fifty by making hatch marks on my belt with a sharp piece of shale I'd found in King Haakon Bay. But I had never walked up a mountain as steep or as high as the spine that makes up South Georgia, and so I had to assume I'd be off as much as a couple hundred steps per mile.

All along, Keane walked next to me, cheerfully singing, or tiredly singing, or just humming under his breath. It is a marvel, to not have to explain oneself. To not be questioned. It is also a trifle unsettling. And yet, isn't this what I wanted all along?

I misnavigated badly once. We stood atop the spine of the creature, looking down at what I was sure was the correct bay, only to look more closely at the map through our sleep-addled eyes and see we would have to retrace our steps so that we could reach Stromness in its bay. We could see the lights of Stromness by then, but they were impossible to reach for the massive stretch of water in our way.

I sighed in frustration and made to sit down in defeat. "Never you mind, Clara," said Keane, gripping my elbow so that I couldn't sit down without losing grasp of the map, "Not long now; we can see it."

When finally we came within sight again of Stromness, having lost sight of it temporarily as we retreated to the interior to make the crossing, I felt I was seeing one of Higgins's lantern slides. There was so much to take in. Buildings of a sort I hadn't seen for nearly half a year, straight walled and not flapping at all. The timber that makes up these walls. The red, red sides of buildings, somehow seeming like a red I'd never experienced before. The white of the roofs seemed foreign as well, a different white than the snow I was so used to seeing. I had to narrow my eyes to look at it all; it will be some time before I can see straight on, instead of looking sideways at everything; everything is so bright, nearer to magic and fairyland than I've ever experienced. In the distance, I could see whaling ships and two great whale carcasses floating in oily water that was both gray and red from blood. Great crowds of men, it seemed, swarmed over and around the bodies, working at them. Such a great many men, after our crew of twenty-eight.

We walked for some time, closer and closer before anyone noticed us, and then it was a man in a suit. He seemed familiar, and I made a mighty effort to remember his name and did, just as he fell to his knees: "Clara, is it you?"

"You remember!" I said, remembering at the last minute to straighten up. The Boss would have wanted us to present ourselves well. "My crewmate, Keane."

Carl Anton, stationmaster of Stromness, was still on his knees, and I, given permission by his own posture to sink from exhaustion, dropped to his level. "Yes, of course I remember," said Anton, sounding reverent. "The sole woman on an Antarctic expedition, how could I forget? My wife and daughters could speak of very little else after you left on your expedition. How are you here? We had given you and your crew up for lost!"

Wife and daughters. Other women! I shook myself. "We are not lost," I said, standing and offering him my hand. "We are here, but we are only two. We have four more at King Haakon Bay, and another twenty-two on Elephant Island."

Anton muttered to himself in Norwegian for a moment. "Come, come," he said finally, "we must see about getting you warm and fed, and getting back to fetch the rest of your crew."

He led the way, a neat figure in dark wool. He reminded me of a penguin, and I burst out laughing. Keane glanced at me and squeezed my elbow. "We've done it, Clara," he said warmly, and I'd have answered, except someone was calling down the street, and my ears felt as if they'd explode in joy.

"Carl? Can it be her?" It had been so long since I'd heard another woman's voice. Carl Anton's wife was running down the street toward us, her skirts bunched in one hand to be out of the way of her boots. For a moment my vision blurred, and Andrine's face took on Mrs. Pankhurst's face, and my mother's face, and the faces of all the women who have worked so hard in the places assigned to them by this world and yet still hope for more. I shook my head, trying to focus, and Andrine came clear again, running toward us in her housedress, making a mess of her skirts in the January mud.

Andrine was the first and only to tell me she thought I'd find life on the ship "charmingly challenging." I'll never forget the sardonic twist of her lips. Her eldest, busy at the sewing machine trimming my socks to fit my feet better before our expedition, nodded solemnly and then laughed out loud.

There is a sisterhood, I think, among we women who choose these climes, these adventures. I didn't know if Andrine knew that her marriage to Carl would take her to these far reaches, at near-opposite pole to her home country, but she told me she relished the idea of anything that was different and new to what she'd said was a cosseted life in Norway.

There have been many moments on the ice wherein I have longed for the company of the other suffragists. But when Andrine came close to me, holding my face in both hands and then throwing both arms around me, knocking Keane's grip off my elbow, I finally realized how much I had just missed the company of other women.

At the Anton home, Andrine quickly bundled me into the house and up the stairwell while Keane was led in another direction. "Wait, wait," I said to Andrine, and called back down the stairwell. "Keane, muster in half an hour, please."

Keane's answer sounded half-choked in laughter. "Yes, marm," he said. "Understood."

I ignored the frivolous tone. "Thank you," I called back.

Andrine smiled at me. "Leading the expedition, are we?"

I pondered that for a moment. "Not really. Just doing a job." Andrine nodded and helped me to maneuver the narrow stairs. Stairs! We'd not encountered steps for some time.

"Now," she said, opening a door and guiding me

through it, "it's time for a bath, wouldn't you say?"

"Not too long of one," I said. Panic had started scratching at me. We'd told The Boss we'd be back in a day and a half, two, perhaps, and time was moving too fast. "There's so much to do still."

My voice seemed to bounce. I looked around at where we were. A porcelain tub and sink and a proper flushing toilet were arranged around a room. There is a different quality to one's voice when it is surrounded by walls.

"You need to bathe," said Andrine. "Surely you can take time for this."

"Not too much time," I said again.

Andrine nodded and sat on the edge of the tub. She turned a tap. Some gurgling sounded in the walls of the house and steaming water began to pour out of the tap. I momentarily forgot my urgency. "Is that . . . is that hot water?"

"It is." Andrine turned the cold-water tap a little. "Now, what do you need done?"

I chewed my lip, thinking. "Please could you ask Mr. Anton if there is a whaling ship at liberty to take us back to King Haakon Bay, as soon as possible?"

She nodded. All efficiency. I thought of Mrs. Pankhurst's daughters, taking orders from her. I thought of myself, learning how to be a woman at Mama's knee. "I will make sure of it," she said. "When will you want to leave?"

"As soon as we've had a bath and something to eat,"

I returned. I sat down on the lip of the tub and began to unlace my boots. I took off my socks. They were so stiff that they did not collapse for some time. "You may want to—" I gestured at my overall filth. "I absolutely reek."

She laughed outright. "I live among whalers," she said. "But I'll leave you. Think nothing more of your forthcoming tasks; I'll get it all settled for you."

I nodded. Privacy seemed a bizarre luxury now.

Andrine turned for the door.

"Wait, Andrine!"

She turned back.

"Where did they take Keane?"

"Oh, there are tubs in all the dormitories for the whalers. Don't worry, he'll soon be just as clean as you will be." She gestured at the vanity. "There's a fresh bar of soap there, and some towels here, on the rack. You take your time." She grinned suddenly. "Well, don't take more than fifteen minutes. I have some clothes here that will fit you, if you like. I'll be back soon with something for you to eat and drink."

I nodded. There didn't seem to be much to say to all of that.

A bath is a thing not to be overlooked. The water seemed cleaner than any water I had ever seen before, which is ridiculous because water from an iceberg melt is the purest thing, truly, so long as there are no penguins about. The steam rose off the top, and I dipped my hand into it, feeling immediately warm. My skin, my entire body, looked absolutely filthy against the porcelain of the tub. I was overtaken with a need to immerse myself entirely in that water.

I grabbed the bar of soap off the vanity and set it on the little stool near the tub, which also held a generous-looking towel; I stripped everything off fast, fast, fast, catching little unsavory whiffs of myself as I did so. Each layer was like a different layer of smell, and when I got to the last layer, I noticed with a kind of delayed shock that my hands and feet and face were an utterly different color from the rest of me.

I got into the tub and experienced a sensation that made me groan out loud.

"Clara?" called Andrine from the hallway. "All right? Can I come in?"

"Very, very all right," I said, and then dropped the soap in the tub when I saw what Andrine had come in with—fluffy-looking baked goods and some hot herbal tea.

Herbal tea! Not the builder's tea that we've been drinking, not the Trumilk I never want to see again, not hot Bovril. Herbal tea. Chamomile. I drank the tea sitting in bathwater, which was slowly going a grayish-brown from the dirt on me, with the bottom of the teacup sat in the water, and I'd never felt so decadent. Andrine smiled and passed me a cookie scented with cardamom and cinnamon, two spices that had seemed in abundance before I got to the ice. Cook is good at what he does, but he isn't cardamom and cinnamon by a long shot.

I bit into the cookie, and crumbs drifted into the bath-water. Butter, fresh butter, melted onto my tongue. My mouth, so accustomed to hardtack and pemmican and hoosh, was temporarily flummoxed. I'd forgotten how to chew something so delicate. I didn't know how to swallow it. Had I taken too big of a bite? How could something taste so velvety and yet be so crisp at the same time?

For someone who'd been pining for "normal" food, eating a biscuit suddenly seemed truly complicated. There seemed to be so many ingredients involved.

I ate every cookie on the plate.

Andrine left the room again, and I was left with myself.

My hair was still short from the last haircut I'd been given, but it carried with it the funk of many months of not washing. It took me four scrub-and-rinse cycles before I began to feel like I'd washed off my own bodily grease and the seal blubber grease and God knows what else had collected in my hat.

I washed all of me once, and the water was already use-less for further cleaning.

"Andrine? I'm going to need to run another tub; is that all right?"

"Yes, of course!"

Draining the tub left a significant ring around it. A ring of myself, of my dead cells, of Antarctic grime.

I filled the tub again and started the whole process all over.

I ended with my feet and hands, getting under my nails and around their beds as best I could. Finally, there emerged a person I didn't quite recognize—scrubbed pink, with freckles where there had once been a smooth coating of dirt and soot that had resisted even drenchings of seawater.

But really, looking deep into my own eyes in the mirror, I recognized myself just fine.

Andrine had laid out a set of her own trousers and a set of her own woolens. She'd brought me a heavy coat, the kind you might wear if you are going on a short boat journey, and my heart lifted, not for the color of the coat, a bright yellow, but for the thought that this would be a short journey, in waters that were well known. We would rescue our men, and in time, too.

I stared at myself in the mirror. Fringe cut in typical hackneyed, Per-and-Blackburn-directing-each-other style; back of head cut in "I don't trust anyone but myself to do this anyway, so I might as well do it blind" style. Freckles everywhere, eyes sunk deep into my face as a result of dehydration and malnutrition, I shouldn't wonder. Skin flushed happily with warmth and feeding instead of cold and hunger. With a pang, I thought of the men back in King Haakon Bay and on Elephant Island.

I turned away from the mirror. I'd had six, seven, eight delicious biscuits and a generous cup of delicate chamomile tea; if I was predicting right, the men were still on Trumilk and omelettes with salt and pepper, unless Cook had found a way to make seasoning out of kelp. I could hardly stand it. How were Blackburn's toes? Was Thomas making a nuisance of himself even now? Was Givens painting anything, and if so, with what, since we had used so many of his oils to caulk the *Dudley Stanwick*?

How was The Boss? Was his sciatica any better? What of Amos? Has his system finally righted itself? And Captain Phillips? Was he navigating in his sleep? How about Burch? Had he stopped having nightmares???

I felt sick, as if the biscuits might come up at any moment, but instead what happened is that I started crying out of sheer homesickness, not for London or for Bucks County or even for Mama, but for my boys, for the men who had taught me so much and given up so much and had worked so hard to look beyond the very basic fact that I was a wrench in the works.

I wanted nothing more but to get back to them. There was no time to waste, and I had just spent fifteen minutes luxuriating in a tub and eating biscuits.

Andrine chose that moment to open the door.

"Oh, Clara," said Andrine, pulling a handkerchief out of her sleeve—like Thomas!—and blotting my cheeks with it. "Come now. Fret not; everyone will come home safe. You've done what you needed to do."

I groaned. "Not yet. We've left them there, all alone," I said, feeling as if my very insides were cracking open. "We need to go back, now."

My tears were incessant. I could not stop.

Andrine held me close for what felt like a long time, letting me cry.

I think it felt like such a long time only because it had been so long since I had let myself cry in anything but frustration. All I felt now was sadness.

When I was done, I washed my face in the basin, making a wet mess of the new woolens, and went to find Keane.

True to her word, Andrine had indeed found a ship for us. It was a small, sprightly whaler, helmed by a pug of a man who only spoke Norwegian. Anton asked to come along, which we were grateful for, as only a few men on the crew of the ship spoke English, and as it would take the better part of the remainder of the day to get there, we set off straightaway.

Andrine packed us more food than I thought it would be possible to eat, but once we set off in the boat, Keane and I fell on the feast with embarrassing ravenousness. We had to remind each other to not eat too much; months of our limited diet meant regular fare would take some getting used to again.

Even as we were eating our food, the anticipation and nerves that comprised getting this rescue right seemed to eat away at *me*. Most of the time, I stood in the bow of the ship, counting the bays as they slid by on our left. There would be four significant bays before we rounded the northwesterly end of the island, and then we would come upon another bay, and then finally, King Haakon Bay and our men. The sun tracked slowly and weakly across the sky. The albatrosses and skuas flew by all the time, making a racket and in general reminding us that we were near land. My eyes felt a great relief upon seeing the whites and blacks of South Georgia Island; I didn't know if I ever needed to see open ocean or an open Antarctic landscape ever again.

There it was. We were upon it. I stood up in the bow of the ship, called for Keane. "Keane! Is that . . . ?"

Keane stood next to me, stuck a hand up in the air, waved madly. "It's him. It's The Boss, and the others. He's standing. He's all right. We're there. We're *there*."

When one weeps in the Antarctic, one's tears freeze on one's face. This is something I seem to struggle mightily to remember.

I thought we'd all sleep for a solid day. But when I got up again, and went in search of The Boss, I found him already at work, hunched over the stationmaster's desk.

He'd shaved and washed; the skin on his face where his beard had been was a delicate pale that I'd forgotten ever existed in men.

"Boss?"

"Ah, Clara. Just a moment." He tapped out a few more strokes on the telegraph machine and turned to me finally. "Well, Clara, that's more like the young lady who came in to see me so long ago. I'd wondered if we'd ever see her again." He smiled, looking bittersweet, gazing at the dress I'd chosen to put on that morning. His words sounded to me like an odd proclamation of nostalgia for a time I would not choose to visit again, and I regretted putting on the dress, regretted the moment of vanity I'd chosen to indulge.

The Boss cleared his throat and took off his spectacles. "Er. I've just sent a note off to the papers in England and to our sponsors and the Metropolitan Police, to let them know we are safe and sound. The police should let everyone's families know that we are arrived on South Georgia Island."

"Oh. That's exciting, sir," I said, sounding stiff even to my own ears.

He looked at me for a minute longer, as if waiting for me to come clean about how I was really feeling, but I wouldn't have been able to tell him right then and there, anyway. I was too mixed up, too worried about what we'd find when we got back to Elephant Island.

I cleared my throat. "Erm. What else are you working on, sir?" My dress itched. I scratched at my neck and wondered how soon I could bolt upstairs to put my trousers back on.

"Oh, just trying to set things in motion here." Before I could ask what he meant, he said, "Andrine says they'll have a fine feast for us prepared in about an hour."

"An hour! What time is it?"

"Late afternoon," he said, absently. "Won't a full meal be nice!" He rubbed the bridge of his nose and put his spectacles back on. "Just imagine it, Clara. Tablecloths. A table, even! Chairs. Silverware and china and teacups. What a change it will be."

I nodded, but part of me felt truly bereft.

"Now, Clara," The Boss said, "don't be doing that."

"Doing what, sir?"

"Missing what we had there. The wet sleeping bags. The drafty tents. The single tin cup. The Trumilk, the hoosh, the pemmican."

"The crew, the teamwork, the camaraderie," I countered. "The sense we were a part of something together. Something huge. Something that would change the world." I turned to look out the window. The crew of the whaling station, who had been so excited to see us back with the living, had already gone back to work. They were busy flensing whales, dismantling them, bloodying the pristine Antarctic waters. I felt like throwing up.

The Boss came to stand by me. "Must do something about that. They're going to empty the ocean of whales," he muttered, and then, "Clara, why do you think most people sign on to these expeditions, or even try for a berth on them?"

I didn't much care what the answer was.

He went on as if it didn't matter whether I'd answered or not. "They do it exactly for the reasons you've just said— to be a part of something really big, truly world shifting."

I mustered some interest, if only to be polite. "Is that why you did it, sir?"

He shook his head. "No. I did it because I was bored."

I turned to look at him. "Sir?"

He twinkled at me, as if remembering the first time he hit upon the idea of exploring the Antarctic. "I'd seen men in all kinds of situations. I wanted to see what they'd be like at the ends of the world. And once I saw it, and witnessed what you've just talked about—the way everyone nearly forms one body, the way everyone pulls together to see an expedition through—I was no longer interested in trafficking among ordinary men in ordinary situations. I have seen what immense good men can do when they are pressed to the very ends of their capacities." He sighed.

I waited. Finally, he said, "This expedition, I have seen what evil man can do. I have witnessed how just one man's actions can tear an effort apart, no matter how much steam that effort has already built up."

"Sir, I—" He started to talk over me, and then thought better of it, it seemed. "Sir, I think—the question must be asked. Do you think the evil you speak of would have occurred if there had not been a woman on board?"

The Boss turned to gaze at me. I scratched at my collar. "I do," he said. "It may not have come to pass in the exact same way, but the bad would have outed itself sooner rather than later, I believe."

It is hard to quantify the relief that saturated my body. It is hard to quantify the rage that flooded me at the same time. The Boss smiled uneasily at me, potentially sensing that this was not the entirety of the answer I wanted to hear. He took a small step backward, away from the window, as if turning back to the telegraph machine, but I like to think he was retreating from my incipient anger.

"Sir! I must ask." I took a deep breath. "Why, why, if you understood Hotchkiss was not a good man—why did you lock *me* away, and not him?"

I'd never seen The Boss gobsmacked before. He opened and shut his mouth several times. "Why, Clara, we separated you from each other. We wanted to give you time to recover from your ordeal."

I stared. The Boss stared back, placid, bovine practically, to my eyes. The silence lengthened while the thoughts swirled around in my head and finally got themselves into order. "But how . . ." I started out stammering and eventually locked into what I needed to know. "Why would you not think to *ask* me what I needed? I didn't need time or space to recover. I needed my *friends*!"

By then I was verging on yelling. My throat felt on fire with outrage, with unfairness.

"*How* could you *possibly* know what a woman wants, if you never, ever asked?"

The Boss turned; the other side of the sweet coin that had been mooning about tablecloths and silverware just a moment ago. He roared. "Enough!"

Another silence. I swallowed and took a step closer, feeling as if I were channeling Emily, stepping straight into the path of a thundering racehorse, risking being trampled to my death—but this one did not shy. We each stood our grounds then.

"I agree, sir, enough," I said. "The next time you want to know what a woman wants, I suggest you ask her."

It would have been appropriate in one of my novels if

I had turned on my heel and left the room (and I was even wearing a dress that I could exit dramatically in!), but I had moved beyond that, somehow, in my head. This was my commander I was speaking to, the leader of our expedition, the reason we were here. Some part of Thomas's military rumblings must have washed off on me, because I found myself unable to turn my back on Sir Douglas Henderson, Commander of the Royal Victorian Order.

We faced each other, each of us, I dare say, feeling exhausted beyond our bodies. The Boss seemed permanently slumped, bringing him to my eye level; I, despite my freshly scrubbed skin and floating, light skirts, despite the weight I know I'd lost from what felt like a lifetime of penguin livers and hoosh, felt tethered to the ground by my heart, for I knew now with certitude what I was feeling—this fight I was in would never be an individual undertaking. In my moment of greatest need, my single—and singular—voice would never be as loud as the voices of a thousand women, shouting all together for what we alone knew we needed.

The Boss shook his head and righted his chair again. He sank into it. "Clara, we need to start thinking about going back to collect our crew. I'm meeting with Anton here in a minute to see if he can spare any whalers; can you find Keane and make sure the men are presentable for dinner?" He glanced at me. "He's in the kitchen, if you—erm, if you don't mind going there."

I nearly laughed out loud. Of all the things, The Boss was worried about how I'd feel being sent to the kitchen again. Instead, I just nodded and tried to remember where Andrine had said the kitchen was.

2/3 February

I'm finding it so hard to try to put my thoughts about tonight's dinner and feast into perspective.

Everything is skewed; everything is confused; I hardly know where to direct my thoughts, much less comprehend that we ate sitting on chairs and were served multiple courses.

Ham was had, whole chickens, even a roast beef Wellington. Mushrooms and vegetables like squash and aubergine and fresh runner beans from the greenhouse in the center of town, seasonings beyond mere salt and pepper. When we first arrived at the table there were multiple forks and knives laid out, and all six of us shared panicked glances that very clearly read, "What do we do with these?"

Andrine took pity on us, but not without laughing out loud first, and went around the table removing all but one fork, one spoon, one knife. A big heave of relief was felt all the way 'round.

When I sat down, I remembered to keep my knees together. My ankles relished the soft swoosh of dress hem against them; even the very feeling of a chairback to lean on was delightfully foreign. My fingers seemed to want to rest upon the cool silver and china of the dinnerware forever; I thought I'd never want to see tin plates and forks ever again. We served ourselves from dishes set in the center of the table; the Antons might have the best in indoor plumbing, but they'd stopped at importing maids and footmen to South Georgia Island.

We all said grace, holding hands around the table, elbows on hard, solid, polished wood. I imagined I could feel the slick of the varnish through the fine fabric of my sleeve. In my left hand, the soft skin of Andrine's youngest girl; in my right hand, the hand of Andrine herself, rougher from work and age, but still soft to my chewed-up paws. I could not help but compare.

What is beauty, after all?

The men had forgotten how to chew with their mouths closed. I had not, and I savored every bite, going between meats and veg, experiencing the different textures and flavors as if for the first time. Beef Wellington is a marvel; delicate pastry crust overlaying the firmer meat! Very little was said the first fifteen minutes, as we all lived the moment we had talked about so often together—our first meal back, together.

Keane asked, very politely, for ale, before being reminded this was a dry camp. A kind of resigned sigh around the table, but then Anton leaned over to whisper in his wife's ear, and Andrine returned with a bottle of port and one of sherry. Restrained cheers all the way around, The Boss's gimlet stare on us all, reminding us there was still work to be done.

"Well, Henderson, what now?" Anton finally asked, after sherry had been poured and the pace of eating had slowed down.

The Boss blotted at his lips with a linen napkin before answering. "We will try for Elephant Island as soon as we can stock the ship you've managed to source for us—many thanks." A murmur around the table, except for from Captain Phillips, who obviously already knew. The Boss turned to all of us. "It is a tidy, steam-driven whaler with a steel reinforced hull for driving through ice."

I did some quick math in my head: we will not have so long a ways to go in order to reach Elephant Island. It will not take so very long to reach there as it did in our dinghy, and with the benefit of sails and engines far stronger and more reliable than our own poor muscles, we should make good time. Three days, maybe five, to make it to Elephant Island, if the ice cooperates; the cold is unrelenting. "Good whaling," said Anton. "They like cold water."

The Boss cleared his throat. "It'll take maybe two days to get everything squared away, and then we'll be off."

A moment of silence. I was thinking of how long the men could hold out for, but then Amos turned the talk to the war.

England has sent tens of thousands of men abroad

already. The United States is largely a topic of derision—they've not stepped in yet despite calls to do so. I've never been so glad I lied to get onto this expedition.

The situation changes week by week, Anton said.

I was afraid to ask, but I finally screwed up the courage to do so. "And the women?"

Andrine answered me quickly. "Accomplishing amazing things," she said. "I'd have expected no less."

My heart lifted. Perhaps now I could encourage Mama to England, so that she might understand what it means to have a voice. "Ah! We've got the vote then, finally!"

Dead silence, and it began to dawn on me that this was not what Andrine meant.

She put her hand over mine. "The women have stepped in where the men have left work to be done," she said, sounding steely. "Just as they said they would." She shook her head, although I hadn't said a single thing yet. "Some English villages are bereft of men entirely. The women are taking care of farms, of shops, of making artillery for the war effort. Everyone," she said, "is pitching in. Everyone."

Andrine's eyes were shining, but I didn't feel the glow. "Women," she said proudly, "are keeping the world running."

"Hear, hear!" said someone down at the end of the table, and I heard water glasses clink in a toast to women—a marked improvement over "Wives and Sweethearts."

"Women are keeping the world running," I said, feeling

bitter, "And yet, no one wants to acknowledge our right to the vote?"

Andrine looked at me, and I'd never felt so pitied in my life, as if I've been out of step for all of my belief. She shook her head. "My dear," she says, "what good is the vote if there is no world to vote in?"

Another silence, and then Burch said, "We need to get Milton-Jones back for the war then, don't we? He'll want to reenlist right away, as will I."

The crew began to ask more and more questions about the war effort. Andrine smiled beatifically at me and leaned in close. "I understand your disappointment," she said, tête-à-tête. "Women are fighting two war fronts. But one must take precedence over the other."

Around us, the crew's voices were pitchy with enthusiasm and joy and pride. Andrine's words, Gwendoline's rebuke, and Mrs. Pankhurst's exhortation that we pick up the mantle of responsibility for our nation while our men were sent to the war front all rang in my ears, in Mama's exhausted timbre. Had I been so busy fighting to get along in the world of men that I had failed to really listen to women?

This bed is too soft, the noises of Andrine and her children cleaning up after our dinner too strange; the fresh air is only a wall away and yet too far out of my reach. The window is cracked open—I imagine only a slice of fresh air coming in. It's a far cry from sleeping practically in the open, with the gently billowing—and sometimes outright snapping!—tent walls, a testament to the existence of the elements.

Pillows. I have pillows, two of them, both to myself. I can bury my whole face in them. I can sleep without my woolen hat on and my many layers of clothing. Tomorrow when I awaken, it will not be to the snuffling and breathing of my tentmates.

Amos, Burch, and Keane are bunked together. I am driven to distraction with jealousy of the sleepy conversation I know is going on right before one drops off, of the soporific sound of my tentmates. There is no one here to talk to about my thoughts; no one here to noodle over the steps we are to take next.

Once again, I feel utterly alone.

3 February

I dreamed of the crew on Elephant Island last night. They are
having a tea party. My mother and Gwendoline are there. It
was a strange, disjointed dream, with the men drinking tea
out of fine china but with their same ratty clothes on, and
someone has carted in a pianoforte made entirely of seal-
skins and gutstrings, so it sounded like eighty-eight pitched
drums instead of a pianoforte. Figgy was plinking away on
it very well, but he's picking out a sea shanty, and I was
watching from behind a rock, as if I no longer belonged to
the crew.

Suddenly, a huge wave crests behind the party. I'm the
only one that sees it. I call out *Wave! Wave!* And they all
finally look at me, but someone points out that it's a wave
made of frothy dresses and meringue, and then everyone
is rolling in sweet, sticky stuff and lace, and no one cares
about drowning.

I awake, sweating.

Since our arrival, we've been run off our feet. We've been down to see the boat and have sat in countless meetings, trying to figure out what we'll need for the run back to Elephant Island. All along, the clock in my head—and the clocks on the walls of every room here!— remind me that the crew is surviving on hope and whatever rations they have left, whatever birds and snails and kelp there are to eat on Elephant Island.

Just back from the stationmaster's office. The Boss was in there, sending more telegrams.

"One for you, Clara," he says, holding it out.

It's from Mama. "Glad you are safe. Surely it is time to come home." I put it in my pocket.

I pulled out a stool and pulled in close to The Boss. "How close are we to leaving?" He grimaces. Grunts.

"Working on it," he says.

I felt a sudden, irrepressible urge to challenge him. "Have a pity, Boss. The sooner the better, surely. What is our best-case timing?"

But The Boss was already back working on something

else, and I had to wait for him to answer me. "A few days," he said, finally, "and then our best-case scenario for getting back to Elephant Island might be five or seven days—or it could be months."

I gape, open-mouthed in dismay. "We told the men it'd be a matter of mere weeks!"

The Boss scrubs his face with his hands. He looks infinitely tired. "I know," he says softly. "The seas may not cooperate."

I shudder, remembering the angry grip of the ice on our *Resolute*, and then The Boss says, "I am working on a second ship right now."

I squawk. "*Two* ships! What do we need two for? Is the first one not fit for all our men and us? Surely it'll take more time to source two!"

"No, love," he says, and I shift at the endearment, bristling at the sudden tone in his voice. I look more closely at him. He seems worried. "You have a choice to make."

"Oh?" I'm perplexed. What choice? Surely the choice is null. It is only when we can leave to get our crew back. Tomorrow? The day after? "When" is the only question.

I hitch up my trouser legs. The delicate swishy feeling around my ankles that had so captivated me at dinner just two nights ago is nothing to think of now. Never again, I think to myself.

"I'm looking for a second ship," The Boss says finally, "because Amos and Burch have made it known to me that they wish to return home from here and enlist in the war effort immediately. To fight for the Allies. They do not want to wait for the uncertainty of fetching the rest of the crew home.

"So, two ships, Clara," he says now, and I understand finally the tenderness in his tone. "One to take me and anyone else who will join me back through the pack ice to collect our crew. And another to send whoever wants to go back home, home." He smiles crookedly. "Well, first back to Punta Arenas. And then home. Or wherever they want to go. If you, say—" He clears his throat, and I think he's going to tear up, but he bites it back. "If you wanted to go home to Philadelphia, then I'm happy to pay for your passage there."

There is a long silence. I cannot believe what I am hearing. Not once have I considered that not going back to fetch my friends could be an option. Not once did I ever imagine anything but pulling up in a big friendly ship, steel hull and everything, power and might beneath my feet, the thrumming engine working with me and my five other crewmates. I never pictured anything but a reunion.

I would be the first off the ship.

I would clamber into the dinghy and be the first to set foot on that guano-infested rock; I would gather Per and Blackburn into my arms; I would never let Thomas go; I would eat all of Cook's hardtack biscuits, just to hear him grunt approvingly at me again.

I would be laden down with sweets and blankets and soap and cold chicken. I would be the one to tell them, *Well done!* and I would mean every word.

But of course, it wouldn't be me anyway. The men would want to see The Boss first. It would be his congratulations that would mean the most.

I would be there, though. And perhaps that would be the only thing that counted.

My friends would be happy to see me. But they would be just as happy, perhaps, to know that I had gone on to do something else. And if Amos and Burch were going back to join the war effort . . .

"Clara?"

"Hm?" I shook my head. The Boss is sitting there, leaned forward, waiting for me to say something.

"Sorry, I was thinking about something else." This part, at least, is true.

"You don't have to answer me now, but it should be soon," The Boss said then. "That icebreaker may be ready for us tomorrow, and I'm happy to take you, but I need to know soon."

∽

I found Keane sat in the sunshine, eyes closed, enjoying a smoke on the hill just above town.

I sat down next to him.

"Clara," he said, without opening his eyes.

"How'd you know it was me?"

"General air of must-do-something anxiety," he said. He smiled at me.

"Ah."

I sat for a while next to him. Below us, the waves pushed the blood of whales in and out, onto shore and back out again. The great bodies lay still in death, unpeaceful. My stomach lurched. "Keane," I said, "why aren't you going back to join the war effort?"

He took his pipe out of his mouth and gazed at me. "I will do. But I need to see this out first. Finish this job."

I swallowed. "Do you think I should finish this job too?"

He didn't hesitate. "Depends on what you think your job is, Clara, doesn't it?"

"I . . ."

But Keane had turned back to the sun again and closed his eyes, and when I sought to speak again he was lightly snoring. I left him there, on the hill.

All my life I've wanted to be more than I am. All my life I saw my mother struggle for what she rightfully deserves as a functioning, and in some ways, foundational member of society, not as "just a woman."

I have seen what it is to fight for what you think you deserve. I have seen what it is to walk uphill, pushing against wind and ice berms and ravines, and even against your own crewmates. I have seen what it means to contribute to a greater effort.

And now I have seen Andrine and her daughters again. I have been reminded that I fight on not only to remind men that we deserve the vote, but also to give other women the strength to carry on in an unjust system.

There is only one answer.

"You go, Boss," I tell him when I come back from visiting with Keane. "You send the men my love, and you tell them I'll see them back in London. The women there need me."

This is a good place for me to tell you about **ENDEX**, or **End of Exercise**. Thomas told me the military uses this phrase in training, and some days, thinking of hearing this neat little phrase from The Boss's mouth was the only way I got through another day on the ice.

I have come to the end of my exercise here in the Antarctic. Tomorrow, I board a whaler bound for Punta Arenas along with Amos and Burch, from which we will continue on to England.

I know not what I will find when we land in Plymouth; I know only that I will search out Gwendoline first, and the WSPU offices second. I cannot imagine that Pankhurst will have closed these down; there must be a way for the British populace to find women who can help.

One might argue that there is no real ENDEX in the kind of endeavor we women are undertaking. That even if we get the vote, there will always be something else to do—or someone else to lift, to elevate, to their rightful station.

But I know now my place is not to soldier on alone,

charging forward in weak leads as if I were *The Resolute* herself. I know my job is to muster with others—other women—to keep the world moving toward what we eventually hope it will be for us.

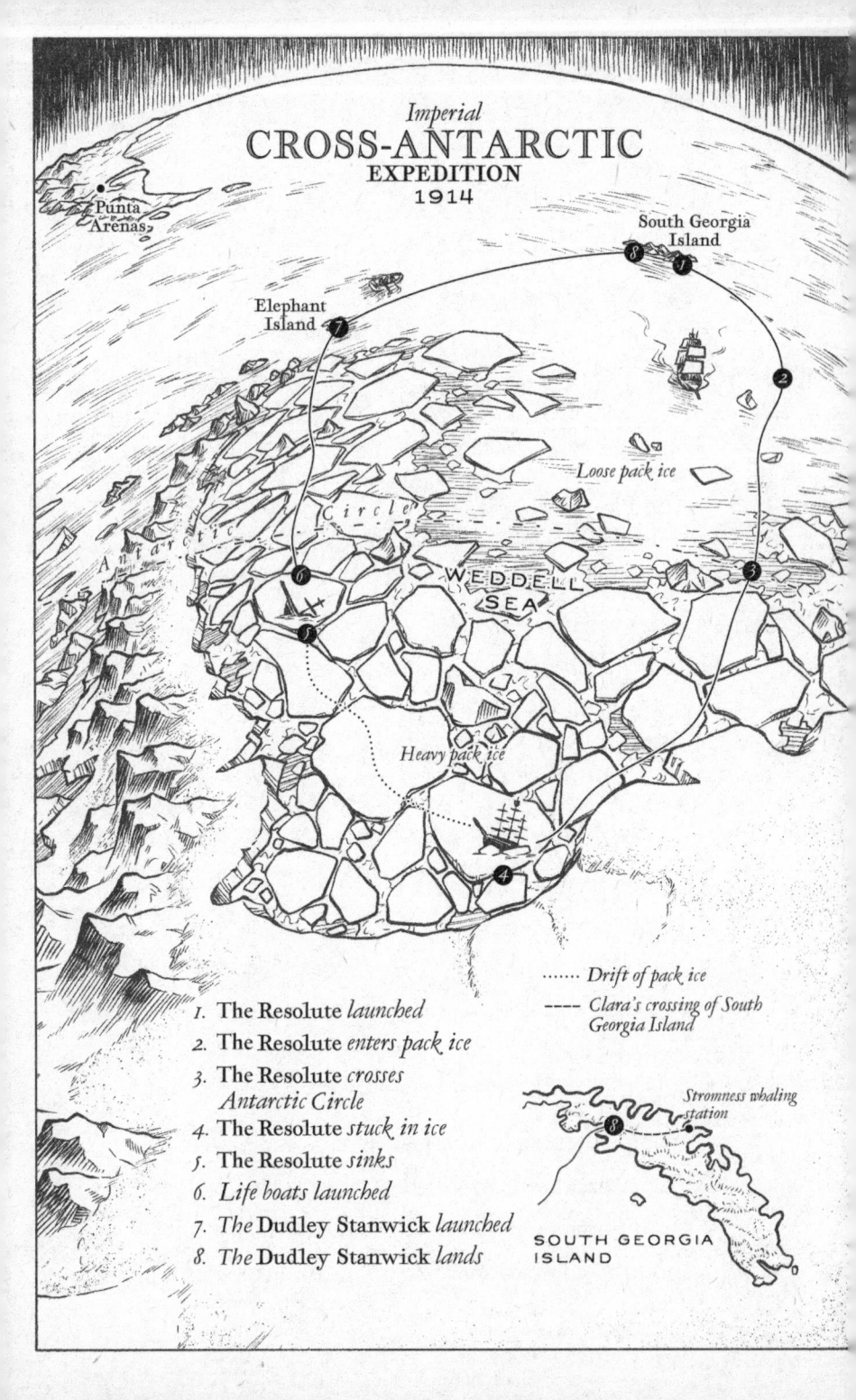

Imperial
CROSS-ANTARCTIC
EXPEDITION
1914

Punta
Arenas

South Georgia
Island

Elephant
Island

Loose pack ice

Circle

WEDDELL
SEA

Antarctic

Heavy pack ice

...... *Drift of pack ice*
---- *Clara's crossing of South
Georgia Island*

1. The Resolute *launched*
2. The Resolute *enters pack ice*
3. The Resolute *crosses
    Antarctic Circle*
4. The Resolute *stuck in ice*
5. The Resolute *sinks*
6. *Life boats launched*
7. The Dudley Stanwick *launched*
8. The Dudley Stanwick *lands*

*Stromness whaling
station*

SOUTH GEORGIA
ISLAND

Author's Note

This book's events are pegged to the events of the Imperial Trans-Antarctic Expedition of 1914, in which Sir Ernest Shackleton and twenty-seven other men embarked on an attempt to cross the Antarctic continent on foot. After their own ship, the *Endurance,* became locked in ice, they tried to march to Paulet Island and eventually sailed to Elephant Island. Shackleton and five other men got into their 22.5-foot lifeboat, the *James Caird,* and sailed the eight hundred nautical miles to South Georgia Island, where three of them made the overland crossing to Stromness. He told the crew on Elephant Island he hoped to be back in three weeks. *Four months* later, after trying three times in different ships, each time getting stymied by pack ice, Shackleton was finally able to charter a sturdy icebreaker, the *Yelcho,* and rescue every man.

Although the expedition had to abandon their original planned overland crossing, every single one of them did make it home, with only one casualty: Blackborow, the inspiration for Paul Blackburn here, lost all the toes on his left foot to frostbite after their passage to Elephant Island.

There has been an immense amount written about Ernest Shackleton and his powers of leadership, but in my research (reading the crew diaries, visiting Antarctica myself, courting an unhealthy fascination with teamwork and what makes a team *go*), I find myself more compelled by his crew and the leadership capabilities *they* had to leverage to play their part in the story of Shackleton's leadership. It is scientifically proven, in study after study, that good leaders know how to step aside when the time is needed. And when you have a headstrong leader like Ernest Shackleton, you need to step aside and let The Boss do his work, by supporting him.

I didn't write this book to counter the myth of Ernest Shackleton. There are whole courses on leadership you can take at top business schools based around study of this leadership, but I've always argued that today's mergers and acquisitions will never require the amount of leadership it takes to save twenty-eight men's lives. I also had no desire to spend more time around the reek of machismo that often encounters retellings—and re*enactments*!—of the expedition. Anyway, Shackleton was not about that.

I wrote this book to shed a light on the crew. On the work they had to do; on the small actions of support they made toward one another; on the tight, interpersonal relationships it takes to pull something like this off.

Most obviously to you by now, I also wrote it to pay homage to the women who were *also* explorers, the women who did not go out and find sponsors and publicity for the cool things they were doing, because that would have put them unfavorably in the spotlight, where they would have been branded as doing what they were not supposed to do.

Women like Edna Brush Perkins, who, in the early 1920s, drove a wagon across the Mojave Desert with her best friend and a guide. Women like Lucy Walker, who became the first woman to climb the Matterhorn, way back in 1871. And, even further back, women like Maria Sibylla Merian, who had the advantage of coming from a wealthy Dutch family who were happy to let her go off to what was then Dutch Guiana to paint flora and fauna and make live studies of these creatures, while her male counterparts were busy shooting, stuffing, and pinning things in order to make them sit still so they could make more accurate pictures.

Women like Edith Garrud, who taught whole bands of suffragists jujitsu so they could defend themselves against folks who did not want to see women get the vote. Women like Emmeline Pankhurst, whose life of public service made it very clear to her that decisions about women should be made *by* women.

At a dinner for friends I was hosting in the early 2000s, a dinner guest said she hadn't voted yet. My friend Jody was absolute: "You must vote," she said. "Women died for your right to vote." To wit: Emily Davison was trampled to death beneath the hooves of the King's racehorse while attempting to hang a "Votes for Women" flag on the horse as it sped its way to win the Epsom Derby. In some places, the story of her death is co-opted to fit the narrative of an hysterical, suicidal woman, bent on playing the martyr.

Ida B. Wells and Alice Paul are real women; the 1913 march on Washington really took place—and Wells, a prominent Black journalist and suffragist, was indeed asked to march in the back of the parade by the leadership of the National American Woman Suffrage Association. Paul, who was a staunch advocate of the move toward a *federal* mandate guaranteeing votes for women, was also a student of Emmeline Pankhurst.

Although many of the expedition events recounted here did occur, and although I have pegged some of the personalities here to men who were on the crew. No one in this book actually exists, but Carl and Andrine Anton did. Carl Anton established a whaling station at Grytviken in 1904; his wife's name was indeed Andrine. The character of Thomas Milton-Jones is most closely found in Thomas Orde-Lees, who was indeed a Royal Marine, and who was notoriously fastidious—enough so that the crew dubbed him the "Old Lady."

Which is—what, is that supposed to be an insult? Come on, now, men. Do better.

Nota bene: the "Wives and Sweethearts" toast was finally formally written out of the British Navy's repertoire in 2013.

Claremont, CA
February 2022

Acknowledgments

People picture writing a book as a solitary endeavor, but nothing could be further from the truth. I owe so much.

This book would literally not be what it is without Roz Ray and Rachael Warecki, the Fiesta in the Corner. The folks who read my drafts and gave valuable feedback—Jackson Brogan, Borchien Lai, Valerie Polichar, Shey Lyn Zanotti, Kelly de Vos, Ken Pisani, Penny Walker, Mandy Wallace, Mike Smith—I am so lucky to count you among my friends and my colleagues. Matthew Bolin and Larry Curran fielded my first excited phone calls about this idea and encouraged me to go on. Mike Smith, Lesley Garside, and Nicola Hinds provided a second ear on English and Irish colloquialisms and dialect—thank you.

Tremendous thanks to Susan Day, Morgan Yates, and Claire Smith, who taught me how to work with archivists; and to Calista Day, the archivist at Dulwich College, who welcomed me into the Ernest Shackleton papers there. The work of the good people at the Scott Polar Research Institute can also not be underscored. Thank you for preserving this part of history for us. These archivists and historians tried their best to help me on my research quest; any mistakes are mine.

Whilst visiting the *James Caird*, the dinghy that took Ernest Shackleton and five crewmates across the Southern Ocean, I met Tony Ellison, whose father had served on a later Antarctic expedition, and whose papers Tony shared with me. Reading William Albert Ellison's letters was transporting. Meeting Tony and his family is, however, the more memorable upshot.

Nicola Jones provided invaluable research help, friendship, and support; and Graham and Mary Henderson will forever be linked to my writing of this book, as I drafted many scenes in their warm Cornish seaside village, knowing I could retreat up the hill whenever I liked for friendship, tea, dinner, or just a good natter.

Wichitaw Busby and Tim Osburn helped with their knowledge of firearms; Ian Neal talked me out of what would have been a disastrously wrong water-rescue scene. Steve Crabtree helped me to find a good place to write, and to connect with the writing community in Cornwall, whilst I was beginning to work on this book.

Katharine Fick and Peter Bilton seem to never, ever waver in their beliefs that whatever I'm working on will get made; and Sue Nelson—oh, Sue. My friend and teammate Sue, who has been to Antarctica *five* times, and who is a pioneer in so many fields—this book is for you too.

Leanna James Blackwell, director of the MFA program in nonfiction at Bay Path University, understands the intricate relationship between fiction and nonfiction, and encourages me every day to make that connection to my students; Wayne Ude and Bruce Holland Rogers, whose faith in my ability to tell stories on the page is as tangible as teeth.

My agent, Kate: our friendship necessitates a novel in and of itself, and this book is the best HEA anyone could have ever asked for. My editor, Kristie Choi, whose informed, spot-on readings and edits make me a better writer. And whose messages always make me smile.

The entire production team at Simon & Schuster and Atheneum: Publisher Justin Chanda and editorial director Reka Simonsen; designer Karyn Lee and cover artist Beatriz Ramo; production editors Clare McGlade and Kaitlyn San Miguel; production manager Tatyana Rosalia—their work has produced the gorgeous volume you now hold in your hands. Copy editor Andrea Martinez's fine work is a key reason I don't look like an utter fool in multiple places.

Alfred Lansing and Caroline Alexander, whose retellings of *The Endurance* expedition first enthralled me over twenty years ago; and John Thomson, whose editing of Thomas Orde-Lees's diaries unlocked a new story in me. And, of course, every crew member of *The Endurance*, whose diaries allowed me myriad dimensions to the expedition.

My teammates on the ShelterBox Response Team: by now you have all heard some version of this book on long rides to faraway sites—during airport layovers, after our nightly debriefs—your presence is welcome.

My neighbors, Suzanne and Jeroen, Marjie and Subbie, Aurelia and Jim, who literally flank me in a web of constant support.

Kelly ver Duin, whose spirit of literary community inspires me; Kate Kante, whose guidance in early research shaped the kind of help I'd look for when crafting this book. The women of the Giant XLB, my Taiwanese sisters in creativity, writing, life, and love—*thank you.*

You, the reader. The librarians, who are consistently my personal heroes; the booksellers. Everyone involved in the fight to keep reading fundamental to our lives. This book is for you. You might not be reading this novel if it weren't for the hard work of the sales and marketing and publicity teams, whose influence often goes unsung—thank you.

My husband, Jim, who has always answered, "Why not?" whenever doubt slouches into my life. My parents, whose unique definitions of bravery and moral code have shaped my own. My brother, my sharpest critic; my sister-in-law Laura, whose door always seems to be open for complaining, for creative help, for safe haven, for contrary opinion.

For KV, this book is in part a memorial to your grit—but it is also a celebration of your continuing joy.

And my dog, Huckleberry, you remedial creature, you tester of patience. You'd be terrible in traces, but you're an inspiration in your own way.